THE UNLUCKY GUARDIANS

THE UNLIKELY DEFENDERS BOOK 3

LILY SKYY

First Edition: August 2023

ISBN 978-1-956525-04-5 (ebook)
ISBN 978-1-956525-78-6 (paperback)

Published by Books to Hook Publishing, LLC.
www.BooksToHook.com

CONTENTS

PROLOGUE

Amberly McHenry had always had it all; she was the most popular girl in her high school and she was beautiful. All the girls coveted her smooth, long blonde hair and all the guys drooled over her piercing ice-blue eyes and toned athletic body. She was the head cheerleader at St. Bernard High as well. It was a very coveted position and only made everyone more envious of her.

But envy wasn't the only thing that made Amberly McHenry so popular, and envy wasn't the only thing that put her at the top of the school.

Amberly was so high above everybody else because everyone at St. Bernard High seemed to fear her. They let Amberly do whatever she wanted and nobody stood up to her. Nobody told her no; everybody acted as nice as they could to her because they didn't want to face her wrath if they did otherwise. Nobody liked being on Amberly's bad side, you could simply glance at her the wrong way and she would put you at the top of her list of those to mess with. And for the other students at St. Bernard High, it was easier just to let her rule than to risk getting attacked by her or her boyfriend, Trace Henderson.

Amberly loved being on top, she loved being feared, and she loved everybody thinking she was as perfect as perfect could get. But Amberly had a secret, one hardly anybody knew, and she didn't *want* anybody to know.

Amberly McHenry was *far* from perfect, and she was far from having a perfect life.

Nobody knew what her life was like outside of school. She never let anybody in to explain it to them. She never let anybody see. Not until recently, when she admitted a horrifying truth to the rest of the Unlikely Defenders, Trace, Kaos, Kire, and even Rose. She already regretted it immensely, but there had been no way around admitting the truth. She had been hanging around them too long—protecting the world and whatnot, and they could see right through her. She had no choice but to explain it to them.

The truth was; Amberly had a father who didn't want her, and her mother was in the hospital, sicker than Amberly had ever seen her. Amberly had recently lost her after-school and weekends job. It had been her and her mother's only source of income. She was the only one who supported her small family since her father— who was also Kire's father, didn't want to have anything to do with her. Now she had no money, but she still had a school to stay on top of and a world to protect from the great, powerful, terrible Yash.

Amberly felt pressure from everyone and everything around her. The more pressure she felt, the harder she tried to hide that she was cracking. The more pressure she felt, the angrier she got. The more she made everyone around her fear her. Sure, she had the other four as a support system, but she didn't want to be supported, she didn't want to be pitied. She wanted to have it all.

Amberly McHenry was determined, desperate even, to do whatever it took to make sure she got it.

1

Amberly McHenry felt uncomfortable as she sat in the stiff, plain, tan leather chair next to her mother's bed inside Montgomery's hospital, Great River Community Hospital. She was glad to be there. She was glad that she was by her mother's side. She was even *more* glad that even though Amberly had spent multiple days inside a magical realm known as the Albus realm, her mother hadn't even noticed that she was gone.

The funny thing was that *nobody* seemed to notice she was gone. Nobody seemed to notice that five teenagers at St. Bernard's high school had all gone into the White Forest and didn't come out for nearly three days. But the thing was, it was only three days to *them*—to Kire Hunter, Trace Henderson, Kaos Miles, Charlie Rose, and Amberly McHenry—otherwise known as the Unlikely Defenders. Those five teens were the only ones who felt three days go by. Once they returned from the Albus realm, they were prepared to deal with a lot of worried teachers, parents, and peers, but instead, found that they only appeared to have left this realm— the Earth realm—for a handful of hours.

Amberly grabbed her mother's hand even though Elizabeth McHenry was so out of it that she could not even tell her daughter was there. Not long ago, Amberly had gotten home to find that her mother had collapsed unconsciously onto the floor. She had been in the hospital ever since.

"This lighting does *not* do good for your complexion," Amberly told her mother as she looked into her sunken, hollow face. She and her mother had the same blonde hair, blue eyes, and an oval-shaped face. It made her realize, "If it doesn't look good on *you*, then it must not look good on me either." Thank God there weren't any mirrors around. Amberly didn't even want to try to fathom what kind of state she was in right now. She just had to hope that when she finally left the hospital room for the night and retreated to an empty, rundown home, nobody would spot her.

After she got out of the portal, she only went back home to change into something that wasn't soaking wet so that she could hurry to Great River to get to her mom and see if she was okay. It had killed her to be gone those three days and not know the state that her mother was in. So she thought she was more relieved than most to find when she returned that time didn't work the same in both realms and that only a few hours had gone by. Still, Amberly had been determined to make up for the lost time.

When she had talked to the doctor and the nurses, they had been blunt with her and told her that things weren't looking good. That her mother was really sick and that they were glad Amberly was there to keep her company. They asked if she had anybody at home to stay with, and she lied and said she was staying at a friend's house. In all truth, she didn't exactly want to be alone inside her house while her mom was here in the hospital, but what other choice did she have? It wasn't exactly like she was the type to just go up to her boyfriend or one of the other Quintets and ask if she could stay at their house. She had way too much pride to do that.

She was glad to be out of the magical realm now, though. And she was glad it hadn't taken them multiple days to get back. After that strange man inside that crumbling castle suddenly started talking to them, his frosted blue eyes no longer frosted—but *glowing*. Amberly and the others knew they had to get out of the castle as quickly as they could. As she sat there in the hospital, she couldn't stop herself from thinking back about it.

"He's coming," the man had said. The Quintets didn't know for certain what the man meant by "he," and when they tried to ask him, he went back to having frosted eyes and not being able to say anything at all. So, assuming the worst, the teens figured it was Yash. Maybe he was making his way to the Albus realm. And they weren't prepared to fight him yet. Not when they had just spent so much time battling various creatures, and not when one of their own, Rose, was as weak as she was. Everybody needed some time to regain their strength before they were ready to take on the evilest and most powerful being in all of the realms.

"Where do we go?" Rose asked, her eyes wide with fear after the mysterious man started speaking.

"We need to get back to the portal," Kaos said.

That was when Halo started moving. Kire opened up the book and saw that she was writing something to them inside.

"She is telling us to go somewhere in the castle. She's writing out directions of where to go."

"And we should trust her?" Amberly asked, not sure, since they hadn't had her very long, that she would really help get them out of there and away from whoever the "he" was.

"Of course, we should," Kire snapped. "Come on." And then he took off running. The others had no choice but to follow him. It would just have been worse if they got separated.

They ran through the castle, looking over their shoulders at every turn in case they were going to be attacked again. They followed Kire and were led outside a room high up in one of the towers. The wooden door to it was locked. But Amberly had no trouble putting on her gauntlet, Gomorrah, and punching through the wood, something she hadn't known her gauntlet could do until that moment. With a normal punch, she probably would have put a small dent in the door and splintered her knuckles. But this punch took the door right off of its hinges, and they were then able to go inside the room.

"What is that?" Rose asked. In front of them, there was a pedestal. It was the only thing in the entire room. That, and the royal blue rock that sat on top of it.

"Halo led us to a rock?" Kaos asked skeptically. Trace had pulled out his flaming sword, ready to fight anything around. But it was clear there was nothing around them.

For now, at least, Amberly thought.

"Hang on," Kire said, holding Halo open and reading something as she wrote in her unreadable language. It was unreadable to everybody except for Kire. It was his gift. He was the one who plucked it out of that cave when they had all been trapped in it several weeks prior.

"What's it saying?" Trace asked. "What does Halo expect us to do with a stupid rock?"

Amberly didn't think the rock looked stupid. It was beautiful, like a combination between a geode and a crystal. Its sparkles glimmered around the entire round room, bouncing off the stone walls. It was almost mesmerizing to look at.

"According to Halo, that rock will teleport us back to the portal," Kire finally answered. "It can teleport us anywhere, as long as we've been there before and can think of it clearly in our head."

"Great," Kaos said, stepping toward it. "How are we all supposed to use it at once?"

"Hang on." Kire read some more. "As long as the first person holds it, and we all hold onto each other, we can all be teleported."

"What is that going to feel like?" Amberly asked, deeply unsettled by the idea of teleportation. Her whole body disappearing and reappearing at a completely different location miles and miles away? She had seen it in movies and read about it in books, but as far as she had known, it wasn't a real thing.

But neither were werewolves and cyclops and banshees.

But, apparently, in this realm, anything could be real.

"I don't know," Kire said. "I haven't ever teleported before."

"You haven't?" Trace asked sarcastically.

"We don't have time to think about what it's going to feel like," Kaos said, stepping in and taking charge. "All we know is that we gotta get out of here."

"Yash isn't coming now," Rose said. "He wouldn't, Albus said we had time. It's much too soon."

"You're probably right," Kire said. "But we need to get back home anyway. You need to rest and we need to let our parents know that we're still alive."

Rose crossed her arms and mumbled something that nobody could understand. But Amberly was pretty sure it was something about how her parents wouldn't care if she was alive or not. She chalked it up to Rose just being dramatic. She was certain that she had a family who loved her. She was sure she was the only one who lived a sad, miserable home life.

Kire picked up the rock. "All right then. Everyone grab on to someone."

Amberly grabbed onto Trace, Trace grabbed onto Rose, Rose grabbed onto Kire, and Kaos grabbed onto Amberly. His grip was firm around her hand. And it made her wonder if he was just as nervous as she.

Kire put Halo back in his backpack. Then he cleared his throat, stared at the stone in his hand, closed his eyes, and began to concentrate.

Amberly squeezed her eyes shut, terrified of what was going to happen next. Then her stomach flipped, the ground fell away from under her feet, and the next thing she knew, she and the other four were slamming into the ground in the middle of nowhere. They were at the portal.

A NURSE CAME into Elizabeth McHenry's room to make the beeping on the machines stop and to change out some of her medication.

"Is she going to wake up?" Amberly asked. She was exhausted, but she didn't want to go home if there was any chance she was going to get to talk to her mother.

"She's pretty heavily sedated," the nurse replied. "And she really needs her rest." Amberly nodded.

"Is there anything I can get you?" the nurse asked, her voice soft and concerned "anybody you need me to call?"

"What I *need*, is for you guys to do your *jobs* and make my mom get better. Don't just stand there with sad eyes when you should be working hard to fix her." She had turned her sass on, and she had turned it on *thick*.

The nurse seemed surprised by her sudden attitude. Instead of saying anything, she just backed away from Amberly and left the room.

Amberly sighed and got to her feet. She paced around the room and looked out the window. She had to check that Yash hadn't made it to Earth yet. Outside the blinds, she wasn't going to see the world in total destruction as far as she could tell. Everything was still; everything was normal. The world kept turning, even if to her, it felt as if the world had stopped. She *wanted* the world to stop. She wanted it to stop, and then it could resume again once her mother was healed.

If only her gauntlet could make that happen, she sat back down. The chair she was in reclined, and she wondered if maybe she should just spend the night with her mom. Did she need to go home for anything, anyway? She was nervous about tomorrow.

ONCE SHE AND her friends had made it to the portal, they had Amberly go through it first. They knew the portal was located at the bottom of the lake inside the cave in the White Forest. Amberly was the only one who could make that water part so that the others could get out of the lake without drowning. So Amberly stepped through the portal and then was underwater, unable to breathe. It was scary at first because it was pitch black and she had no idea which way was up. But she forced herself to mentally calm down and concentrate on her gauntlet. Then she made the water part, creating two walls of dirty old lake water with a narrow pathway between them for everybody to be able to walk through. She had no way of letting the others know that she had done it correctly at first, so it took a couple of minutes before, finally, Trace appeared through the portal.

"Awesome, Amberly," he said to her encouragingly. "Just hold it there, and I'll let the others know it's clear to come through." Then he went back through the portal and returned with everybody else. Amberly had to walk behind them and keep her focus on keeping the walls of water up. She was drenched from head to toe while all the others got to remain dry. It irked her. But this was what her ability called for.

Once they were out of the lake and out of the cave, they walked through the White Forest cautiously. Rezin, one of Yash's minions who had been tormenting them in the Earth realm, could be around. He could've been notified about their return to the Earth realm. He had been chained to Earth, and even though he was more powerful than all the beasts they had fought in the Albus realm, he hadn't been able to go through the portal to try to join the other minions in their battle. He had to stay on Earth, so he was waiting. The reason Amberly kept thinking about that walk through the White Forest after they made it back through the portal was because of Kire.

"Well, we're back on Earth," Kire said as he walked alongside Amberly. On the other side of him was Rose. Amberly couldn't help but notice that, out of nowhere, Rose no longer seemed like she hated Kire. They are very on-again-off-again, she started to realize.

"And?" Amberly asked Kire, sneering at him. Just because they had come to an understanding while making their journey to the castle on the volcano in the magical realm, it didn't mean they were suddenly besties who made small talk with each other. Amberly could tolerate Kire now. She could be okay with letting him be a part of their friend group. But that was as far as it went.

Kire looked at her as if she were stupid for not understanding what his comment meant. "And... I'm going to keep my promise, Amberly."

"Oh." Her stomach knotted. Now she realized what Kire was referring to.

"I'm going to tell my dad as soon as I get home," he said.

"Good." She kept her head high. She didn't need Kire to know how incredibly nervous she was. She knew that her father, Gerald Hunter knew she was alive, but she also knew that Gerald wasn't aware that she knew. She wasn't sure what his reaction was going to be. But she was eager to let him know that she knew. She was eager to hopefully have another parental figure in her life. One that could take care of her since she could hardly even take care of herself now that she was out of a job.

"I'll let you know how everything goes at school tomorrow," Kire said.

"Fine," she replied. Then she walked ahead so that she was next to her boyfriend and Kaos instead of them.

Tomorrow was coming up quickly. It was already almost midnight. Amberly thought it was so strange that she had just spent *days* fighting unimaginable beasts and monsters, and now she had to resume her normal-everyday life and go to high school. It felt so much more insignificant now that she knew she had an entire world to protect. Two worlds, even. No one in their group wanted the Albus realm to be destroyed by Yash and his minions. They had all come back to the Earth realm, but Amberly had a feeling they weren't going to remain there for long. After all, they still had a job to do.

They had to find Albus, protect the Albus realm, figure out how to close the portal, and they had to defeat Yash, or else, all of humanity was doomed. It was up to them.

2

Amberly wanted to stay in the hospital with her mom all night long. She really did, but she had school early and she was exhausted, so she didn't trust herself to be able to sleep at the hospital and then get home to shower and get ready in time before school started the next morning. So eventually, she left the hospital and told the doctor to call her straight away if her mother woke up or if she got worse.

It had been awful to be home. The old, unkempt bungalow with the overgrown front lawn had a sense of abandonment and forlornness to it when she walked up the two flights of stairs to the front door. She felt as if the old house reflected the way she felt inside. And she was terrified that the way she felt inside was showing on her outside. What she was most afraid of was anybody seeing the real her.

When she walked inside the house, it smelled like her mother. But her mother wasn't there. Amberly was alone.

She walked through the foyer into the living room and paused at the only picture hanging on the wall. The one of her and her mother. Amberly was just a baby in the photo, and she and her mother looked so happy in it. Amberly had been too young to know how truly horrible her life was. To know how sad and depressed her mother was at having been abandoned by Gerald Hunter. At having been abandoned by him so that he could go be with another woman. Kire's dreadful mom. It made her sad to look at the photo. Her eyes even started filling with tears, but Amberly McHenry didn't cry.

Instead of standing around feeling sorry for herself and her mother, she focused on one task at a time. Taking a shower. Brushing her teeth. Doing her skincare routine. Braiding her hair. Putting on cute pajamas. And then finally, crawling into bed.

When Amberly woke the next morning, she felt groggy and confused. She had tossed and turned all night, and when her alarm went off, she was certain she had set it for the wrong time—it couldn't possibly be time to get up already.

But then, when she remembered that today was the day Kire was going to tell her how it had gone with telling their father that she knew about him, suddenly, she was more awake.

Quickly, she grabbed her phone off of its charger on the night-stand, sat up in bed, and yawned as she composed a text to Kire.

Amberly: So, did you talk to him?

Then, as she sat there in bed thinking about what had happened the day before, she remembered that Kire had been trying to show them something in one of the books inside the castle. So she sent him a follow-up text.

Amberly: Also, what was inside that book that you were trying to show us?

She hadn't gotten to read it because the creepy frosty-eyed man had shown up sounding all prophetic and scaring the crap out of her.

Kire didn't reply right away, but she also figured it was because he didn't get up nearly as early as she did. She had a lot to do to get ready for school in the mornings. She showered again, where she exfoliated herself raw, shaved her legs, and deep-conditioned her long mane. Then she had to get out, towel herself off and put lotion on her legs, and blow dry her hair to perfection. After that, she had to do her skincare routine again. And her makeup took forever too.

A lot went into being perfect.

Still, even after Amberly was fully ready for the day, she had some time. That had been her goal in the first place. She left the house and made the long walk back to the hospital. She wanted to see her mom again before she went to school. She felt this need to constantly check on her. For some reason, she was nervous that the nurses and doctors weren't telling her anything and that they weren't giving her enough updates. So she had to go to her mom and see for herself.

"Hi, Amberly," a nurse said as she saw Amberly walking past her station to get to her mom's room. "I was just about to call you." And the only reason Amberly believed her was because the woman had a receiver of a phone in her hand.

Her stomach dipped and she stopped walking. "Why?" she asked the nurse. "What happened?"

The nurse smiled. "Your mom just woke up a little bit ago. She's still pretty out of it. But she was asking for you."

Amberly didn't bother saying anything else to the nurse. She ran inside her mom's hospital room.

It was true. Elizabeth McHenry was awake. Her eyes were only barely open to slits as she stared at the news on the TV screen.

"Hi, Mom," she said as she approached her bedside. Elizabeth slowly-ever so slowly turned her head to her daughter. Then the faintest of smiles showed on her lips.

"Amber," she said. Then she coughed. A lot. But Amberly didn't think anything of it. Her mom had also coughed a lot at home before she fell unconscious and was transported to the hospital.

"Are you feeling better?" she asked.

Please say yes.

"Loads," her mom said. Amberly smiled, thrilled to hear it.

"You'll be getting out of here and back home in no time," she said reassuringly. She checked her phone that buzzed in the back pocket of her designer jeans, the ones that made her butt look extra good, and hoped to see that Kire had finally replied to her texts. But it wasn't Kire. It was just a text from Trace.

> Trace: Hey, where r u? Kaos and I swung by ur house 2 pick u up but u weren't there. U good?

She rolled her eyes and didn't reply. She wasn't frustrated at Trace as much as she was just annoyed that the text hadn't been from Kire instead. She wanted to know what happened.

"Everything okay?" Her mom asked, watching her reaction to her phone.

"Don't worry about me," Amberly said, reaching out and brushing some hair away from her mom's face. "I have everything totally under control. Like always." But in all honesty, Amberly's mother didn't even know that she had lost her job yet. That they had absolutely no income coming in to pay any of their bills.

"The nurse told me that you've been staying at a friend's house and that you're not home alone. That makes me happy," her mother told her, changing the subject. "Which friend?"

Her stomach dipped. She didn't want to lie to her mom any more than she had to. But this was another instance where she felt like she had to.

"Angela," she lied. Angela was another cheerleader at St. Bernard, and even though the two of them weren't exactly close, she had been sitting at their lunch table a lot lately when she and Kire had been dating, before Kire made a stupid move and broke up with her. Didn't Kire know better? Dating a cheerleader was the best way to show off your popularity. And Kire's popularity because of how good he was at soccer was relatively new. He wasn't very good at keeping the status quo.

"Good," her mom said.

Amberly stayed in the room with her mother a little bit longer, but then, unfortunately, she had to get to school.

"THERE YOU ARE," Trace said to Amberly as she showed up outside of the school just a couple of minutes before the bell rang. He threw his muscular arms around her shoulders and pulled her in close. She hugged him, inhaling the overwhelming scent of his manly-smelling body spray. He always reeked of it first thing in the morning, and it eventually faded away into a dull smell by the end of the school day.

"Sorry. I had stuff to do," she decided to say. She was aware that the others knew her mom was in the hospital, but she didn't want to remind them. She wanted them to forget about it completely, in all honesty.

"We were worried about you," Kaos said. He was wearing all black as usual, and he had on black sunglasses, concealing his attractive facial features. His auburn hair was slicked back, but it was getting a little long. Amberly could understand why they hadn't exactly had much time for haircuts lately.

"Where is Kire?" Amberly asked, ignoring Kaos. She didn't need people to be worried about her. Even if they were her friends. Amberly was fine. She could handle anything.

"Who knows?" Trace said. "Probably off somewhere with Rose. I think the two of them might have gotten back together."

"What a downgrade from Angela," Amberly said.

"That's what I said," Kaos agreed. Then he smiled darkly. "I know Rose is part of our group, but... she's sort of a nobody. And Kire is a god at soccer. There's no point in even trying to deny it. I feel like he could do much, much better than Rose."

Amberly looked at Trace and waited for him to agree. He suddenly looked slightly uncomfortable, like he didn't want to. It was weird because Trace was usually always ready to throw insults at anybody. She didn't like that he wasn't insulting Rose.

The bell rang and Amberly retreated to English with Kaos and Trace. Once they got inside the classroom, they saw that Kire was already in his seat. But there weren't any open seats around him, so Amberly couldn't sit next to him and demanded to know why he hadn't texted her back. And when she walked into the room, Kire wouldn't even look in their direction.

When the final bell rang, Mrs. Goody was eager to start her teaching and walked up to the front of the class.

"Now that the papers have all been turned in from our last book assignment, it's time to move on to the next one," she said, her lips pursed tightly like they always were and her black and white hair in its tight bun like she always wore it. Mrs. Goody was an older army veteran who sometimes seemed like she hated her job and the teenagers that came with it. The only time she ever softened up was if she could tell that a student needed her help.

The class groaned collectively. Nobody likes starting a new book reading. Amberly felt stressed; she could hardly handle homework on top of dealing with everything else going on in her life.

She had better things to be doing.

"We're starting 'The Odyssey," Mrs. Goody informed them. Amberly had never heard of it.

Her teacher continued. "It's an exciting tale about Odysseus, the king of Ithaca, making the journey back home after the Trojan war."It sounded miserable.

"It's many small stories put into one. We'll learn about nymphs, Laestrygonians, cyclops, gods, and goddesses. There will be lots of fighting."

Amberly looked at Trace and Kire, who looked at her in return. She was a little more interested now. A story about the main character fighting mythical beasts? The Unlikely Defenders had just returned from doing something very similar to that. In fact, they had even just killed a cyclops.

"You can check out a copy of the book at the library, buy your own, or I have a good handful here that you can rent out," Mrs. Goody told them. "Please figure out how to get your hands on a copy before tomorrow."

When class ended, Kire was quick to get out of the room.

"Is it just me, or does it seem like Kire is avoiding us?" she asked Trace and Kaos as she crossed her arms. They walked out into the hall, where they were constantly bombarded by people saying Hi to them or giving them some sort of compliment. This was how it went every day for Amberly. Normally, she reveled in it. But now, she wished everybody would leave her alone so that she could find Kire. She was worried that he hadn't told his dad after all and that, for some reason, he didn't want them to know what was in that book.

Trace rested his arm on Amberly's shoulder as they walked. He had such an effortlessly cool-guy air about him. He was a total jock, while Kaos ruled in a more mysterious, rebellious way. "Don't worry, babe," Trace said to her as they walked through the halls. "We'll see him at lunch. He can't hide from us forever."

When lunch rolled around, much to Amberly's surprise, Kire walked over to their table after getting his lunch in line. Amberly wasn't going to eat. She didn't have much of an appetite, even less so when she thought about her mom stuck in that hospital room forced to eat plain yogurt and gross, greasy fried chicken strips. To add to Amberly's surprise, Kire had Rose in tow with him.

The two took a seat at the table, no one bothering to point out that Rose was sitting with them when it wasn't really her place to do so. She wasn't as high in the popularity ranking as the rest of them were. She didn't exactly belong at their table.

"*There* you are, dude," Trace said to Kire. "Hi, Rose."

"*Hi, Rose*?" Amberly glared at Trace. He didn't see her expression, however, because he had already started digging into the meatloaf.

"What?" Trace asked. "Rose is one of us, baby."

"I doubt the rest of the school thinks that," Amberly said.

"Look," Kire joined in, puffing his chest out and sitting up straight in the seat across from Amberly. "Rose and I... we're sort of... Well, I don't know exactly what we are. But I want to sit with her. And I want to sit with you guys. And we're all a group, ya know? So whether you like it or not, I think Rose should get to stay."

"I'm not trying to steal your popularity or bring the ranking down," Rose added, her cheeks flushing. "I just want to be able to spend time with Kire on my lunch break."

Rose just looked so... plain. Slightly strange too. She had flowers in her hair. She was wearing green overalls and pink Keds that she seemed to have hand-painted little yellow flowers all over.

She wasn't even that pretty. Not that Amberly thought Kire was the most attractive guy in the world and he *was* her brother after all, but since he was a star soccer player, didn't he know that he could get someone prettier than her? Didn't he *want* anyone prettier? *Once a loser, always a loser,* she thought to herself.

"Whatever," Amberly snapped, tossing her hair back and taking a sip from her water bottle. She was self-conscious. She felt like everyone around the cafeteria was looking over at their table. At the fact that Kaos, Trace, and Amberly, the three most feared people at St. Bernard, were letting someone like Rose sit with them.

"It's, like, a million degrees in here," Trace said as he fanned himself with one of his school folders. "Kire, dude, how are you even wearing a jacket right now?"

Kire shifted uncomfortably in his seat. "I don't think it's hot," he said. But Amberly knew it was a lie, she could see perspiration building up at his hairline. She squinted at him.

"*Hello*? Don't you have something to tell me?"

Kire was busy digging into his frozen bean and cheese burrito. How her friends wanted to eat the disgusting lunch that the school served, was beyond Amberly.

"I'm starving," he said with his mouthful. "I'll tell you later. Let's just make it through the school day first."

She crossed her arms and glared at him some more. "Did you even tell him?"

"I said we'll talk about it later."

Amberly wanted Trace to step in and say something. To demand that he tell her now. To tell Kire he couldn't treat her this way. But Trace hadn't even heard the exchange, for he was in deep conversation with Kaos about their plans to make some more cash. They always had plans to make money. Amberly didn't exactly understand why because Kaos came from a wealthy family. He didn't need it. Maybe Trace did so that he could buy Amberly presents to spoil her and show what a good boyfriend he was.

The thought of that made her a little less annoyed at him.

LATER, at cheer practice, Amberly was mad at herself because she wasn't doing as good of a job as she normally did. She was distracted. Flustered. She wasn't on time with the movements and when she went for a back tuck, it turned into a backhand spring because she didn't give it enough force to be able to flip without her hands.

When they took a water break, Charity, one of the cheerleaders who Amberly suspected longed to be more popular than Amberly, casually walked up to her at the drinking fountain where Amberly was refilling her water bottle.

"So, *Amberly*," she said, tossing her brunette hair back and giving Amberly a slight smirk. "Was I hallucinating today at lunch, or did I see *Charlie Rose* sitting at your lunch table?"

Amberly's stomach dipped. She should've known this would happen. Was she actually getting insulted by somebody beneath her right now?

She was not about to put up with it.

"Oh my *God*, Charity," she said with a fake smile. "Am I hallucinating, or did you seemingly gain ten pounds overnight?"

Behind her, she could hear some other cheerleaders giggling, clearly on Amberly's side.

Charity, who had taken a protein bar out of her gym bag, paused in the middle of tearing it open and flung it back into her bag.

"Whatever," she said to Amberly. Then she walked over to some other cheerleaders and it seemed as if she wasn't going to try to bring anything like that up to Amberly again.

But what if somebody *else* did? What if people kept giving her a hard time for letting a nobody like Rose sit at her table? What if it made her lose some of her popularity status? What if it let somebody like stupid, ditzy Charity be the new queen of the school?

Amberly couldn't let that happen.

3

The cheerleaders held their practice outside in front of the soccer team who was doing their practice. As Amberly tried to focus on cheerleading and on being the best at it, she couldn't help but notice that out on the field, Kire was wearing track pants and an athletic jacket. Sure, it was slightly chilly outside, but with all of the running and drills they were doing, everybody else on the team was in a T-shirt and shorts. She wondered if maybe he was getting sick. It would also help make sense as to why he didn't seem to be playing that well today. He wasn't running as fast, and she also wondered if maybe he fell at one point and she missed it because it seemed like he was also limping a little too.

Amberly had other reasons for keeping her eyes on Kire during the practice instead of on someone much more interesting, like her handsome hunk of a boyfriend, Trace. Her reasoning was that she didn't want to let him out of her sight. She didn't want him to escape from her.

After both of their practices ended, Kire walked over to the bench to pick up his gym bag and head into the locker room, but Amberly stopped him immediately. She had known he was going to try to make his escape. She knew he was still trying to avoid her so they didn't have to have this conversation.

But the time was now. Amberly wasn't going to wait any longer.

"*Hold* it, buddy," she said venomously, holding her hand out in front of his chest so that he couldn't keep walking. Trace approached her to chitchat like he always did after practice, but she held up her other hand's pointer finger to him. "Trace, later," she snapped.

"All right then," he said with his eyebrows raised. "Good luck, Kire." Then he walked off with Kaos.

"Hey, Amberly," Kire said in a careful tone.

"You promised me after school, and not only is it after school. It's after *practice*. I waited all dang day to hear how it went last night. You can't just keep avoiding me. I don't care if it went bad. I just want to know. Did you even tell him?"

"Why don't we go talk somewhere more private?" Kire said as he looked around them. There were a lot of kids still lingering around. The soccer players were talking to the cheerleaders. Their new coach was individually talking to his players and making his way toward Kire, like he wanted to talk to him, too. Probably about how sucky he was on the field today.

She nodded stiffly, and then they walked over to the bleachers and hid underneath them, out of sight from everybody else.

"Talk," she demanded.

Kire let out a long, slow breath. He didn't seem to want to meet her gaze. "I told him," he finally said.

Hope filled Amberly. But it was quickly replaced with worry as she realized that Kire didn't look happy. He didn't look eager to share the news with her. It wasn't a good sign.

"And how did he react?" Amberly asked, her voice not as confident as it had sounded a moment ago. It wasn't the voice of somebody who ruled St. Bernard High. It was a voice of a scared puppy. Amberly was disgusted with herself for it.

"It went just like I knew it would go, Amberly," he said,

sounding slightly irritated with her. "I told you I didn't tell him before to protect you. And I meant it. But you wanted this, so I did it for you to make you stop hating me."

"Okay..." she trailed off, worried about what he was going to say next.

"He didn't take it well."

"What do you mean?" she asked. "How did he not take it well? You can't just leave it at that."

He ran a hand through his damp-with-sweat dark hair and finally looked at her. "I mean he was furious. He said I didn't know what I was talking about and that I needed to shut my *bleeping* mouth. Then he went into his office and started throwing things around. It was scary, Amberly. I don't know why you even want him to know that you know. He is your dad in the first place. He's not someone to want as your dad."

Amberly's heart fell. But she didn't want Kire to see it. "Yeah. You *don't* know because you don't know what it's like to not have a dad in the first place," she said. Her heart felt broken. Her hope was gone. This was not how she had expected the conversation to go. "Does he... does he even want to talk to me?"

There was a pause, but then Kire slowly shook his head.

A lump formed in Amberly's throat. "Oh," she said.

"I'm really sorry, Amberly. But I promise you, you don't want someone like him in your life anyway. My dad is..."

"Whatever," she said suddenly, holding her head up. She was Amberly McHenry. *Nothing* bothered her. "I wanted him to know, and now he knows. You've completed your end of the deal, so consider yourself no longer hated by me. Now, if you'll excuse me." She turned sharply on her heel, kicking up a bit of dust underneath her feet, and then she stormed out of the underside of the bleachers before Kire could say anything else to her.

And before he could see her cry.

AMBERLY GOT a ride home from Kaos in his snazzy red car with Trace, and she was able to hide from the guys as she sat alone in the backseat, staring out the window and wiping her eyes. So far, she had done a good job of not letting them know that she was upset. And they were busy talking about sports and other stupid boyish things that didn't interest her, so they weren't curious as to why she wasn't joining in the conversation with them.

"I'm still coming in with you, right?" Trace asked Amberly when they pulled up outside of her bungalow.

Amberly had completely forgotten. During one of their classes today, Trace asked if he could come over after practice. She had agreed. They *were* boyfriend and girlfriend, after all. What kind of boyfriend and girlfriend didn't hang out with each other after school? What kind of girlfriend didn't feel like hanging out with her boyfriend? Amberly was dating the buffest, most threatening guy in school. What kind of girl *wouldn't* want him over at her house after school?

"Duh," she said, plastering a fake smile onto her face. "We'll see you later, Kaos."

"Fine," he said. "I didn't want to be invited in, anyway."

Amberly smiled, shrugged, and got out of the car. Trace got out of the passenger seat and turned back to his friend before he closed the door.

"Sorry, my man," he said. "Sometimes you just need a little alone time with your girl, you know? You should consider getting one. It's pretty great."

"I'll get right on that," Kaos said, rolling his eyes. Then Trace closed the door and followed Amberly inside her lame house.

"Is it okay if I raid your pantry?" Trace asked, already heading into the kitchen as Amberly looked at the photo of her and her mother on the wall again.

"What?" she asked, not having heard him fully. She wanted to go visit her mom again. But she didn't want to bring Trace with her. And she didn't want to kick him out. She would just hang out with

Trace for a little while, then she could go see her mother later. Maybe get some homework done in the hospital while her mom slept. Maybe apply for some new jobs, too.

"I'm raiding your pantry," Trace called. Then he reappeared in the living room with a toaster pastry. Without toasting it first, he ripped the bag open and shoved a huge bite into his mouth.

Amberly rolled her eyes and flopped onto the couch. "You're such a slob."

He shrugged and joined her. She turned on the TV, but she didn't care about what they watched. She wasn't going to pay any attention to it. She was still distracted by her thoughts of what Kire had told her earlier. And her thoughts about her status at school. And, of course, her thoughts about her mom. With all this going on, she could hardly even think about the fact that she was supposed to save the universe.

"Amberly?"

Amberly looked up at her boyfriend to see that he was holding an arm out, waiting for her to curl up into him.

"Sorry," she said, tucking her legs under her and resting her head on Trace's chest as he stroked her arm and continued eating his after-school snack.

"What's on your mind?" he asked her.

"Lunch," she said simply. The only way she knew to avoid not having to admit how upset she was by being let down about her biological father was to talk about something less significant.

"Lunch?" Trace questioned, raising one of his bushy eyebrows as she looked up at him. "Because you didn't eat today? Do you want me to make you something?"

"No," she replied. "I'm talking about lunch in the *cafeteria* today."

"That's weird. What about it?"

"Um, did you forget?" she snapped, pulling away from him and sitting up straight again. "Rose sat at our lunch table. People stared. People totally judged us."

"Oh. To be honest, I didn't notice, Amber."

"Well, I did."

Trace leaned slightly away, too. "Okay? Did you forget what we talked about before? I thought we were going to start including her. I thought we were trying to be a team here and that we were trying to make sure no one was left behind. You have to remember what Albus told us, Amberly. It makes us stronger that way. We're so much stronger together."

Is he seriously defending her right now?

"We're including her in our 'saving the world in our spare time' group, right? Fine. Then consider her included. I think I have done a decent enough job of doing that. But does that mean we have to include her at school, too? Because I was never made aware of that, Trace. I didn't know that's what it entailed. I don't even *like* her, and I know you know that. Having to be around her when we're fighting monsters and protecting the world from devastation and whatever is already more than enough."

He shrugged. And then, with one more big bite, his toaster pastry was gone.

"Trace. Come on." She had to get through to him. "We don't want Rose at our lunch table. She seriously brings down our average. She's... weird. She's not like us. She doesn't belong at that table. Everyone at school thinks it. I know I am not the only one, here."

"Oh, *you* come on, babe. What is so bad about her sitting there? She's not, like, hideous or anything. And she's nice. When has she ever not been nice to you? She keeps to herself. She doesn't bother anyone. She doesn't even want to sit at the table to be popular. She just does it because she likes your *brother*."

"What are you trying to say?" Amberly made it evident with her tone how appalled she was. Why wasn't he on her team? Trace was always on her team.

"Maybe you should talk to Kire about it, then," Trace continued, not seeming to understand her tone and that she was upset at *him*, not just at the situation they were discussing, "if it bugs you so much. The two of them are together... or whatever. Kaos and I like having Kire at our table. He has officially turned cool, ya know? Everyone in school thinks so. What with him being a super killer soccer player and all that, as much as I hate to admit it. He's the reason why Rose even wants to sit with us in the first place."

"I think what you're supposed to say *as my boyfriend* is that you'll talk to Kire about it. That you'll handle the problem and that you'll do whatever you can to make sure I'm happy." Amberly crossed her arms and glared at him.

He jutted his head back, and an irritated expression crossed over him. "Amberly. What is your deal? Do you... do you think I like her or something? I don't like Rose. I'm not interested in being with Rose. I like being with *you*. There's a reason you're my girlfriend. And the Amberly I know and cherish and worship doesn't let someone like *Charlie Rose* make her feel threatened."

The words were nice. And yet, Amberly still wasn't satisfied. She just wanted Trace to agree with her like he always used to do. Still, he wasn't telling her that he would get rid of Rose. He was making it seem as if they were going to be stuck with Rose sitting at the table every day. He was making it seem as if Amberly was going to have to get used to her being around and get used to people giving her looks and questioning why she was letting her popularity sink.

Amberly had to be in control. She had to make sure she kept her popularity. With everything going on with her mom, she felt that it was the *one* thing she could manage. The one thing she had a good grasp on. Or at least... it used to be that way.

She got to her feet.

"Where are you going?" Trace asked, making a move to get up as well.

"I have to go visit my mom," she said shortly. She fumbled around her house, looking for her bag and an umbrella in case it started raining during her walk to the hospital.

"Now?" he asked. Finally, he stood, but it looked very much like he didn't want to go anywhere. "But I just got here."

"Yeah. And now, you have to go."

"I thought we were going to hang out?"

"I need to go see my *mom*, Trace. She's in the hospital, remember?"

"Amber, are you mad at me?"

She turned to him slowly. It wasn't even worth it to admit that she was mad and hurt that he wasn't taking her side. "No. I'm fine."

And as clueless as most guys often were, Trace seemed to believe it. He nodded and put his hands in his pockets. When he spoke again, his tone was soft.

"Okay. Do you want me to come with you at least?"

"To the hospital?" She arched a perfectly tweezed eyebrow. "Absolutely not."

"Why not?" he asked. "I'm your boyfriend, and I want to be supportive. And I was looking forward to spending time with you today. Besides. I think your mom likes me."

Amberly rolled her eyes. Her mom hardly even knew that Trace existed. She had spent most of the past six months completely out of it.

She continued getting ready to leave and didn't say anything to him. He followed her around the house like a puppy.

"Trace, I'm *fine*," Amberly tried. She walked outside the house, and Trace followed. Despite realizing the TV was still on, she didn't bother to turn it off. She was a glutton for punishment. So what if the cable bill was high? It wasn't as if she had a job to pay for the bill on it anyway.

"Okay," Trace still pressed, "how about this: let me at least walk you?"

She locked the front door and tried to pretend as if she hadn't heard him. But when she turned away, he was staring at her intently.

"It'll make me feel better if you let me," he continued. "I don't like you walking around this town alone. Especially with..." He trailed off so that he could look around them as if he was making sure nobody could overhear. Then he looked back at Amberly and finished the sentence. "Especially with Rezin around." His voice was a whisper.

She was silent for a moment. Then finally, she caved. "Fine."

But the only reason she agreed to it was that Trace was right about one thing. It was probably dangerous to be out on her own with Rezin, who could be lurking around any corner. Who could be waiting to make his next attack at any moment?

Satisfied, Trace threw his arm over her shoulder and they descended the steps of her porch together. She could sense that Trace thought the argument was resolved and that things were going to be just fine between them now.

But Amberly didn't feel that way at all.

4

There were no nurses in the hospital room when Amberly went to go see her mother again after exchanging an awkward, stiff goodbye hug with Trace outside.

"Hi, Mom," Amberly said with a sigh as she sat down in her usual spot beside her bed. She couldn't tell if her mother was asleep or sedated.

Her mother didn't answer her.

"I'm sure you're tired," Amberly said, opting to believe that she was just asleep. She needed her rest if she was going to get better. "So I'll just talk. Keep you distracted. Um...cheer practice was horrible today."

Would she really be telling her mom all of this if she was awake? Would she be admitting that she felt like that? As if she had failed at practice? Let people down? It wasn't normally the sort of confession Amberly would have made to anyone. Even her mom.

Still, she continued. "I was completely distracted. Everybody noticed it. And Mom, there's this annoying, stuck-up, goody-two-shoes, plant-loving brat that has decided it's okay to sit at our lunch table. People judge me for it! I mean, can you even believe her audacity?"

Every time she thought back to it, it only made her think about Trace and how unsupportive he had been when she complained about all of this to him.

"It's because she's seeing Kire and Hunter," she told her mother, making a face. "Yeah. *The* Kire Hunter."

Her mother's hand twitched. But that was it.

Amberly held onto it, deciding to take it as a signal. That was what her mother wanted, just to feel her daughter's touch. To feel that her daughter was really sitting there next to her and that she wasn't just having a dream about her being there.

"I'm here, Mom," she said sadly. She wished her mother would just open her eyes and say something to her. She wished she could talk to her about what Kire had told her at school earlier, too. But she couldn't bring herself to admit it. Her mother had warned her that Gerald Hunter didn't care about her. That no matter what Amberly tried to do about it, it wouldn't change.

And go figure. Her mother had been right.

Amberly rested her chin on the side of her mother's bed. She wasn't quite sure what else to talk about. And she felt exhausted. Her eyes started drifting closed, but the moment they were fully shut, some buttons started mechanically beeping on the machines on the other side of her mother's bed.

Amberly snapped her eyes back open and looked around. Was a nurse or a doctor coming in? All those beeps didn't sound good. And her mother, even though her eyes were still closed, had her face scrunched up like she was in distress.

Amberly shot up and ran out into the hall. "Is somebody coming?" she hissed loudly. And she could see as she spoke, that somebody was already on their way in, walking at a brisk pace. Amberly tried to follow her back into the room, but the woman stopped her.

"I'm just going to have you wait out here."

Then she went in and closed the door in Amberly's face.

As she stood there, tears streaming down her face because she didn't know what was happening to her mom, more doctors rushed in and out. A "code blue" was called over their speaker system, but Amberly didn't know what it meant. Not until she was ushered into a private waiting room with just her inside of it. Did Amber become fully aware that something was deeply, deeply wrong.?

She didn't sit in the waiting room. She paced profusely until someone finally came in and talk to her. It was an older male doctor with kind eyes. Kind eyes that Amberly didn't want to see right now. She just wanted to see her mother.

"What happened?" she asked immediately, storming up to him. "How is she?"

He hung his head. "I'm afraid your mother's heart stopped. We were able to bring her back. But she's on a ventilator."

"A ventilator? Why?"

"She's having trouble breathing on her own. She's just very sick right now."

"Can I go see her?"

"In just a few more minutes."

The lump in her throat was huge. *A ventilator.* That had to be bad. Her heart had stopped. That meant she... she *died* for a moment?

"Oh God," she breathed out, sinking into a chair.

"Is there anything I can get you?" the doctor asked. "Is there anybody I can call?"

She shook her head. There was nothing she could demand to make this better. Not unless any of these doctors had the magical ability to make her mother able to breathe on her own again.

The doctor timidly patted her on the shoulder and then left her alone again.

IT WAS WELL into the night, and Amberly was still at the hospital with her mom. It was horrible seeing her on the ventilator. She had googled it. The ventilator meant she was on life-support. She sat at the side of her mom's bed again and put her head in her hands. Things really couldn't get much worse. Why were they turning in this direction instead of getting better? Why did this have to be happening to her? Why her?

When a nurse came in a few moments later, she messed with some stuff on all of the poles next to her mom's bed and Amberly could feel her side-eyeing her every so often.

"We don't know for sure, but she might be able to hear you," the woman finally said. "It might be worth it to talk to her a little. So you can let her know that you're here supporting her. To maybe encourage her a little."

Then the nurse disappeared.

"Can you hear me in there?" Amberly asked curiously. She scooted her chair closer so that her mouth could be a little bit closer to her mom's ear as if that would somehow help. "Can you tell that I'm still here, Mom? That I'm not going anywhere?" As she spoke to her, more tears trailed down her cheeks. She didn't want to cry anymore, but there was no way to stop it. She was terrified.

"You can't go, okay?" Amberly tried. "You have to be all right. You have to make it through this. I... I can't be here without you. You're all I have."

When Amberly said that last sentence, something tugged in her chest. It was as if she was getting a gentle nudge from someone. A gentle reminder that maybe that sentence wasn't entirely true. Her mother wasn't *all* she had. Sure, she was the most important one. But she wasn't the only one.

Amberly pulled out her cell phone. She couldn't believe she was about to do this. But she felt helpless. She felt that she couldn't do this alone. That she wasn't strong enough to handle it. She had had such high hopes that when she returned to the hospital today, it would be for good news. It would be to her mom looking healthier and happier.

But that wasn't the case.

"Trace?" she said into her cell phone when her boyfriend answered her call.

"What's going on, Amber?" Trace asked in a gentle voice that made her instantly break down into tears. It was something she rarely did in front of him. But there wasn't any time for her to even be embarrassed about it now. She told him what was going on, then she told him she needed his support, and she asked him to assemble the rest of the gang.

Maybe it was like Trace had told her earlier. Maybe they were all stronger together.

TRACE, Kaos, Kire, and Rose raced into Amberly's mother's hospital room all at the same time. Kaos must have picked them all up in his car. Amberly noticed that he must've been rather quick about it, too, because it hadn't been that long since she had made the phone call to Trace. It made her feel affection toward her boyfriend and her good friend.

Trace hugged her first. Then Kaos wrapped his arms around her too. Kire and Rose, who were not close with Amberly like that, hung back and gave her friendly smiles. Amberly didn't enjoy the idea of Rose being there with the others, but she was trying to keep in mind that the whole crew had to be together for them to be at their strongest. Amberly wanted to feel stronger. Strong enough to deal with what was happening with her mother.

"Thanks for coming," she said. Visiting hours were long over, but she had worked her charm; in other words, she threw a *gigantic* hissy fit and her friends had been allowed to come.

"I'm so sorry about your mom," Rose said to her, looking over at Elizabeth.

"I'm sorry that you have to deal with this," Kaos joined in.

Amberly sat in her seat as the others stood around.

"Her... her heart stopped," Amberly said, unable to bring herself to look at any of them.

"We can stay as long as you need us to," Kaos said.

"Do you want any of us to go get you something?" Rose asked, her maternal instinct kicking in. "Have you had anything to eat?" I can run to a vending machine or get you some coffee, maybe.

Don't do something to make me sort of start to like you.

"I'm fine," she replied curtly.

Rose nodded and pursed her lips shut. Then the gang decided to get her attention off of things by talking about other stuff. Stuff completely unrelated to what was going on with her mom. Trace had a way of almost making Amberly feel, just for a moment, that she wasn't even in the hospital dealing with her mother being on life-support at all.

5

Things only got worse. There was another episode where Amberly's mother's monitors started beeping wildly again. Then all of the teenagers were rushed out of the room and sent to that private waiting room Amberly had been in earlier.

Amberly was numb. She sat frozen as a statue in the waiting room chair as she waited to hear what the news was this time. Why was it that even with the ventilator, her mother's heart was still not cooperating?

The gang all tried to comfort her as best as they could. Trace even got so worried at one point that he gently shook Amberly and asked if she could even hear him. Then Kaos told him to back off. All the while, Amberly sat there and said nothing. What could she say? What could she do? She felt as if she was in complete shock.

Eventually, the doctor came in and told her a whole bunch of mumbo-jumbo that she didn't understand. The only thing she did comprehend was the fact that her mother's heart had stopped yet again. And that they had brought her back yet again.

They were still in the waiting room a little while after that when Trace tried to lighten the mood. "She's going to have a cool story to tell people when she gets better," he said. "I doubt many people who have had their heart stop twice get the chance to talk about it."

He was sitting across from Amberly in the chair. He reached out and playfully nudged her knee, seeming desperate to get her to smile.

She glanced up at him to show that she acknowledged that he was there, but that was all she could do.

When the nurse walked back into the room to tell them they had *the okay* to go visit her mom again, Amberly didn't get out of her chair as the others did.

"Don't you want to go see her?" Kire asked.

Amberly shook her head. "I just... I don't think I can do it right now."

"This room is all yours," the nurse said as she stood in the doorway. "Feel free to come and go from it as you need. You just go see her whenever you're ready. Okay?"

Amberly nodded her head slowly. The other sat back down. It was probably better for them to stay here anyway. At least they had somewhere they could sit, and they didn't have to feel uncomfortable with her unconscious mother just a foot away from them.

She took a deep breath and leaned her head back in her chair. She closed her eyes, just wanting to focus on her breathing and on relieving her anxiety.

When she opened her eyes again, suddenly, she was no longer in the waiting room of the hospital. She wasn't anywhere that was familiar. She was on a cliff side. A cliff side of a mountain she had never seen before. It was cold and it was windy, and she was so high up in the sky that when she looked over the edge, all she could see below were clouds.

"What's happening?" she asked herself as she spun around in circles, trying to piece together how she got there. "Where... where am I?"

"Hello, Amberly."

The voice was so loud. It echoed through her ears and nearly made them ring. It was as if this voice was emitting through a speaker the size of one at a rock concert. It was as if no matter where she ran and tried to hide, she would still be able to hear it just as loudly.

Rezin was everywhere.

Her blood ran cold. "What is this?" she demanded. Her voice was shaky and her knees were wobbly. "Where did you take me? Where is my mom?" She couldn't deal with this right now. Her mom needed her.

"Here, I can make you do whatever I want you to." Rezin's voice seemed to carry on as if he hadn't heard a word she had just said to him. "Here, whatever I want to happen, happens."

"Take me back," she ordered in a careful voice. "Just... stop." She didn't have her gauntlet. Gamora wouldn't be able to help save her in this situation. Especially since none of the other Quintets were here to help her either.

Her feet rose into the air. She screamed. Then she felt herself flying back. She landed on the ground hard on her side, a rock digging into her. She rolled a little way before she was able to stop herself from rolling right off the edge of the cliff.

How is he doing this?

She stood herself back up. "Where are you?" she demanded. She at least wanted to be able to see her attacker. To see which way she needed to run or which way she needed to fight.

"That was easy." Rezin's voice commented.

"Bring me back," she demanded again. She knew her effort was futile. Why would Rezin ever give in to any of her requests?

"What if there's nowhere to bring you back to you?" Rezin asked.

Some fog ahead of her parted, and through it, she could see a bed. She thought it strange. Why was there a bed that high up on a mountain?

And who was that lying on it?

Amberly stepped toward it. The fog cleared more and she saw her mother, still on the ventilator, looking weaker than ever.

"Mom!" she called out. Her mother shouldn't be up here. She needed to be in a hospital where she could get the care that she needed.

Now that she knew it was her, Amberly changed her timid walk to a sprint to get to her mom's bedside.

But the moment it seemed like her mother was within her reach, the bed moved as if on its own accord. It slid away from her, toward another cliff edge.

"No!" she screamed, reaching a hand out pointlessly. There was no way for her to stop Rezin.

"Oh, come on, Amberly McHenry. Don't you want me to put her out of her misery?" Rezin's voice asked. "Before she is forced to face matters far, far worse than this?"

"Leave her alone!" Amberly bellowed.

"At least here, she's comfortable in a hospital bed. At least here, she'll go peacefully." Rezin didn't seem to hear what Amberly was saying to him, or he just didn't care.

Then suddenly, the bed was in the air. It levitated there, and Amberly ran to her mother and jumped as high as she could, but she couldn't reach her.

Rezin chuckled darkly. "Time to say your goodbyes, Amberly."

A hard shaking made Amberly's eyes snap open.

She was back in the hospital waiting room. But all of the Quintets were standing around her with wide, alarmed expressions on their tired faces.

Kaos has been the one shaking her. "Amberly!"

"What?" Amberly asked, feeling out of it as she looked around the room. At least she had only been dreaming. What happened with Rezin hadn't been real.

"Something's going on in your mom's hospital room again," Kaos said urgently.

"A lot of doctors ran in there," Kire joined in.

"*What*?" Amberly got to her feet. She practically shoved her way through her friends and ran out into the hall. She turned the corner and could see through the small window outside of her mom's ICU room. There were about six people in there. They were all moving quickly.

Until suddenly, they weren't.

Amberly watched as the doctor in the white lab coat hung his head.

"Amberly!" one of her friends called behind her. Then they were all at her side. They were there to catch her as she collapsed into them. She knew what had just happened in that hospital room.

She knew her mother had just died.

"Rezin did this," she said in a strange, unfamiliar, high-pitched tone that she didn't recognize. "Rezin...he killed her!"

She began sobbing as her friends tried to help her back to her feet. None of them knew what to say, but she knew she sounded crazy, that dream she had just had. It must've been real after all. Rezin was able to do whatever he wanted. He had told Amberly to say her goodbyes, and then when she opened her eyes, her mother was dying.

She didn't care what anyone else said. She knew the truth. Her mother's death was Rezin's fault.

6

___

Amberly was slowly, slower than the pace at which a snail moves, unpacking a suitcase that sat atop the squeaky mattress of a white iron-framed bed. She was taking all of her clothes and either hanging them up in a small closet or folding them and tucking them away in an empty dresser. She was in an unfamiliar room. It had been three days since her mom passed away. Her aunt had arrived in town. Her name was Lydia, and she was her mother's only sister. Amberly had only met the woman twice in her life, and both instances had been when she was extremely little. Her mother and her aunt never got along with each other, and whenever Amberly tried to ask her mom about it, her mother would never tell her the reason why, and then she would demand that Amberly drop the subject.

Amberly hadn't known what would happen to her after her mom died. She had never expected it to be her aunt who had to come to her rescue.

They were still in Amberly's hometown of Montgomery, just a couple of neighborhoods away from where she normally lived, in a rental that her aunt had got for them. Lydia had told Amberly that she didn't want to make anything harder than it needed to be and that since she worked from home, she had the flexibility to not have to make Amberly pack up all of her belongings and head to Wisconsin to live with her.

"There's nothing to see or do in my town, anyway," her aunt had said to her when they first met. "And nothing was keeping me there either."

Amberly hadn't talked to the woman much yet. She wasn't interested in getting to know her, for one. If her mother didn't like her, then why should she? And two, she was too devastated about her mother's sudden passing, and too busy feeling like it was all her fault, to really want to put in any effort to do anything. She hardly even had the effort to unload her suitcase. She'd been at this rental for two nights already. Her aunt hadn't let her spend a single day alone in her house before she was forced to leave it and come here.

There was a soft knock on her door, which was cracked open, and then her aunt Lydia peeked her head inside her room. She was very pretty, with blonde hair a little bit lighter than Amberly's.

Amberly assumed it was the result of getting it colored weekly at the salon. Her eyes were green instead of blue, but they shined brightly, especially when she smiled and showed her perfectly straight white teeth. She was younger than her mother had been, but she still looked very similar to her at least, similar to when her mother had been healthy all the same.

"Amberly?" she asked in a light tone. "You've been in here a while, and I just wanted to check in."

Amberly said nothing and continued unpacking.

So her aunt continued. "You started unloading your stuff! That's great."

Still, Amberly pretended that is if she wasn't even there.

"Well... I'll have dinner ready soon if you'd like to come down and have some. We could also..."

The only reason Amberly turned to acknowledge her this time was because of the way she had trailed off in her speech. What was it she was hesitant to tell Amberly they could *also* do?

Her aunt swallowed before she continued. "We could maybe talk a little more about her funeral."

Amberly's stomach rolled violently. There was no way she was going to want dinner. She didn't want to plan her mother's funeral. That would only make it more real.

"I know it seems soon," her aunt said. "But these things tend to move relatively quickly. The funeral home can only hold her body for so long."

"*Okay*," Amberly said dramatically. Saying the words "her body" had taken it too far. Amberly had heard enough. She just wanted to get her aunt out of what was apparently her new room.

"Just let me know if you need anything." Lydia gave her a sad smile before she left Amberly alone again.

Amberly hadn't gone to school since her mother died. She had hardly talked to anybody. Sure, her friends had called and texted her, but nobody knew where she went. No one knew she was with her aunt. Amberly was keeping everyone very much in the dark about it. She wasn't ready to talk, and she wasn't sure when she would be.

That short conversation with her aunt Lydia had taken it out of her. Amberly stopped unloading her suitcase and flung herself down on the bed next to it. Her hair sprawled out all around her as she crossed her hands over her stomach and stared at the ceiling. *Her body.*

She thought about how weird that statement was. How you only referred to somebody like that when they were dead. You wouldn't just say, "Her body is upstairs in bed," to refer to somebody who was simply just taking a nap. *Her body* meant she was dead. Her mom was dead.

Amberly was exhausted but couldn't go back to sleep. It was nearly impossible to get any rest. Because of her exhaustion, it was nearly impossible for her to move, and for her to think. Sometimes, she felt like she had to remind herself to even breathe.

She sucked in a deep breath then and forced herself to sit up.

She picked her phone up off the bleached wooden nightstand beside her bed and saw the new texts coming in. Things like Trace saying, *Please just let me know you're OK,* and *I'm so worried about you, Amberly.*

There were also texts from Kaos saying, *I'm here for you, whatever you need.*

She was certain that the news had spread like wildfire through the school about her mother's death. She also had a ton of text messages from people she had never talked to, giving their condolences and asking if they could attend the funeral in support of her. To those, she didn't even bother to reply.

Eventually, Amberly made her way down the small hallway into the dining room and then into the kitchen. Her aunt had been right about dinner almost being finished. She was just pouring what looked like a pasta dish into a serving platter when Amberly walked in. The smell of garlic bread wafted in through her nose. Her stomach growled in reaction, but still, she didn't feel like eating.

Lydia smiled at her, and together they set the table, even though it was just the two of them eating. Amberly plopped some pasta onto her plate and pushed it around with her fork. She'd at least let her aunt think she was trying.

"Look," Lydia said after a while of silence. "I can't imagine how hard all of this is for you. If you want me to do everything, to take care of the funeral and all of it, I will. You just say the word. I just don't want you to think I've stepped in and taken over. Just because, well, you knew her best. You would know what she would want." Amberly nodded stiffly.

"Would it be okay if I went over some of my ideas? I've had to help plan a few funerals before, with mom and dad."

"Sure."

And so her aunt talked. She used a gentle, almost soothing voice that sounded nothing like the phlegm-filled one that her mom used when she got sick. Also, unlike her mom, Lydia didn't have to constantly stop coughing every twenty seconds. It almost made the house feel quieter not to hear it ringing in her ears.

But Amberly didn't need quiet. She needed her mother.

She listened to Lydia speak and nodded her head when necessary and said a simple yes or no whenever she asked her questions about funeral stuff. About how her mom would want everything done. When it was clear she wasn't going to eat, Lydia tilted her head and smiled sweetly. "You don't have to eat, Amberly."

Grateful, she pushed the plate away.

"I'll leave this in the microwave for a little while longer in case you change your mind. The leftovers will be in the fridge."

A tapping noise on the window to Amberly's right made her aware that it was pouring outside. The rain was angry. The wind was heavy and loud. A tree branch kept screeching along the top of the window pane. Amberly thought it almost looked a bit like a creepy arm reaching out.

"I know it will take some time to get used to being here. But I really think it's better for you to be here than... than in that house."

"I like my house," Amberly said, still staring at the tree branch outside the window. She would much rather be there. Where it smelled like her mom and where all of her mom's things were.

"I know it's what you're used to, but Amberly, that house is old and dirty. I honestly think it would just make you sadder to be forced to stay in it. Think of this as a way for you to have a fresh start. If you want it."

"Can I go to bed now?"

Her aunt looked disappointed. It was clear she didn't want Amberly to go. But anyway, she nodded her head yes. Amberly leaped out from her chair and quickly retreated into her bedroom. She didn't want a fresh start; she didn't want to be in this house. She didn't much want to be *anywhere*. The more she thought about it, the more she wasn't opposed to the idea of Rezin and Yash ending the world. What was the world anyway, without her mother in it?

7

Then Amberly woke up one particularly dreary, dark, cloudy day; it wasn't just the weather that was making her not want to get out of bed. It wasn't that she was overly comfortable on her springy mattress underneath her too-lightweight comforter, either. She just hardly had the energy to get out of bed because today was a hard, hard day. Probably one of the hardest days she was ever going to experience in her life. Almost as hard as the day she actually lost her mother.

Because today was her mother's funeral, today was the day they would be laying Elizabeth McHenry to rest.

Amberly's alarm had gone off several times, and she had hit SNOOZE for all of them. But she hadn't hit SNOOZE so she could go back to sleep. She kept hitting SNOOZE so that she could stare at her ceiling a little bit longer and try to get herself to stop crying. She didn't want her aunt to see her like this. She didn't want *anybody* to see her like this. She wanted to be calm and collected and put together when it was time to go to her mother's service. People from her school would be there, after all. And as queen of the school, it was important that she didn't look vulnerable. She didn't want anybody thinking they had a chance to swoop in and take her spot. Being on top of the school was the only thing she felt she could keep controlling. So she needed to do just that.

Amberly knew her aunt wanted her out of bed at a specific time so that they could get to the venue early. But even as Amberly continued to hit the SNOOZE button on her alarm and not get up, her aunt didn't come to her door to bang loudly on it and tell her to get up and move. Lydia seemed to understand what a hard day it was going to be for Amberly and that she was going to need a little extra time to get herself ready and out the door.

How did anyone ever make it through getting ready for their own mother's funeral? Especially as a teenager?

Aunt Lydia did, however, come to the door with a soft knock as Amberly was slowly starting to get dressed in her all-black ensemble a little while later.

"Amberly?" she asked on the other side of the door. "Are you awake yet in there?"

"I'm getting changed," Amberly said, her voice more snappy than she wanted it to be. Aunt Lydia was talking in such a sweet, gentle tone. Amberly didn't know why she was being so harsh with her. She knew her aunt's sole purpose for being here was to help Amberly now that her mother was no longer around to do so. But Amberly still couldn't stop thinking about the fact that her mother and her aunt never seemed to get along. And Amberly heavily disliked that she was living with this strange, unfamiliar woman when she didn't even know the reason why.

"Okay," Aunt Lydia replied, still using the same gentle voice. "Um, there's no rush, but somebody is at the door to see you."

"Who?" Amberly asked, zipping up the back of her dress.

"Oh… he didn't give me a name. Do you want me to go ask?"

Even though Amberly hadn't given her new address out to anybody yet, she figured word would've gotten out by now about where she was residing. Everybody in Montgomery always noted when a new person came to town. And everybody did everything they could to figure out why that new person was here, too. They were an awfully, nosy bunch of people. It was a miracle no one had seemed to find out about the Unlikely Defenders yet, or about all of the secrets that lay in the White Forest.

Amberly knew it was a boy at the door, so she assumed it was Trace, finally here to demand that she speak to him in person instead of just giving him vague text responses anytime he tried to check in on her. Was she ready to talk to him in person yet?

It didn't matter if she was or not. She didn't seem to have any choice. Now that Trace knew where she lived, it was unlikely that he was ever going to leave her alone. She could tell just in the texts he sent her *alone* how worried he was about her. It was sweet, but she didn't really care to be worried about it.

"No, it's fine," she told her aunt. "I'll be at the door in just a moment."

She heard the sound of her aunt's retreating footsteps. She hadn't done her makeup yet, so she swiped her eyelashes with some mascara and quickly put her hair in a side braid. Then she walked out of her new room then went to go see Trace at the door.

To Amberly's surprise and confusion, it wasn't Trace at the door after all.

It was Kire Hunter.

He looked out of sorts, standing there on her new doorstep like that. He looked as if he wasn't sure if he was at the right place or if he should even be there at all. Amberly wasn't sure, either.

"Kire?" she asked, crinkling her nose at him.

"Wh-what the heck are *you* doing here?"

He had his hands behind his back, and at first, Amberly thought nothing of it. Not until wordlessly, he removed his hands and revealed that he was holding a slightly crumpled brown paper bag. He slowly held it out for her to take from him.

"Here," he said simply as he did so.

Amberly stared at it and was afraid to touch it. Afraid of all the contents that might have been inside of it. "What is this?" she demanded.

"Just take it. Look inside and you'll see."

"Do I even want to know?" Still, Amberly felt distrustful. She noted how Kire was wearing all black and had his hair gelled differently than he normally kept it at school. She decided he looked more put-together than she had ever seen him. Like he was getting ready to go to a school dance or something. But then it dawned on her that there was no school dance to go to. That Kire was planning on going to the funeral in support...of *her*.

"I think you *do* want to know," he replied to her. So carefully, she took the bag out of his hands and unraveled the top of it so that she could peer inside and view its contents. What she saw made her intake a quick breath.

"What the heck?" she gasped.

"Told you so," Kire said in response. When she glanced up at him, she thought that there was the slightest hint of a smirk on his lips.

She looked back down inside the bag. She could not believe what her eyes were beholding. "What is this, Kire?" she asked quietly. Was this some kind of trick? A joke? Something he had collected from some charity to help pay for the funeral costs? How had anyone even known she needed financial help?

Inside the bag was cash. A giant stack of it, from what she could tell. Not only did she see $20 bills, but she also saw $50 bills and $100 bills.

"In light of recent events, I think our father has had a slight change of heart," Kire explained, itching the back of his neck. "He still doesn't exactly want to be involved in your life, Amberly. But I really do think this should at least help a little."

This was from Gerald Hunter? Her father?

Amberly opened and closed her mouth repeatedly. She didn't know what to say. She normally would have said something smart to Kire about how she didn't need a stupid handout, and she would have told him somewhere *else* he could stick that money...

But things were different now. After all, this had been one of the reasons she wanted her dad to acknowledge her existence in the first place. To get the financial security she and her mother had longed to have. And now here she was, finally receiving it. Apparently, all it took was for her mother to pass away for her to get it."

She closed up the top of the bag and stood up straighter. She would take the money with dignity.

"Oh, "she said, her nose in the air. "Well, then. Thank you for bringing it by."

Kire nodded like it was no big deal. "There's more where that came from," he assured her.

Would she be getting more than just this?

"Good," she said simply.

Kire scanned the front porch and the view he could see behind Amberly into the house. "This is a much better place than where you were, Amberly."

She felt insulted and slightly embarrassed, but she didn't have it in her to do anything about it. Besides, Kire had a sincere look in his eyes.

"Are you doing okay?" he asked her.

Kire Hunter being sweet and considerate to her... It was revolting. Certainly, not something Amberly thought she would ever get used to.

"You're the first person that's been here," she said, not really knowing why, and she definitely did not want to answer his question.

"Oh. Well, everyone's been talking about it. Saying that you are living with your aunt now?"

"It's true. That woman you spoke to is my Aunt Lydia."

"Good. I wondered what would happen to you after..."

There was an awkward silence for a moment that hovered in the air between them, but then Amberly cleared her throat. "Speaking of which. Are you coming to the service?"

"I... I was planning on it. I didn't know how you would feel about it, so I was also going to ask you if it was okay. Rose would like to come, too. To pay her respects."

"It's fine," she decided. "So many people who haven't asked my permission are going to be there anyway. The more the merrier." Her tone was flat as she spoke. She wanted to make sure the sarcasm she was using was evident.

He smiled softly. "Great then. I'll see you there."

She awkwardly waved goodbye and closed the door, then she leaned up against it. She couldn't believe it finally happened. After all these years, she was finally getting somewhere with her father. Sure, he didn't want to see her or be a part of her life, but she was finally getting the financial support she desperately needed and definitely deserved.

8

As beautiful as the service for her mother was, Aunt Lydia had really done a wonderful job putting it together; Amberly had a hard time enjoying it and appreciating it to the fullest because of what a nervous wreck she was.

Eventually, the time had come for her to stand up from her seat and walk over to the podium. She had to stand in front of the massive crowd that had gathered to give their condolences and pay their respect to Amberly and her mother. She had to stand in front of them all, and she had to say a few words. If she could dance and shake her booty in front of the entire school wearing a promiscuous outfit, then talking to a room full of people should have been an easy task. That's what she tried to tell herself anyway as she made the seemingly never-ending walk over to the podium. She didn't even have anything prepared. She hadn't written anything down. She hadn't wanted to. Because writing down a speech for her mother's funeral made it feel much too real. But nothing would feel more real than this did.

She cleared her throat as a microphone gave a bit of feedback while she stood at the podium, scanning the audience and seeing everyone who had attended. Among them, she could see the rest of the Unlikely Defenders. Trace looked handsome in his button-down and slacks, Kaos looked the same as he always did because he always wore all black, Kire was still wearing the same suit he had been in when he showed up at her house earlier, and Rose was wearing a floor-length black skirt and a black lace blouse. Amberly was slightly surprised Rose wasn't wearing something covered in flowers with vibrant spots of green. She even looked hard to make sure it really was black that she was wearing and not just a deep, deep shade of green. Her signature color.

Amberly shook her head quickly. She needed to focus. All of these people were waiting for her to say something, "*Short and sweet*," she told herself.

"Thank you all for coming," she started, like other people who had spoken into the microphone before she had done. "My mother would have so loved to see all of your faces in one room like this. It's unfortunate that she didn't have the time, health, or energy to have a get-together like this so that she could see all of you and talk to all of you before she went." Amberly could feel that familiar lump in her throat that seemed as if it hadn't left since her mother passed. But she would not cry in front of everyone. She would be strong, just like her mother would want her to be. "My mom was a wonderful lady. She raised me all by herself. And I don't know about you, but I think she did a pretty good job."

There were some smiles and scattered clapping around the room. She was glad to see that they all seemed in agreement about her statement. Not that this was really the time or place for them not to.

"She worked hard her whole life. So hard that oftentimes, I felt that I was missing out on really getting the chance to have her as my mother. She didn't have time to spend with me because she was busy working. And then when she got sick, *I* didn't have the time to spend with *her* because *I* was working. I wish more than anything that in her last few months, I had gotten to be around more. I wish I had gotten to be by her side more. I love her very much and... I guess I'll just say that I cannot wait until we are finally reunited again in the future, however far away that may be."

That was it. That was all she had in her. The tears were going to fly out of her eyes if she continued. So she simply stepped down from the podium and bowed her head slightly to signal that she was done. The crowd applauded and some wiped their eyes with tissues. When she sat back down, she pretended to be digging around in her purse for something so that she could let her hair fall in front of her face and quickly wipe the tear that had fallen.

AT THE RECEPTION that followed the funeral, countless people came up to Amberly to tell her how sorry they were, and to tell her they loved her short speech and that she had looked beautiful up there on the podium. She appreciated their words but didn't want to talk to a bunch of people she didn't care for. All she wanted to do was be around Trace and Kaos, but there never seemed to be an opportune time for her to make her way over to them as they sat at their round table eating the finger sandwiches and other hors d'oeuvres that had been laid out for them.

At one point, when a member of the Quintets finally did get to come up to Amberly, it wasn't any of the ones she wanted to talk to.

It was Charlie Rose who had approached her.

"Hi, Amberly," she said in a friendly, quiet voice.

"Oh. Hi, Rose."

"I'm really sorry again about your mom," she said. "Thank you for letting me be here. I know we haven't always been on the best terms..."

"Yeah. It's whatever." Had she been expecting Amberly to say that they were on better terms now? Because that wasn't about to happen. Not today. Maybe not ever.

"Um..." Rose looked down at her feet, cleared her throat, and tucked some of her hair behind her ear. When she looked back up and met Amberly's gaze, she seemed nervous about something. "There was something kinda unrelated to all of this that I wanted to talk to you about while I had a moment of your privacy."

"Something you want to talk about *now*?" Amberly asked, looking around them as if she was trying to get Rose to realize and remember where they were. There were still a lot of people that were waiting to talk to her about her mother and the funeral service they had just been at.

"I know, I know. But I won't take long," she said.

"Fine." Amberly crossed her arms and couldn't believe Rose's audacity. "What is it?" She could only imagine that Rose wanted to say something to her about the lunch table situation. And she thought the girl couldn't have picked a more inappropriate time to do so.

"It's about the money that you're getting," she blurted out quickly. "From Kire and *your* dad."

Amberly's eyes widened. She was surprised and a little annoyed, if she was being honest, that Rose knew about this. "What?" she snapped.

"Kire told me about it. That your dad wants to give you money to help with everything now that you don't have your mom around. But... something is fishy about it, Amberly. I don't think you should accept it."

"Are you kidding me?"

"Have you seen the way Kire's been acting? The way he's been moving around? He seems like he's in pain. I... I haven't been able to get it out of him directly, Amberly, but I think Gerald beat him for confronting him about you. I think he's hurt."

Amberly stepped closer to Rose and lowered her voice to a venomous whisper. "Of all days, Rose. You had to turn this into something that's about someone else *today*? Are you kidding me?"

"I just asked."

"No," Amberly interrupted harshly. "Not today, Charlie Rose. If there was ever a time for you to seriously mind your own business and butt out, it would be today. Got it?"

"I'm sorry, Amberly, but..."

"Get out of my face," she demanded. "Now."

Rose gave her one last desperate, helpless look, then she turned on her heel and scampered back off to Kire and the others.

The reception went on, and as Amberly talked to other people that resided in the town of Montgomery, she did her best to ignore what Charlie had told her. There was no way it was true. Kire would've told her if Gerald had hit him. Rose just wanted to create drama for no reason. She couldn't bear to have attention on Amberly.

That had to be it.

Now. If only Amberly could get rid of this new strange feeling she suddenly had in her gut that refused to leave.

9

Amberly wasn't certain that she was ready to go back to school when the time finally came at the start of the new week. Sure, when she looked in the mirror, she knew she *looked* ready. She looked fabulous, even. She was wearing a snakeskin skirt with sheer tights and black, furry boots along with a soft off-the-shoulder gray long-sleeve with a black coat over her shoulders. Her hair was freshly blow-dried and it shined brilliantly. Her makeup was done expertly, and she looked like a million bucks.

Now, if only she *felt* like a million bucks, too.

As she looked at herself in the mirror, she tried to think about if her mother was still there. What would she say to her if she saw Amberly in this outfit headed to school?

"You look absolutely beautiful," Elizabeth McHenry would've said. "Stunning. Gorgeous. The most beautiful girl at St. Bernard High. I'm absolutely sure of it." Her mother always had a way of lifting her up. Making her feel like she was perfect. There was nobody there to do that for her now. Nobody to reassure her that the outfit choice she had picked out was a good one. To assure her that she was going to remain on top of the school and that everybody was going to wish they were her. That all of the boys were going to wish they could date her.

"You're on top of the school," Amberly decided to say to herself. If her mom couldn't be there to tell her this stuff, then maybe giving *herself* the pep talk would work. "All of the girls want to be you. And all of the boys want to date you." Then she looked at the small picture of her and Trace in a photo booth at the mall that she had pinned up on the mirror in the corner. "Not that I *want* all of the boys at school to want me. I don't want anyone else but you." Then she kissed her pointer finger and tapped it on Trace's small face in the photo. When she reevaluated herself in the mirror again, this time, she felt a little bit better. A little bit more confident and ready to take on the day.

When Amberly walked into the kitchen to grab a protein bar, something she had requested her aunt get her at the grocery store over the weekend. She saw her aunt enjoying a cup of tea at the dining table.

Aunt Lydia's eyes widened when she saw Amberly in her attire. "Wow," she said. "Would you look at you?"

"Thanks," Amberly said, flipping her hair behind her shoulder and deciding to take it as a compliment.

"You always dress like that to go to school?"

"Always."

She noticeably nodded slowly. "You know, I did see that there were a lot of people at that funeral. Way more than I thought would attend. I almost thought we were going to run out of snacks at the reception. I thought it had been your mother that was the popular one somehow. But now it's making much more sense. *You're* quite popular around Montgomery, aren't you?"

Amberly grabbed the protein bar out of the pantry and ripped it open. Then she took out a bottle of water from the fridge. "I guess you could say that," she said modestly.

"Aren't you going to be cold? Those tights don't look very... warm."

Amberly glanced out the window and saw that it was another gloomy, miserable day outside. It looked like it was sprinkling a bit, too. She shivered, just imagining how cold it was going to be outside. But she figured it was a price she paid to look this good.

"I'll be fine," she claimed.

"Do you want some tea?" her aunt asked.

"No thanks. I better be heading to school. I always like to get there early." *So that I have time to see Trace and let everybody ogle over my outfit of the day,* she wanted to add but decided not to. Her aunt didn't need to know specific details about why she made the decisions that she did.

"Oh. All right, then. I'll just be working from home all day. So please call me or text me if you need *anything.* If you're deciding that it's too soon for you to go back and you want to be picked up, you just say the word. I can get you in a heartbeat, Amberly. I mean it."

Amberly appreciated the words, but she didn't want to seem weak. "I won't need you," she said dismissively. Then she gave her aunt a quick wave and disappeared out the front door. At least in this new neighborhood, she was incredibly close to the school. The walk would take her just a couple of minutes.

Amberly hoped when she arrived at school that she would find the popular kids hanging out with each other. She didn't want to see all of the Unlikely Defenders in a group together, waiting for her arrival.

But once she arrived by the school steps, she found exactly that.

Outside of the school, in the freezing cold, the Quintets all stood around talking to each other. That instantly stopped when they saw her approaching, however. All of them turned and gaped at her as she arrived at the circle, an annoyed expression evident on her face.

"Morning," she said shortly.

"You look gorgeous," Trace said, giving her a quick hug and kiss. "I wish you would've let Kaos and I pick you up this morning. We saw the funniest thing while we were driving. Lance from Gym was riding his bike and when he checked the time on his watch he totally rode right into a tree."

"It was pretty hilarious," Kaos added.

She rolled her eyes. However, she was glad that they weren't checking in on her. She was glad they weren't giving her puppy dog eyes and asking her if she was doing okay. They were treating her like everything was back to normal. Like her mother hadn't even died. Like she hadn't been missing from school for the past few days.

"I like your jacket," Rose offered. Amberly went to answer her, but then she decided she was better off pretending she hadn't even heard her. She wanted Rose to feel like she wasn't wanted around them, at least at school. She wanted her and Kire to just disappear and go hide under a rock somewhere until they needed to do something related to saving the world.

"It's good to have you back," Kire said casually.

"True that," Amberly agreed confidently. "I'm sure you all missed me. How did the school event go on without me here?" She smiled like a princess and flipped her hair again. Trace beamed at her. Kaos chuckled. Rose and Kire stayed silent.

AT LUNCH, Amberly's luck wasn't any better. There were Kire and Rose again, sitting at their table in the cafeteria.

I guess I'm just going to have to grit my teeth and bear it.

She sat down next to Trace, nothing on her tray except for a side of Caesar salad and an unsweetened iced tea. Trace looked like he had enough on his tray to feed a small Third World country.

"Now, babe," Trace said as the entire group of teens looked at only her. "I know this isn't your ideal lunch situation, but there's actually a reason we are all sitting together today."

"There is?" Kire asked, his eyebrows crinkling.

"What is it?" she asked, peeling back the top of her Caesar salad and eating it without the dressing.

"We know you had a rough week," Kaos said. "So we sort of put things with You-Know-What on pause. But... I think we need to get back to being focused on that. Making sure Yash isn't close to arriving on Earth. In our realm. I know Halo said we have time, but we still don't know how much. And we still don't know how to go about keeping him from getting here."

"I'm sure he's not gonna be here anytime soon," Kire said quickly. It made everyone look at him.

"Did Halo say something?" Trace asked.

"Uh... no. She hasn't actually talked to me much lately. Things have been sort of... crazy."

Amberly thought briefly about what Rose had told her at her mother's funeral. *Were* things crazy at Kire's home? Were they... okay? Was he?

He's fine, Amberly, she said to herself. *Don't let Rose's words get to your head.*

"Yeah," Kaos agreed with Kire. "They have. And things will only get worse if we don't do something about it. We need to get back to being the defenders. We need to get back to figuring out how to defeat Yash."

"I'm down," Amberly said confidently. "I could use a distraction," she added when everybody gave her a surprised look. None of them had seen Amberly seem so excited at the prospect of being an Unlikely Defender before. It was the first time she had heard herself sound this way, too.

"Great," Trace said, turning to Kire again. "So, about what you were trying to show us before that weird prophet dude popped up out of nowhere in the other realm...?"

The tips of Kire's ears turned pink. "What do you mean?"

"What do you mean, what do we mean?" Kaos snapped, leaning in so that Kire could hear him more closely. "You were showing us something in a book. Remember? We've only been asking about what it was for, like, ever now?"

Kire scratched the back of his head and looked utterly clueless. "No, I don't remember."

"Are you serious?" Trace asked. He looked angry.

"Sorry, guys. But whatever was in the book, it was probably nothing important if I can't remember it."

Amberly exchanged looks with her boyfriend and Kaos. She didn't believe what Kire was saying. She didn't believe it for one moment.

Amberly decided to let Kaos give her a ride home after school that day. But she also made it very clear that he was not allowed to give Kire or Rose a ride. That it just had to be him, Trace, and her. Her reason for this was that she needed to get some alone time with them. She needed to talk to them about what had happened at lunch that day.

"I don't believe it," she said to the guys as they started their drive. She was in the front seat, next to Kaos, and Trace was in the back, sitting in the middle and leaning forward so that he could be a part of the conversation.

"I don't either," Kaos said. "It was clear he was avoiding us when we tried to ask about the book before. And now he's just claiming that he doesn't even remember what was in it at all? He's full of it."

"Want me to beat it out of him?" Trace asked, putting his fist into his hand.

"You might have to," Amberly said, not completely hating the idea.

"Or maybe not," Kaos said as he gripped the steering wheel tight and got a focused look on his face.

"What are you talking about?" Amberly asked. Since when was Kaos not in the mood for Trace to beat somebody up?

He glanced over at Amberly with a sinister smile on his face. "We know how to get back to the portal. We don't need Kire, or even Rose for that matter, in order to get back into the magical realm. We can go back to the castle and find the book for ourselves. I don't exactly remember what it looked like, but I'm sure I can figure it out. I know there was something in that book that he wanted us to see, even if he's changed his mind about it now. And I think it's up to us to figure out what it was he didn't want us to know about any longer."

"I think it's important that we figure it out," Trace said. "I think it's important to know why Kire changed his mind about it."

Amberly wasn't thrilled about the idea of traveling back into the magical realm. It had been a completely different experience being inside of it. Seeing magic and seeing all of those mythical beasts come to life. In other circumstances, it would've really been cool to be there. But with the world under fire and monsters trying to fight them at every turn, it hadn't been as cool as it could've been.

"I'm in," she said anyway. Kire could try to keep his secret all he wanted. The three of them were not going to let that happen.

10

The next day, Amberly felt as if she was about to go to a secret drug deal. It was kind of like that, anyway.

Kire had texted her and told her that he had some more money to give her from their father. And in order to do the exchange at school, Amberly requested that they meet somewhere in secret. She didn't want any of her peers to see her being handed a brown paper bag like that. She thought they would find out that she was being given money like a handout, or they would think she was doing drugs. And she couldn't have that. She didn't want anybody to find out what she was up to and how she was getting her money. Nor did she want anyone to find out that her father was Kire Hunter's father.

For the second day in a row since going back to school, Amberly made herself look fabulous. This time, instead of walking the quick journey to school, she let Kaos pick her up with Trace. She put on a happy face and acted like the queen bee she always was. Sure, a lot of the time, she thought about her mom and how much she was missing her, and it made her stomach hurt so badly that she thought she needed to run to the restroom or find a trashcan to throw up in. But she would never let anybody see that. To everyone else, she was perfectly fine.

Amberly had decided that she and Kire would make the handoff in between classes. They would go to the back of the school, out of one of the only back doors that were constantly left unlocked for kids to sneak out of class if they wanted to. Amberly got to their meeting spot first between two of their block periods. When Kire showed up, he weirdly had his hat on and was completely covered up by his long-sleeve jacket and pants. They both made sure nobody was around and then Kire pulled the brown paper bag out of his backpack and handed it quickly to Amberly, who already had her back open so that she was prepared to quickly shove it inside and zip it up. No one saw a thing. And again, Amberly had a huge wad of cash. More than she ever thought she would get if her mother formally took Gerald to court.

"We good?" Kire asked quickly, his eyes not even visible underneath his hoodie.

Amberly wasn't ready for him to leave yet.

"What's going on with you?" she asked quickly.

Kire had been turning to leave, but with her question, he stopped and turned back to her.

"What do you mean?"

"Why are you dressed like that? And why are you being so short with me?"

"Um... I think you're just being paranoid," he said to her. Amberly figured he was probably right. That she had let Rose's words get to her head just like she hadn't wanted them to. She was standing there worried that Gerald was beating him up for what he did for Amberly and that Kire just wasn't telling her about it. But if that had happened, Kire would have told her. There wouldn't be any reason for him to keep that a secret.

Still, she could remember his words when he told her that he had finally confronted his dad about knowing that she existed. *He didn't take it well.*

Then when Amberly had tried to ask him what he meant by that, he hadn't given her a good enough answer.

And now there he stood, covered head to toe in clothing with his eyes obscured. It didn't seem right.

"Amberly, we are as far away from my next class as possible. I really got to get going."

She grabbed his shoulder and prevented him from leaving yet again. Was she crazy, or had he winced when she had grabbed him?

"Wait," she said.

"What?"

"Are you okay?" It felt weird to ask the question. Since when did Amberly ask about *anyone's* well-being?

"Everything's fine, Amberly. What is with you? Since when do you ask if I'm okay?"

"I don't know," she said with a shrug.

"Is it because I'm giving you that? That money? Now you're being all nice to me?"

"Kire..."

"Don't worry. I'll have more for you next week."

"I was actually wondering," she continued quickly before he could try to leave again, "what exactly was it that made Gerald change his mind?"

"Oh..." He looked like he really didn't want to answer the question. "It's like I told you. Circumstances changed. You know."

"No, I don't know."

"Like, with your mom... and stuff. He's decided to help you. At least with money, if he can't help you in the fatherly figure aspect. But don't feel bad about that. He can't even act fatherly around *me*."

"But, Kire..."

"I seriously gotta run." He darted back inside, so Amberly followed in after him. Some of her peers and other girls on the cheerleading squad tried to say HI to her as she walked, but she ignored them. She was too focused on Kire and why he was acting so strange.

She was even more focused on him when all of a sudden, he shouted, "Hey!" at someone down the hall and then took off at a run. When Amberly looked up to see who it was he was shouting at, and what the problem was, she saw another group of girls from her cheer squad surrounding none other than Charlie Rose. They were all laughing while Rose held textbooks tightly to her chest and looked like a frightened wild animal.

Immediately, Amberly could tell what was going down. The girls were tormenting her. And as she got closer, she could hear some of the words they were saying.

"You try so hard to be cool, *Charlie*," one said. "You make everyone call you *Rose* because of your stupid boy name. And yet, you're still a loser."

"Back off," Rose said, looking like she wanted to push through the crowd but couldn't. She was trapped by them.

"You sit at Amberly McHenry's lunch table and think she and her friends actually want you there," another one said. "But they don't. And they never will."

"Leave me alone," she tried. But her voice was coming out all squeaky.

"You're just a pathetic little wannabe who will never have any friends and will never be cool," the third one said.

This was when Kire finally reached the group and inserted himself into the situation.

"Don't you guys have anything better to do? Back off of her!" he shouted at them, his face red and his eyes full of hate.

They all backed away from her and giggled some more.

"Kire to the rescue," the first cheerleader said. "What is it, Kire? What is it about Rose, here? Is she *paying* you to be with her or something?"

"Did you lose a bet?" another girl asked.

Amberly hung back, watching the scene from afar. Luckily, it didn't seem like Rose had any idea that she was standing there.

Then all of a sudden, they made direct eye contact with each other. She could see the desperate, pleading look in Rose's eyes. But yet, Amberly did nothing about it. She just simply stood there and watched.

"Mind your own business and leave us alone," Kire said to them coldly. "What is wrong with you?"

They all giggled some more, and then when they saw Amberly, they smiled and waved at her.

"Come on, Amberly!" one of them called over their shoulder, motioning for Amberly to walk with them.

Amberly knew right then and there that she had a choice. She could go and join her cheerleading squad. Or she could comfort Rose and tell her that those girls were stupid and that she should just ignore them.

But how was doing the latter going to help her stay on top of the school? After all, the cheerleaders had just been defending Amberly.

So she did what the head cheerleader was supposed to do. She went and joined the rest of her squad.

11

Amberly returned home that day and was greeted by her aunt Lydia, who was sitting at the table on her laptop, working diligently at her work-at-home job. Her hair was swept up in a loose ponytail and she was wearing comfortable-looking pajamas, and still, she looked very pretty and put together. Amber noted how when her mom spent every day at the end of her life in pajamas and with her hair up, she didn't look nearly as nice as her aunt Lydia did. It often saddened Amberly to see that, because her mom had been very pretty when she was younger, it's where Amberly had gotten the majority of her good looks from. She had seen some photos of Gerald Hunter over the years and noted that he was handsome for an older dude, but she couldn't see any of herself in him. Yet, it didn't stop her mother, Elizabeth, from mentioning how much she thought she looked like her dad.

"Hey, Amberly," Aunt Lydia said from the table, smiling brightly at Amberly as she closed the door and hung her backpack up on the hook on the wall.

Amberly was annoyed to see her aunt sitting there like that, looking happy and fine. How could she be so happy and fine when her sister just died? How could she be all cheery toward Amberly and expect her to be the same way back?

Amberly decided to hardly even look in her direction as she started making her way to her bedroom.

"Hello?" Aunt Lydia asked, her voice starting to get a little bit of attitude in it. "Amberly?"

Amberly stopped walking and turned to her.

"I said *hi*," Aunt Lydia said when they made eye contact.

"Okay... hi."

Aunt Lydia frowned. "Is everything all right?"

Amberly crossed her arms. Where would she even start it, if she were going to give an honest answer, anyway?. "Yeah. Why?"

"You just seem..."

"I'm sorry. Do I seem like my mother just died or something?" Amberly challenged.

Aunt Lydia sighed and got to her feet. "Look, I know that you having an attitude with your mother might have been okay. You might have been able to get away with it. But all I've been trying to do since I got here is help you, look after you, and make sure you're okay. I'm trying my best here, Amberly. I don't know why you're being so cold to me, and I really don't appreciate it."

Amberly had to admit to herself that she had not been expecting her aunt to confront her like that. The vibe she kind of got from her was that she was a bit of a pushover. Her mother had been a bit of a pushover, so Amberly supposed she just assumed they would be similar and that way. The way her aunt Lydia was talking to her reminded her a little bit of... herself.

"Well, *excuse* me," Amberly said, her voice full of attitude in return. "Sorry, I'm dealing with a lot and it's not easy for me to be nice and fake-cheery toward you. I don't even know you."

"I know you don't," she said. "And I'm trying to change that. I'd like us to get to know each other. I've always wanted that, Amberly. I hated that just because your mother and I didn't get along, I didn't get to be a part of your life. But I'm here now. And I want things to be different between us. Don't you? Don't you want to chance to get to know me?"

Not really.

"I don't know," she said.

"You don't know?" Aunt Lydia looked hurt. "Fine." Her voice was getting quieter. "Fine. But at least be a little more respectful to me, will you? I just wanna take care of you and help you through this hard time. That's all I'm trying to do. Just meet me halfway. Or at least a little bit."

Amberly intensely fought the urge to roll her eyes, then she nodded slowly.

"Thank you," Aunt Lydia said.

Thankful that the conversation seemed to finally be over, Amberly walked quickly into her bedroom before Aunt Lydia could say something else that required her to go back and continue their conversation.

She closed the door and leaned against the back of it. Then she let out a long slow breath.

One single tear left her eye.

She desperately missed her mother a little bit more right now than she had before.

WHEN AMBERLY WENT BACK out into the living area later that evening, she saw that her aunt Lydia was no longer there. She could hear the sounds of the shower in her bathroom running inside her room with the door closed. Thankful that she wasn't around to have another awkward confrontation with. Amberly walked over to the notebook beside her computer and went to a blank page where she scribbled a quick note:

Going to hang out with my boyfriend. Won't be late.

Then she threw on a jacket, put on some warm boots, and left the house.

The truth was, she wasn't going to visit her boyfriend, but she didn't want her aunt Lydia to know where she was really going. She didn't want Aunt Lydia to feel sorry for her when she found out that Amberly just wanted to go to the graveyard to visit her mother's headstone.

The graveyard was eerie. She had never been the kind of person who went inside one. She had driven past it many times, but she never thought she'd have any reason to go inside it. Not unless she was a part of some ridiculous high school dare.

And yet, here she was, going in through the black wrought iron gates of her own accord. No one was daring her to do this. She wanted to be here, as crazy as it felt.

The cold air mixed with the humidity created a foggy mist that floated through the atmosphere. Lights were sprinkled about here and there, only creating a glow every so often, making the graveyard otherwise incredibly dark in other patches. There were winding cement pathways and green metal benches to sit on. There were big old oak trees that seemed to hold many secrets about what they had seen at the cemetery. Amberly didn't see anybody else around, and she didn't feel comforted by that fact whatsoever. She knew maybe it would be better if she came back during daylight, but what if she felt differently tomorrow? She was sad and wanted to talk to her mom *now*.

She walked over to the plot of land where the fresh headstone had been placed. She trailed her fingers across her mother's engraved name and felt the huge lump forming in her throat.

"Hey, Mom," she said, feeling sort of like she was back in the hospital when she had been told talking to her mom might be a good idea, even if she couldn't hear her. Could her mom hear her now? Was talking to her really pointless?

She decided to believe that it wasn't.

Amberly wanted to sit down on the grass but noticed that it was damp. It was also cold out, but she didn't want to just be standing there hovering over the grave. She knew she was going to be here for a while because she had a lot of things to say to her mother. So she decided to take off her jacket, which propelled water and spread it out on the ground so that she could sit on top of it.

Then she sat down and got to talking with her mom. She filled her in on how things had been going ever since they last spoke. And how it had been living with Aunt Lydia. She asked her mother a few questions, like about what had happened between them and why they were never close, but of course, she didn't get any answers from her.

Amberly found herself completely losing track of time as she talked and talked and talked.

She was so invested in the conversation she was having with the headstone that she no longer paid attention to the ominous atmosphere around her. She didn't see the shadow slowly getting closer until it loomed over the headstone and darkened it.

Amberly's blood ran cold.

Rezin?

Gulping audibly, she slowly turned her head and nearly screamed.

But it wasn't Rezin who was hovering above her.

It was Kaos, wearing his crown and giving her a mischievous smile.

"Oh my God, *Kaos*," she said snappily, jumping to her feet. "What on earth are you doing here?"

"I *thought* that was you," he said. "I like to come here."

With his all-black ensemble that he always wore and the sinister expression that was usually on his face, it suddenly made sense to Amberly. A cemetery seemed like just the kind of place Kaos would like to hang out in his free time.

"Why?" she asked, turning her nose up at him. She hoped he couldn't tell that she had been crying while talking to her mother. She also hoped he hadn't been hearing the things that she had been saying.

He sneered right back at her. "Not that it's any of your business, but I like to practice with my crown here. I practice controlling people and reading their thoughts. And I'll have you know, I'm actually getting much better at it."

"You are?"

"Don't sound so surprised."

"I'm sorry. That's... that's great, honestly, Kaos. I know that the crown has been giving you a lot of annoyance lately."

"Whatever. Are you visiting your mom?" He seemed more than eager to change the subject.

"I... yeah," she said, knowing there was no point in lying because they were standing right in front of her mother's headstone. "I am."

"It's kind of dangerous for you to be out here alone at night, don't you think?"

"I could say the same thing about you," she replied.

"Touché. Are you okay?"

Amberly was about to quickly say yes like she always did, but something about the genuine look Kaos was giving her made her decide otherwise. "I don't know. Not really." Why would she even be visiting her mom at the graveyard this late at night if she was okay anyway?

"What's on your mind? Anything I can help with?"

"No." But then, as Amberly thought more about it, she quickly changed her mind. "Actually, maybe you can." She shivered, missing her jacket but wanting to sit back down on the ground. She did so; then she patted the small patch of jacket next to her that could easily fit Kaos's butt. He sat next to her and they had to be pretty close together for both of them to fit.

"What's up?" he asked.

"I just... I've been having kind of a hard time since my mom passed. And I thought that being the good boyfriend that he is, I would hear from Trace more. Do you... do you know why I haven't really heard from him?"

"Oh," Kaos said. "I don't know, Amberly. I would try not to think too much about it. I think he's just busy right now, you know?"

"Busy?" she asked, furrowing her brows. "Busy doing what?"

"Well, he's trying to make money. And he's trying not to flunk out of school. He's got a lot going on, just like you do."

"I don't think it's really comparable," she said.

"Maybe not," Kaos said with a shrug. "Maybe he just doesn't know how to act around you. Some people aren't really the best at being comforting about this kind of stuff."

She frowned. "And are *you* any good at it?"

Instead of answering her, Kaos got this far-away look in his eyes. He still had his crown on his head as his eyebrows clashed together and he got worried creases on his forehead.

"Kaos?" she asked.

It took him a moment before he answered. "I... I hear something," he said, suddenly leaping to his feet. He held out his hand and helped Amberly get to hers as well. "Amberly, I think I hear Rezin's voice. That means he is in the graveyard somewhere. And he's getting close."

Amberly's heart skipped a beat. "Rezin is here *now*?"

"If my crown isn't wrong, yes."

"What do we do?"

He looked around, and Amberly did, too. She couldn't see anything lit up by the small lights sprinkled about, nor could she see any shadows in the darkness.

"It's just the two of us; we're missing more than half our group. I don't think we can take him on our own. And you don't have your gauntlet with you, do you?"

"No," Amberly replied fearfully.

Kaos nodded. She could see plainly that he was also scared. "Then we need to get the heck out of here."

12

The next day, Kaos and Amberly decided that they all needed to meet at good old Aunt Marg's after school. Aunt Marg's was where they had met up a few times before, a grocery store in the front by the door that led to a large room in the back with tables and chairs where tea and cookies were often served.

Kaos had given everybody a ride after school, so they all arrived at Aunt Marg's at the same time and went into the back room, and took a seat around one of the cloth-covered tables. They were the only ones in there, as they usually were, so it provided the perfect place for them to talk about things related to Rezin and the other realm without being overheard.

"So, what is this meeting about?" Kire asked.

"Well, we need to decide something," Kaos said. "First off, I just wanted to talk to *you*, Amberly."

"What about me?" she asked, crossing her arms and holding her head high and confidently. Sure, she had been vulnerable toward Kaos yesterday, but she wasn't about to keep acting that way around him today. Today, she was back to her old self.

"How are you doing with everything? Are you ready to go back and check things out in the magical realm? We need to see how things are going over there. What the state of it is."

She hated that he was checking in on her. "I'm fine," she said. "Don't try to say that *I'm* the only reason we haven't gone back yet. I could've gone back forever ago."

"No one is saying that, Amber," Trace said, sitting beside her and reaching over to give her knee a quick squeeze. Amberly leaned away from him slightly. She was still sort of mad at him for the lack of talking they had done. Even at school today, he had seemed as if he was avoiding her and like he was too busy to talk to her. She didn't understand it.

"I'm not opposed to going back to the Albus realm," Kire said. "What about you, Rose?"

"Whatever," Rose replied.

Amberly squinted at her. Rose had her arms crossed, too, and was looking everywhere around the room except any of them. Was she seriously in a bad mood? What reason did she have for it? Because Amberly hadn't saved her yesterday? Because she was sick of getting teased at school?

Newsflash, Rose, there are bigger problems in the world.

"Yeah. I still would like to find Albus," Kire said. "It would be nice to hear from him again." He didn't even seem to realize that Rose was being snotty toward him.

"And if it seems that the world is completely destroyed, then that means that Yash is going to be trying to come over into our world at any second," Kaos said.

"I'm ready to fight," Trace said. "I've been practicing in my backyard with my sword after everyone goes to sleep."

"I've been practicing, too," Kaos said. "We all should be." Then he snuck a look at Amberly. Amberly quickly looked away from him.

"Rose, how are you doing with your powers?" Kaos asked.

"Fine," she replied.

"Rose is killing it," Kire complimented. "She's got them down.

She's getting stronger. And she'll only be stronger if we all continue to work together."

"I said I'm doing *fine* with them, Kire," she argued. "I'm not amazing or anything. You're being dramatic."

Geez. Even Amberly thought it was rude how Rose was behaving toward her boyfriend.

What was Rose's problem? *Is this girl seriously never satisfied?*

Was she still deciding to feel like an outsider even though the gang clearly decided to include her in everything, *including* their lunch?

As Amberly sat there, she found herself getting more and more annoyed with Rose.

"We also need to get back in the mindset of figuring out how to destroy Rezin," Kaos continued.

"Let's kill him," Trace said, pumping his fist into his other hand.

"I wish it was that simple," Kaos said.

"What do you mean?" Trace asked.

"Well, he never seems to exactly show himself, does he?" Kire joined in.

"Exactly," Kaos said. "In fact, just last night, Amberly and I sort of had a run-in with him."

Amberly's stomach dipped. She hadn't told Trace that she had been at the graveyard last night with Kaos. And now it was being announced to the entire group. It made her slightly irritated with Kaos because she didn't want everyone to start questioning her. Wondering what she was doing in the graveyard in the first place. She didn't want them to know that she was still mourning her mom and that she wasn't back to her normal self yet.

"What do you mean you had a run-in?" Trace asked.

"I had been practicing with my crown, and I caught wind of him," Kaos explained. "I could hear... something. I don't know exactly what it was. It wasn't like I could hear his full thoughts, but for some reason, I just knew that it was him. That he was getting closer to us. And I knew Amberly and I wouldn't be able to take him on just the two of us, so we ran for it. Luckily, we weren't attacked or anything. But it could've been bad."

"Yeah. Sounds to me like you two could've gotten yourselves killed," Kire said irritably. "This is why we're supposed to stick together and not go out at night. Don't you guys have any idea how dangerous it is?"

"He's already tormenting us in our dreams as it is," Rose said.

Was it happening to her, too?

Kire nodded.

Was it happening to him, as well?

Was Amberly, not the only one being messed with in her dreams?

"Fighting Rezin is different than fighting Heno and Jago," Kire said. "We could see them. They were tangible and fightable, physically. With Rezin, we only ever feel his presence. He does things without us even being able to see him doing them. Not until it's too late and we're already being attacked by something, anyway."

"We need to have a brainstorming session. We all need to go home and do some thinking on our own and then we'll reunite and figure out how we can defeat him if we never see him," Amberly said. She felt good about contributing a little bit. Usually, it was always Kaos and Kire coming up with the ideas.

"I agree," Kire said. "I say we tackle one thing at a time. The first on the list will be to brainstorm Rezin's ideas. The quicker we have him out of the way, the safer we can travel to the portal to the Albus realm without worrying about having to deal with him."

"Fair point," Kaos said. "Then we'll go to the Albus realm and check things out soon. As long as Halo doesn't give you any sort of warning that Yash is coming sooner than we're anticipating."

"Great," Trace said, getting to his feet quickly. So quickly, that Amberly was slightly startled by it. "Then I guess this meeting can be adjourned for the day?"

Everyone looked around at each other.

"I guess so," Kire said, getting to his feet next. He offered to help

Rose out of her chair, but she ignored his help and got to her feet on her own.

Kaos seemed to notice that Amberly noticed it, too, and they both exchanged the look that said "What is her deal?" Then they smirked at each other.

"Amberly," Trace said, "want to walk home together?"

"Uh…" Amberly wasn't sure how she felt about spending time with Trace right now. Why did he suddenly want to hang out with her after ignoring her all day long or for the past couple of days, for that matter? "Actually, I was going to walk by myself."

"Guys… I have a car," Kaos said. "I can drive us."

"I'm good," Rose said even though Kaos hadn't exactly been addressing her. Then she walked out of the store. Kire gave the others a look that said, "Help me," and then he turned and dashed out of the store after his girlfriend.

"You guys want a ride then?" Kaos asked.

"No," Amberly said. "I said, I want to walk. And my aunt's house is literally so close to here."

"Let me walk with you then," Trace said.

"No, I'm good," she said.

"Why?"

"Because, *Trace*," she said, losing her patience. "I'm just… I'm tired, okay?"

Suddenly, Trace's eyes clouded over. He looked a little tenser than usual.

"What?" she asked.

"Nothing."

She rolled her eyes and turned to leave.

"It's just funny that you're too tired to hang out with me today," he said, apparently changing his mind about having nothing to say. Amberly turned back around. "But yet yesterday, you were apparently not too tired to hang out with Kaos."

"Dude," Kaos said in a whiny tone.

Amberly stared at Trace down. Was he seriously starting this fight with her right now? After the way, he had been treating her?

"I'm not doing this with you, Trace," she snapped. When she spun on her heel this time, her ponytail flung behind her and she left the tea room.

When Amberly got home that night, it was another long evening of her lying in bed and crying herself to sleep.

13

In all truth, Amberly has been completely lying when she told the rest of the Quintets that she was fine and ready and able to handle going back into the Albus realm. The truth of the matter was that she wasn't fine. She was still incredibly, overwhelmingly sad over the death of her mother. She didn't much feel like doing anything other than lying in bed. She didn't want to sleep. She didn't want to eat. She hardly wanted to even talk to anyone, especially her aunt, no matter how much she tried to feel otherwise. She knew that yesterday when she had that meeting at Aunt Marg's with the others, she had been the one to come up with the plan that they needed to go home and brainstorm ways to defeat Rezin, but yet, since she had been too busy crying herself to sleep last night, she hadn't thought about it at all. And now, she was dreading going to school and seeing her friends again.

For some reason, when she first went back to school after her mom died, it had been much easier to fake it and get ready and look like the glam queen that she normally was. But that morning, when she got out of bed and thought about getting ready, dread filled her. She didn't want to do all of her hair and makeup. She didn't want to pick out a trendy outfit.

She didn't want to go to school and pretend like she was on top of the world and put on that fake smile. She knew the school was the one thing of her she felt like she could control, but today, she didn't much feel like controlling it whatsoever.

So when she did finally get ready, she did it half-heartedly. Her outfit was one she had worn before so she didn't have to think about it much. She only did a light bit of makeup, enough to where she still looked pretty and put together. She put some product in her hair and scrunched it up for an effortlessly messy look that took two seconds.

When she looked in the mirror, she simply said, "Good enough."

Then as she walked to school that morning, in the chilly cold air with bits of snowflakes sprinkling down every so often, she devised a plan. A way to get her out of the fact that she hadn't brainstormed what to do about Rezin yesterday. A way to get her out of doing pretty much *anything*.

When she met up with Kaos and Trace out front of the school, they looked concerned all over again. She had once more ignored them when they offered to give her a ride earlier. She didn't have the energy to come up with an excuse as to why she ignored them. Instead, she coughed dramatically and sniffled.

"Are you okay?" Trace asked, raising one eyebrow.

"I feel like death," she replied, coughing some more. It wasn't true. She didn't feel sick. But this way, they would at least stay off her case. They would understand why she hadn't planned out anything with Rezin and why she wasn't in the mindset to do stuff that had to deal with the Quintets. She hardly even had the mindset to be at school at all, but she didn't want the others to know that.

"You're sick?" Kaos asked, looking concerned. "Why don't you go home?"

She shook her head. "I can't miss school. I already did after my mom… you know. I can't miss any more or else I will just fall more behind."

"I could help you catch up," Kaos said.

"Of course, you could," Trace replied.

"What is that supposed to mean?" Kaos asked.

Trace shrugged and shook his head, The bell rang and they left for class.

Somehow, Amberly was able to make it through the whole school day without saying much about anything Quintet and Albus realm-related. She continued faking being sick and she avoided pretty much everyone at school. She took the halls that were less busy in between classes so that she wasn't forced to stop and make conversation with her friends. She sat at the lunch table but kept her head down and ignored everyone as they talked. And no one tried to ask her any questions, too, because they knew she just needed her rest.

Then when the bell rang, signaling the end of the school day, Amberly walked out with Trace and Kaos toward the soccer field, where they had soccer and cheer practice.

"Aren't you going to head to the lockers?" Trace asked Amberly.

She shook her head. "There's no way I can go to practice today," she said. "Not when I feel like this."

"Okay," he said. "Well, I have to head that way. Make sure you go home and get lots of rest, yeah?"

Amberly nodded, and then she accepted the hug that Trace gave her. He looked like he wanted to lean in for a kiss as well, but she put her hand over her mouth and shook her head quickly. "It's best if we don't," she said, then she fake-coughed some more.

"Oh," Trace said, making a look of disgust. "Right."

Trace started walking toward the lockers; then he turned around to Kaos. "You coming?"

"I'll be right there," Kaos replied.

Trace rolled his eyes and continued on his way by himself.

"Are you really not going to cheer practice?" Kaos asked, looking like he didn't quite believe her. Like it was totally out of character for her to do so.

She shrugged. "I just don't really have it in me to go today," she said. And this time, she wasn't lying.

"And you're going home, then?"

"I was planning on it. Why?"

"I didn't know if maybe you were going back to the cemetery to visit your mom again."

"And what if I was?" she asked.

"Well... I was going to come with you."

Amberly stood there and stared at him for a moment as kids from all around walked past them and either went to their after-school activities, got in their cars, had her parents pick them up, or walked over to the school buses. Outside, it was no longer snowing, but there were a few patches of snow on the ground where it had stuck on and off throughout the day. The sun was barely peeking through the clouds now, and Amberly knew that the snow on the ground wasn't going to stay there long.

"But you have soccer practice," Amberly finally said.

"So? You're not the only one who's allowed to play hooky."

Despite everything, Amberly found herself smiling at him.

"All right, then. I don't wanna go to the cemetery. But if you want to skip, too, then we can hang out."

He smiled back at her, and then together, they left the school campus. They didn't have anywhere, in particular, they were walking to. They just walked around their town and talked. Amberly almost forgot that she was supposed to be pretending that she was sick, and every time she remembered, she threw out a quick cough or a fake sneeze.

"I feel like I should just take you home," Kaos said after a while.

"No," she said quickly. "I'll be fine."

Then they walked in silence for a little while.

"So," Kaos finally said, changing the subject. "How have things been with Trace? Still off?"

"What do you think?" Amberly asked. "You've seen us together."

"Well, I know that you've been feeling sick today. I didn't know if that had anything to do with it or not."

"It does... and it doesn't," she said. "You saw how mad he got yesterday when he found out we had hung out together. How unfair was that?"

"I don't really think I should be getting in the middle of this," he said.

She rolled her eyes. "You were the one who asked."

"Yeah, but still. Trace is my best friend. My *guy*, you know?"

"I just..." Amberly trailed off, wondering if she should trust Kaos enough to tell him what she really felt like saying. Quickly, she decided that she would. "Things were just so different with Trace and me at the beginning of our relationship."

"How so?"

"We couldn't get enough of each other. We were, like, the hottest thing at St. Bernard High. And we were always together. We only wanted to spend time with each other. I mean... *you* saw. You were frequently annoyed at us, remember?"

"I remember." He chuckled.

Amberly shrugged. "Then... I don't know. Ever since this whole stuff with the Albus realm and us being the Quintets... I feel like a lot of it has changed."

"I kind of noticed it, too," he said. And it hurt Amberly's feelings because she had been hoping he would say something along the lines of, "What? You're crazy, Amberly. Trace is just as into you as he was at the beginning." Her relationship with Trace was not good, and it sucked.

LATER THAT EVENING, when Amberly got a phone call as she was yet again lying in bed, she saw that it was her boyfriend.

"Trace?" she asked when she answered. In all honesty, she was surprised to even be hearing from him.

"Hey, Amberly," he said in his soft tone. If she had any guesses from all of the late-night phone calls they had shared together, she would say that Trace was in his bed as he talked to her as well.

"What's up?" she asked.

"Are you feeling better yet?"

"Not really," she said.

"Can I bring you soup or anything?"

"Do you even *want* to bring me soup?"

He was silent for a beat.

"I'm really sorry," he finally said.

"Sorry?" she asked. "Sorry about what?" She played with her hair as she lay in bed and talked to him. It was weird to hear him apologize. She was almost worried that Kaos had talked to him for her even though she didn't want that.

"For how I acted yesterday. When we had that meeting."

"Oh..."

That's all he wanted to apologize for? For the fact that he had gotten mad that she didn't want to hang out with him yesterday? *Trace, you have much more to apologize for than just that.*

"I talked to Kaos about it later, and he explained that he had only run into you there. Not that you guys had gone there together. I don't know why I assumed, and I guess I just instantly felt jealous because I've been wanting to spend time with you, and it hasn't really seemed like you've been wanting to do the same with me."

"Wait for a second," she said. "Are you serious?"

"What?"

"What makes you think I haven't wanted to spend time with you? Trace, I don't know if you remember this or not, but my mom sort of just died. I've been dealing with a lot. Nothing that's happening has anything to do with you. If anything, you're the one who has seemed to be a little standoff-ish and who has seemed like you don't want to spend time with *me*."

It was strange having this conversation with him. Even though they had been together for a while, Amberly and Trace weren't exactly ever the best at communicating their real feelings to each other. A lot of their relationship felt very surface-level. They were hot; they made a cute couple; they liked each other, and that was that.

"That's not true. I care about you so much, Amberly," he said.

"I care about you, too."

For some reason, Amberly found herself getting a little choked up.

They talked on the phone a little while longer, and when they hung up, Amberly thought she would feel better. But she still couldn't shake the feeling that something was off about her relationship with Trace.

14

Amberly felt like she had no more tears left to cry that night. So as she lay awake in bed, instead of crying, she finally decided to attempt to do some brainstorming over this Rezin situation.

How could they attack an alien who refused to let himself be seen by them?

Well, Amberly thought, *for one, the first thing we have to do is obvious.*

They had to make him be seen. They had to find a way to know his whereabouts so that they knew what they were fighting. So that they knew where to attack. But how would they do that?

Amberly even put her gauntlet on, and still lying in bed, she rearranged everything else in her bedroom by simply lifting her hand. At one point, her aunt Lydia came to the door knocking and asking if everything was okay in there because she claimed to be hearing a lot of thudding noises. Amberly responded, "Everything's fine, Aunt Lydia! Just trying to do some homework." And luckily, her aunt Lydia left her alone after that.

How could Amberly use Gamora to fight against Rezin? How could she use her powers in a way that would make him be seen? If he was just simply invisible, maybe she could take a can of paint and splatter it in different directions until it coated him and made him visible to everyone else. Maybe if she could get a sense of where he was, she could use her gauntlet to summon him to wherever she wanted him to go, locking him there and holding him in place so that the rest of the Quintets could attack.

She only really thought it over for about twenty minutes before her brain felt too exhausted to continue. But she didn't exactly want to fall asleep, either. The only reason she had been able to fall asleep previous nights was that she had cried herself to sleep and therefore hadn't even realized she had drifted off at all. She hadn't dreamed about Rezin those times, and she was grateful for it. But as she lay there now, she just had an overwhelming feeling that it was going to happen again. That the next time she closed her eyes and fell asleep, Rezin was going to be there to attack. That he was going to control her somehow. Once she woke up from her dream, she was going to find that another person she cared about was dead. She still felt convinced that he had controlled her dreams in the hospital, and it had been his way of showing her that he was killing her mother. She still didn't fully believe that it was just her mother's illness that had finally gotten the best of her. Rezin had made her mom die. And if he could do that, who else would he kill? What if Aunt Lydia was next?

With her stress and fear, Amberly couldn't sleep. She didn't *want* to sleep. She was too terrified to sleep. It didn't matter that her eyes wanted to close and that her body felt heavy. She just couldn't let herself do it. If she stayed awake, then Rezin wouldn't be able to mess with her as he had in the hospital. So, staying awake all night was exactly what Amberly ended up forcing herself to do.

AMBERLY WOKE the next morning feeling off. When she got out of bed, she walked over to her full-length mirror and noticed that she not only *felt* off, she *looked* off, too. How much had she slept last night? Maybe combining all the tidbits of sleep mixed in with tossing and turning and staring at the ceiling and daydreaming and thinking horrible thoughts, she figured she probably got about an hour and a half max.

And her reflection showed this clearly. She had dark circles under her eyes. She lacked color on her face. Her skin was waxy. Her cheeks were sallow.

She pinched the apples of her cheeks to try to get a little pink to them. It hardly worked.

Thinking maybe she just needed to have some coffee and eat something, she wandered into the kitchen where Aunt Lydia was already hard at work on her computer.

"Good morning," Amberly said in a sleepy voice as she walked over to the pantry to get herself a protein bar.

"Good mor—whoa."

Amberly turned to see what her aunt was freaking out about. Only, when she looked at her, she found that her aunt was staring directly at her face.

"What?" Amberly asked.

"Are you feeling okay?" Aunt Lydia asked.

"Yeah. Why?" Amberly was lying, of course.

"You don't look so good, Amberly," she pointed out. "Have you felt feverish at all? Did you take your temperature?" She got up out of her chair and started walking toward her.

Amberly was about to refuse to let this lady put the back of her hand to her forehead. She stepped away and turned sharply to the pantry. She used the door of it to block her aunt from getting any closer.

"I'm fine. Honestly," she replied behind her shield.

"Okay," Aunt Lydia said uneasily, halting her steps—thank

goodness. "There's no harm in staying home from school if you're not feeling well. I'm just saying."

"And *I'm* just saying—for the *hundredth* time—that I am fine." She ripped a protein bar out of the box and shut the pantry door a little louder than she meant to. When she glanced at her aunt again, she was biting her lower lip and slowly backing up toward her computer.

It was strange how yesterday, Amberly had faked being sick, and today she actually felt it.

Amberly retreated back to her room to get ready for the day. Same as yesterday, she only put half the effort in because she was simply too exhausted to do anything else. She wished she could go to sleep, but she knew if she even tried to take her Aunt Lydia's advice and stayed home and laid back in bed, sleep wouldn't come to her. Amberly was simply too terrified to sleep.

After she finished getting ready and checked her reflection in the mirror one last time before heading to school, she knew one thing to be true.

She definitely wasn't going to put the act on that she felt unwell today.

JUST AS SHE figured they would be, the other Quintets were worried about her when she arrived at school that morning. Trace checked on her about a million times, and Kaos couldn't look at her without having a worried expression on his face. It was weird for Amberly to see it because Kaos wasn't usually one who wore a worried expression.

She reassured them all that she would be fine and that she couldn't miss any more school, just like she had told her aunt Lydia earlier in the day. But even as she sat in her classes, she felt herself straining to stay awake. She'd close her eyes for a second, then squeeze them shut tight and open them wide as if that made any difference and helped her feel more alert. On a bathroom break, she slapped her cheeks a little to see if that would help her feel more alert. She didn't want to fall asleep. She didn't want to let Rezin take over her dream in the middle of class in case something embarrassing or horrible should happen.

It was a miracle that she even made it to Gym, and as much as she wanted to skip cheer practice again, Angela and the rest of the cheerleaders simply wouldn't have that from their team leader.

"You can't just abandon us again," Angela said with her hands on her hips as she stood beside Victoria and Lindsey.

"Yeah. If you're well enough to go to school, then you should be well enough to make it to cheer practice. We sort of need you," Lindsey added.

"More like we totally *suck* without you," Victoria clarified.

What was the matter with Amberly? Not cheerleading was usually the last thing she wanted to do. She loved to cheer. She loved dancing. She loved showing off how talented she was in front of the other cheerleaders and the rest of the school. Her mother's death and being one of the unlikely defenders were really messing with her personality.

She looked at the other cheerleaders that were standing in front of her. They were voicing that they were angry with her. They were giving her *dirty* looks. Since when did any of the girls at St. Bernard High feel brave enough to do that?

Take control, Amberly. This is your *school.*

"Oh, don't worry; I know you sucked without me yesterday," she said, lifting her nose in the air snootily. "I saw the videos sent to me."

Victoria quickly looked at her feet while Lindsey's eyes widened in astonishment.

"Well, are you going to come today or not?" Angela asked.

"Fine," Amberly snapped. "I can cheer better than any of you, even when I'm having a crappy day like this." She looked only at

Angela as she spoke the next sentence. "And *somebody's* got to help you learn how to do an eight-count."

Angela looked offended but said nothing and simply turned and headed toward the locker room. But Amberly rushed past all three of them to make sure she was the one leading the way there.

15

It was lunchtime, and Amberly knew as soon as she walked into the cafeteria that she was feeling incredibly irritable—that her *lack of sleep* had her feeling incredibly irritable.

So she knew right away that when she saw Charlie Rose sitting at her lunch table again, she wasn't going to be happy about it. And given the way she had treated the other cheerleaders, who were supposed to be her *friends*, she knew she wasn't going to have it in her to be even a little bit nice to Rose today.

I need a nap; she found herself thinking as she opted to skip lunch and just go straight to the table, where sure enough, Rose and Kire were already seated. Amberly needed a nap, but she wouldn't take one. She wondered if she would ever be able to fall asleep again or if she would just live the remainder of her life in this stressed-out, cranky, exhausted state.

Amberly took a seat at the lunch table.

"What's up, Amberly?" Kire asked, casually nodding his head at her. Beside him, his girlfriend said nothing to her.

"Hey," Amberly said shortly, deciding not to even make eye contact with Rose. Then there was a long, awkward silence as the three of them sat there until finally, Trace and Kaos, who had just left the lunch line with their trays full of food, joined them.

When Trace sat down, he kissed Amberly on the cheek and then dug into his gigantic, falling-apart chicken wrap. Kaos gave a cool guy head-nod to everyone and popped open an energy drink.

"So, has everyone been brainstorming this Rezin situation?" Trace asked.

"I'm trying," Kire replied, "but I'm not exactly getting anywhere."

"Same," Trace said. "All I know is that I can attack him with my fiery sword. Maybe get some gasoline and light him on fire? Do you think that would work?"

"It might be worth a shot," Kire replied.

Beside him, Rose scoffed. "Are you kidding?" she asked, giving Kire a dirty look. "How is he going to light something on fire that he can't even *see*?"

Instantly, Amberly was fired up. "Well, at least he *has* a suggestion," she snapped. "What exactly have *you* come up with, Plant Princess?"

At first, Rose opened her mouth like she was going to have some great solution to offer and Amberly was going to be annoyed by it. But then, luckily, Rose shut her mouth again and fell silent.

But still, Amberly was heated. Why was Rose continuously being so rude to Kire? Wasn't he supposed to be her *boyfriend*?

Amberly decided she wasn't done with Rose. She decided she was going to let her crankiness get the best of her. "What is your deal, anyway?" she snapped. "Why are you such a huge brat all the time?"

"Excuse me?" Rose snapped back defensively.

"You heard me, Miss I-Am-So-Afraid-Of-Animals-I-Can't-Even-Talk-To-A-Cat."

"You can't just talk to me like that," Rose said. She looked fired up now, too, it was just the reaction Amberly had been trying to elicit from her. It meant her plan was working.

"That's funny because I think I can." Amberly let out a nasty snicker. "*God*. I don't understand how you even get the audacity to treat Kire the way you do and speak to me the way you are. We don't *have* to let you sit at our table, Rose. We all know what a huge wannabe you are. And yet, here we are, letting you be one of us, even though you don't belong."

"Can you guys just stop?" Kire asked. "Not this again. Seriously, what is it with you two? Why can't you just get along for the sake of the group?" He looked back and forth between Amberly and Rose, an appalled expression on his face. He was no longer eating his lunch. It was as if the two of them fighting again had ruined his appetite.

"Maybe I'd get along with her better if I didn't have to see her all the time—for example, at *my* lunch table! Why can't you just get lost, Charlie Rose?"

Amberly noted how Trace and Kaos weren't backing her up, and even though she could feel herself growing even angrier because of it, she tried to let it slide. This was just supposed to be between her and Rose. She didn't need their backup.

Suddenly, Rose leaped from her chair and quickly stormed away from the table. Amberly was mildly surprised. She hadn't expected Rose to actually listen to her. She had expected her to say something back. To keep the fight going. To refuse to back down like she usually did. But Amberly supposed she should be thankful that Rose finally left.

"Look what you did," Kire said angrily, looking behind him and watching Rose leave the cafeteria before he turned back to Amberly.

"Are you kidding me?" Amberly snapped at him. "I was defending you. You should be thanking me. She treats you like garbage, Kire. Why do you put up with it?" How could he not see that? And how dare he be mad at her right now when, if anything, she had just been helping him?

"She doesn't," he claimed. "She's just... she's going through some stuff. It's none of your business. Just cause your mom died, it doesn't give you the right to be rude to everybody, okay?" Then, before Amberly could say anything else to him to defend herself, he got up as well and also left the table.

"*Finally*," Amberly said, leaning back and crossing her arms as she watched Kire go run after his awful girlfriend. "This is the way it's supposed to be."

Beside her, Kaos and Trace stayed silent. This irked her, so she snapped her head to them.

"*Hello*?"

"Keep me out of this," Kaos said, shaking his head.

"Fine," Amberly snapped. Then she looked angrily at her boyfriend. "Shouldn't you be thanking me? I got rid of her."

"Thanking you, Amberly?" he asked, sounding incredulous. "Are you kidding?"

"What?" She snapped.

"Amberly, Kire was right. What *is* the matter with you? Why can't you just leave Rose alone?"

"Are you seriously defending her right now?" Amberly was appalled. As her boyfriend, Trace was supposed to always take her side.

"It's not about defending her," he said.

"You're right," Amberly replied, feeling the sting of hurt on her face. "You're defending her because you *like* her. Why can't you just admit that? How many times are we going to have this stupid fight before you finally come clean about it, huh?"

Trace pushed away his food tray, suddenly done eating it. Amberly was making everybody lose their appetite today.

"How many times are we going to fight before you finally believe that I don't have feelings for her?!"

Amberly was slightly alarmed at how loud Trace's tone was getting, but she didn't let him see it on her face. "Come on, Amberly! We are supposed to be a team! We have this huge battle ahead of us and if we are not all united, then our gifts aren't going to work as well as they did back in the Albus realm! What part don't you get about that?"

"My powers work just fine!"

"Well, fine isn't good enough! We need them to be at their best!"

"I don't need to get along with Rose for that to happen!"

"Yes, you do!"

"UGH!" was that all Amberly could manage to get out after that? She was too infuriated to think of anything else to say to him. She turned to Kaos. "Care to weigh in on this? It sort of involves you, whether you want it to or not."

"Yeah, dude," Trace joined in, at least agreeing with his girl-friend about *one* thing. "Back me up."

Kaos looked between the two of them before giving them both a casual, apathetic shrug. "I honestly don't much care either way if Rose sits at our table or not. Yes, Rose and Amberly need to get along, but I bet that it's only when it comes time to fight and save the world and whatnot. I don't think it's necessary for us to need to like each other every part of every single day. To be honest, I don't even know if I could ever seriously consider Kire to be an actual friend of mine."

Amberly rolled her eyes. "*Thanks*, Kaos. You're a ton of help."

Again, Kaos simply shrugged.

"Dude," Trace complained.

"You know what?" Amberly said to both of them, slapping her hands on top of the table to propel herself out of her chair. "I don't even know why I am sitting in the cafeteria right now anyway. I'm not even eating."

"Amberly, you need to stop walking away every time we get into an argument," Trace warned.

"Do I?" she questioned, staring him down with as much venom as she could muster. "What are you going to do about it?" She waited for half a second for him to answer, then she rolled her eyes again and left.

AMBERLY DIDN'T NEED to be getting along with everyone in the group for her powers to work just as well as they had been since she received them. Charlie Rose was the only one who had problems with her health when she used hers. Kaos was the one who hadn't seemed quite able to master his abilities with his gift yet. And neither of those things was Amberly's problem.

When school ended, Amberly made sure to speed off campus as quickly as she could before Kaos or Trace could try and stop her. She felt the need to prove herself. So the entire walk home, she thought about in her head just how she was going to do it.

"Welcome home," Aunt Lydia said when Amberly walked into her new house. "How was your day today? Feeling better?"

"Yes, just great," Amberly replied as she made her way to her room.

"I was thinking of making some good, hearty chicken noodle soup tonight for dinner. Does that sound appealing to you at all?"

Amberly shrugged. "Whatever you want to do. Um, I have to go work on a school project with some of my classmates, I just came home to grab something for it real quick."

"Oh," Aunt Lydia said, "no worries. I will have it ready for when you get home then."

"Thanks!" she called over her shoulder as she dashed into her room, grabbed her gauntlet, put it in her backpack, and then headed out the front door again.

Amberly walked all the way to the White Forest all on her own. There was still plenty of daylight out, and what she needed to do wouldn't take long. She didn't have to be afraid of Rezin. Not during the day.

Right?

Besides, she had Gamora. And with Gamora, Amberly was powerful and could at least defend herself against Rezin if she couldn't kill him on her own.

With haste, Amberly entered the dense woods and followed the path she had memorized to get back to those caves she so hated. but this would be necessary. This was going to be the perfect way for her to show how powerful she was with her gauntlet, and she didn't need to be friends with Rose to make it that way.

Getting more and more nervous as she walked along through the woods, she picked up the pace even more until, eventually, she was at a full-blown run, trying to get to the caves as quickly as possible. Sure, there was still plenty of daylight out, but Amberly thought it looked so dark in the woods this deep that it could nearly pass for nighttime.

Or what if the darkness was just a trick Rezin was playing on her? What if he was here somewhere, ready to attack?

Amberly shuddered until she finally dove into the caves. She kept running until she was all the way to the lake that contained the portal to the Albus realm at the bottom of it.

"Finally," she said, dropping her bag to the ground and pulling Gamora out of it, and putting it on. She flexed her fingers in it, feeling the gift become a part of her as it built itself up her arm.

"All right," she said to herself and her gift. "Hope you're ready for this." Then she used her magical abilities to manipulate the water, just as she had done to create a pathway for them to all be able to reach the portal before.

But this time, Amberly wasn't there to make a pathway to the portal. She was there to make it so that she never had to create a pathway to the portal ever again. Concentrating hard and trying to tie her mind to her gauntlet, she grunted out as she used her strength to lift the water completely out of its bed. Miraculously, it was actually working. She was moving the entire body of water as if it were a single entity.

When she felt she had a good strong hold on it, and when she was confident it wasn't going to drown her when she let go, she cried out because of the amount of force she was using as she threw the entire body of water in the direction of the cave's exit. The water blasted through the tunnels, and at first, Amberly was worried that there was too much water and that some of it was going to come back and pull her under, but before it could touch her toes, it leveled out, and then a couple of moments later, it seemed to have dispersed enough to where it only looked like there had been a slight flood inside of the cave tunnels.

"I did it," she said to herself, out of breath, as she smiled down at the gift she had been given. "See? I don't need Rose."

She looked at the deep hole where the lake had been. Down inside it, she could make out the archway waiting for her. But it wasn't time for Amberly to go through it. She needed to first make sure no one accidentally came across this portal.

She walked out of the tunnel and then turned around to face the opening to the path that led to the lake with the portal. Then she used her gauntlet again to pick up heavy boulders, one after the other, to strategically place them over the mouth of the tunnel so that it looked like there had been a cave-in. Rock after rock, Amberly moved the items with her enchanted glove, and the more she worked, the more tired she grew. Still, she somehow managed to fill up the mouth completely. No one would even bother trying to get to the other side of it.

She leaned against the new wall she had made and nearly collapsed from how tired she was. She had done it. She was proud of herself. Sure, it had been exhausting and she felt a little dizzy and out of it and had no idea what time it was now, but she had done it. The reason she was probably feeling off had to do with the fact that she hadn't gotten much sleep and had nothing to do with the fact that she had been using all of her strength on her own while she wasn't whole and connected to everyone in the group.

It couldn't be that. Amberly was certain of it. She didn't need them.

16

When the sun rose again, and Amberly had hardly gotten any sleep, she dreaded another day of school, only to then realize that it was a Saturday morning. Her stomach was rumbling in a way that made her unsure whether she was hungry or just nauseated, so she decided to roll out from under her fluffy pink comforter, put her cozy silk robe on, and wander out of her room and into the kitchen, where she found her aunt already awake and smiling at her. Lydia looked eager to talk, but since Amberly was tired and hungry or nauseated, she was the opposite of her aunt.

"Good morning, Amberly," Aunt Lydia said from over at the small dining table. Amberly was beginning to realize it must be her aunt's favorite spot in the house, for she rarely saw her anywhere else. She worked there, ate there, and apparently preferred to converse there as well. "How did you sleep? Do you like that bed okay? It wasn't the most expensive mattress in the world, so if it isn't comfortable, you can tell me and I will work on getting you a new one. Maybe I can finance it, or if you just gave me a little bit of time to save up..."

"Aunt Lydia," Amberly said, trying her best not to sound exasperated. Her aunt was talking entirely too much for this early in the morning. "The bed is fine." Sure, Amberly would prefer one that was a little more comfortable. Her bed back home was her favorite but she didn't want to say so and risk this conversation. She just wanted to eat some breakfast in silence. At least until she had a chance to make herself feel a little more awake. She knew she needed to sleep ASAP. It embarrassed her to think about how she had fallen asleep in class, but she just was too afraid. Afraid of what Rezin would do next if she did.

"Oh, okay." Aunt Lydia pursed her lips, and Amberly thought it was because the woman could tell Amberly was in yet again another grumpy mood.

Amberly sighed and pulled a protein bar out of the pantry, as well as a banana off the counter and some almond milk out of the fridge. She also could smell coffee in the coffee pot, so she got a mug out and poured herself a cup, and used the almond milk as the creamer for it. She wasn't normally the biggest fan of the taste of coffee, not unless she went to an actual shop and got something super sweet and topped with extra whipped cream, but she needed something to make her feel a little more alive.

Once she had all her breakfast items, she took a seat at the table, wishing she were alone.

Aunt Lydia looked over her breakfast approvingly. "So," she started, making Amberly internally groan. Couldn't her aunt just get the hint that she didn't feel like talking? "I am glad you're up early this Saturday."

"Why?" Amberly asked as she peeled back her banana. The peel had a smattering of brown freckles on it. Her favorite time of ripeness to eat it.

"Because I sort of need you to go to your old house and sort through everything to decide what you want to keep and what you want to donate," her aunt replied.

Amberly almost choked on her banana. "*What?*"

Lydia frowned sympathetically as if it wasn't her who had made this decision, even though it clearly was. "We need to get your house ready to sell. These things move fast. I know it's hard, but the quicker we get it done, the quicker we can… move on."

"You're selling my house?" The bite of banana in her mouth suddenly felt too mushy and overly sweet. She downed some hot coffee, burning her mouth slightly, just so she could wash it down. She felt more nauseated than hungry now.

"Once we sell, the money goes into an account you'll have access to when you're eighteen. It's in your mother's will," Lydia informed her.

Amberly figured most teens would have been excited to hear news about them getting a bunch of money handed to them when they turned eighteen. And Amberly, who had spent the majority of her life with hardly any money, knew she should be excited, too. But the circumstances over which she was getting this money prevented her from being so.

"What if I just want to live in that house?" she asked her aunt.

"You don't want that, Amberly. You need a fresh start somewhere new, not trapped by the bad memories."

Amberly felt triggered by her words and bit out quickly, "I didn't know that someone I've met three times in my life was such an expert on what I need."

Aunt Lydia winced. "Sorry. It's what I *feel* is best for you. And it's too complicated. We can't just save the house until you are old enough to have it. It doesn't work like that."

Of course, it doesn't. Nothing could ever just be easy and simple for Amberly.

She turned away from her aunt. "Whatever."

"So, if you could just decide what to keep and what to sell," Aunt Lydia repeated after sighing, "we can rent a small storage unit if there are some bigger items you'd like."

"Fine." Amberly wanted to be defiant, but what was the point? She had a feeling that the house was going to get cleaned out whether she wanted it to happen or not.

"I can drive you over?" Aunt Lydia offered in the form of a question.

That was the *last* thing Amberly wanted. "I want to go alone. I got it."

Aunt Lydia tilted her head. "Do u have a license?"

"I got it the day I turned sixteen," Amberly informed her snootily. "I just... can't afford my own car."

"Take mine, at least. Maybe see if your friends will help you. So at least someone is there with you."

"I don't need anyone's help," she replied quickly, even though she was very much excited about the idea of getting to take her aunt's car.

"Okay. Well, the keys are on the hook by the door. Just head over when you're ready. Maybe just write a list of what is going to be donated and what you want to keep, and I will have a moving company do the rest."

"Okay." Amberly stood from the table.

"There's no great hurry, Amberly," Aunt Lydia said. "You can finish your breakfast."

"I'll finish it in my room." She picked up the rest of her banana, her protein bar, and her mug of coffee and retreated into the bathroom in the hall, where she threw the food away and gulped down the rest of the coffee. Then she quickly showered and got ready, and before she left, she opened her texts and composed one to Trace, despite what she had told her aunt earlier.

> Amberly: Aunt is making me go clean out my house so she can sell it. Thinking of not going. Can you even believe her?

Trace replied as Amberly sat in her aunt's car, adjusting all of the mirrors and her seating. The car wasn't anything fancy. It didn't even have leather seats, but Amberly was excited to be driving it nonetheless.

Trace: Aw come on babe it won't be so bad. It has to happen sometime. Maybe the sooner u do it the quicker u'll be able to move on.

Amberly was instantly angry about his response as she put the car in reverse and backed out of the driveway. His dumb, unsupportive reply was ruining her driving experience. She had wanted him to be on her side or to ask if he could go with her for support.

Instead, she blasted loud pop music from the radio and drove to her old house—alone. It was borderline freezing outside, and still, Amberly drove with the windows down, her hair blowing wildly around her. She liked being behind the wheel, in control of what she was doing and where she was going, and she found that quickly, she was getting in a better mood.

When she pulled into her old driveway, she realized it never really hit her how horrible and not well-kept her house had been when she had lived in it. The overgrown front yard. The rotting wooden steps lead to the front porch. The windows with broken blinds in them. It looked haunted and abandoned, maybe It was.

It took a while to even get inside the house because Amberly had a hard time finding the courage inside of herself.

Once she stepped inside, her good mood from driving was gone again. She was still exhausted, and the thought of sorting through an entire house, one full of reminders of her mother sounded daunting. And she couldn't believe she had to do it all on her own.

But she'd rather do it alone than have her aunt here helping her.

Feeling overwhelmed, she quickly turned and went back outside. She walked down the driveway and stood on the sidewalk, where she pulled her phone out and snapped a picture of it. At least she could have this to keep the memory of what the house she had lived her whole life in with her mother had looked like. Even if it wasn't much to look at.

"Okay, just get it over with," she told herself. She took a deep breath, tucked her hair behind her ears, and reentered her old home. It still smelled of her mother. Her mother always smelled like she lived in a hospital or nursing home—commercial soap, sterile and slightly like rubber.

She tried breathing through her mouth so she didn't have to smell her mother because smelling her made it feel as if her mother was still there with her, and Amberly hated having to remember that she wasn't. And that she never would be again.

Going through her and her mother's things, it didn't take long for Amberly to start crying, as much as she didn't want to. It was just too hard to look at everything. Her mother's presence was everywhere. Even the indent of her butt in the chair in the living room that she never left made Amberly incredibly sad. She underestimated how hard of a task this would be.

Still, she continued working, despite the tears that constantly blurred her vision. She found a notepad and pen in the kitchen and started jotting down all of the things she wanted to keep. Her aunt did say she'd get a storage unit, so Amberly started marking down that she wanted to keep a lot more than she actually did. She knew it was because she was feeling bitter over the fact that her aunt made her do this. Amberly wanted to force Aunt Lydia to buy the biggest storage unit they could find as her secret sort of payback. Was it ridiculous of her? Maybe. Did she care? Not in the slightest.

The steadily streaming, quiet tears didn't turn into full-blown sobs until Amberly came across a photo of her and her mother taken when Amberly was younger and happy. When she was too naïve to know what a hard time her mother was having to be a single parent. Back before her mother got sick. The reason it made Amberly sob so much was that she didn't know if she wanted to go through life without her mother. Every day was still so hard. Wasn't it supposed to start getting easier? Would that ever happen?

Amberly curled up on her mother's chair and hugged her favorite couch pillow, the one with the daisies on it, and cried for so long she lost track of time.

Eventually, she pulled it together and finished going through the house. She had it all organized into what she wanted to keep and what could be donated. She also had a box of stuff she wanted to bring back to her new house instead of putting it in storage. It was mainly full of pictures of her and her mother that had been in her mother's closet. Amberly hadn't even known they existed.

She picked the box up and brought it outside, where she placed it into her aunt's trunk.

When she closed the trunk, she turned back to her former house to go lock up, but as soon as she took a single step toward it, there was a loud *BOOM!*

Amberly felt her body lift off the ground and heat on her face.

Then, as she flew back through the air, she caught a glimpse of bright orange flames, and then everything went black.

17

When Amberly awoke, she recognized immediately that she was in a hospital, but she wasn't exactly sure how she had gotten there or why. For a moment, she thought she was just back here because she was visiting her mother again. But as she looked around the room, she began to realize that she was the one in the bed, and all of the people in the room, which was still lit up by the daylight outside, were there to see her. She had no idea what happened. But she has a full house. All of the Quintets were there, even Kire and Rose, whom Amberly had been so rude to yesterday. And Kaos appeared to be wearing his crown in public, even with Aunt Lydia in the room.

Amberly realized that no one had quite noticed she had stirred yet, for they were all focused instead on listening to what Amberly's aunt was saying.

"How could this have happened?" Lydia asked her friends. "Being her friends and boyfriend, do any of you know anything? The police haven't told me what the cause of the fire was yet, but I don't know, it feels... intentional somehow."

Amberly slightly cleared her throat, and the Quintets all turned to look at her. Her aunt stared at the gang, still waiting for them to answer her. But when she saw that they had all turned to look at Amberly's bed, she followed their gaze, and her bloodshot eyes widened when she realized with the others that Amberly had come to. Aunt Lydia immediately got off of her chair and moved to stand closer to Amberly in her bed.

"Oh, thank God," she said, "you're awake. How are you feeling?"

Her aunt and the others stared at her, waiting for her reply.

"Confused," Amberly managed to get out. She felt weak and tired, but she wasn't in any pain. She remembered going to her mom's house to pack up. But then... her mind went blank.

"Honey," Aunt Lydia said. "You went to sort through stuff at your mom's, and then there was an explosion. The house went up in flames. I... I am so sorry, but everything is gone."

"What?"

"It's a miracle you're still alive, Amberly."

"My mom's house... all of our stuff... it's... gone?" Amberly didn't want to believe it. But as she lay in that bed, the memory started coming back to her. She had put a box in the trunk of her aunt's car. And then, when she had turned back to the house...

BOOM.

"I don't even want to think about what would have happened if you had been inside of the house when it exploded..." Aunt Lydia continued.

"How did it happen?" Amberly asked. She was in shock. Everything... gone.

"No one seems to have an answer yet," Aunt Lydia explained.

"I'm so sorry, Amberly," Trace said from the foot of the bed, grasping Amberly's shin on top of the blanket that covered her.

Amberly didn't know what to say or do. So she just laid there, not looking at anyone.

"I'm sorry I just... need a minute," Aunt Lydia said in a thick voice. Amberly turned her head to look at her and saw tears in her eyes. Then her aunt left the room, and it was just the other Quintets inside.

"She really cares about you," Kaos pointed out.

Amberly was stunned and a little flattered. "I've never seen her act like that in my life. She didn't even cry at my mom's funeral."

"Huh," Kaos said.

Then the room filled with awkward silence.

Amberly turned her head about the place, noticing that cards and flowers were already everywhere. "Word spreads fast," she decided to say. How long had she been out? It was still Saturday, right?

"People really love you, Amberly," Trace said.

"Or they're just terrified of you," Rose muttered, making Amberly's eyes fly to her. Then Rose's eyes widened. "Did I say that out loud? I totally didn't mean to. Sorry."

Then a nurse walked in to check on her. She looked to be in her mid-twenties and had pretty blonde hair and long eyelashes. It made Amberly feel hideous in comparison.

"All right," the nurse said after checking on a couple of things. "It's time to change those bandages."

Amberly instantly began to freak. *Change the bandages?*

She had the ability to heal faster than a normal person did, and she didn't want the doctors to find out about it and have her committed and made to do all of these studies...

"I don't need them changed," she said quickly.

"Unfortunately, that's not how it works," the nurse told her with an arrogant look. "They have to be changed."

Amberly couldn't let this happen. "I'll be queasy. I'll... I'll vomit."

The nurse rolled her eyes at her. "Just don't look. I'll be fast." Around the room, the Quintets all looked at each other, seeming to realize at the same time why Amberly was acting so worried.

Couldn't they do something?

"I'll...I'll scream," Amberly continued, sounding as bratty as possible. "I'm not kidding. I don't want them changed. I don't need them changed."

"You'll risk getting them infected, though."

Amberly was full-on panicking. She didn't know what it looked like under those bandages, but she had a feeling it was not going to look like what the nurse was expecting it to.

"Another nurse was in here not too long ago," Kaos said, stepping in. "She already had them changed."

"Oh," the nurse said, totally changing her demeanor. "They were just changed. Never mind." Then she walked out of the room.

Amberly was stunned. *What just happened?*

"Did you just do that, Kaos?" she asked as her jaw dropped.

Kaos winked at her.

Trace slapped him on the back. "That's incredible, man!"

"You're getting the hang of this" Kire joined in, smiling big. Even Rose was smiling at him. Everyone was proud that he was getting better at using his gift.

Kaos brushed it off. He seemed embarrassed that they were making a big deal out of it. And to get them to stop gushing over him, he turned his attention back to Amberly. "They're going to be keeping you here overnight for observations," he explained.

"Great," Amberly muttered. She was not looking forward to spending her whole night in the place where her mother had passed away, where she had last dreamed about Rezin.

"Are you okay?" Trace asked. "I mean...*really*?"

"I'm fine," she said quickly, not wanting their pity.

No one looked convinced. Kire stepped forward. "But Amberly, you lost everything."

"Not *everything*." she tried. "I already had brought a bunch of stuff to my aunt's house. I didn't want anything at my mom's anyway." She didn't need them to know that the opposite was true. That she had marked so much stuff to be kept for when she had a place of her own someday.

It was all gone now.

"Okay..." Trace trailed off, looking like he didn't believe her in the slightest.

This annoyed Amberly. And it reminded her about Trace's reply to her text from earlier, and she remembered that she was a little bit angry with him.

"Look," she said, addressing everyone. "I really need my rest. You guys go. Don't waste your whole weekend at the hospital with me again."

They all looked around at each other like they were trying to agree about whether or not they should listen to her.

"I'm serious," Amberly said. Maybe she didn't want to be left alone. But she wanted them to think that she did. She wasn't good at being vulnerable.

Trace was the one who stepped forward and ended up speaking for the group. "If you're sure, Amber."

Amberly's eyes stung with tears that she tried her best to hide. She had hoped at least Trace would say he wasn't going anywhere. That he wanted to stay with her the entire time she was here. That he was going to sleep here, too. That he was going to get her treats and presents and whatever she wanted to make her stay here at the hospital more comfortable.

Not this. She certainly didn't want this.

But would she tell him that? No, she couldn't. Amberly just couldn't do it. She was too afraid to ask for what she really wanted for fear of being rejected. Amberly was not one to take rejection well.

"I'm sure," she managed to choke out. "I'll see you guys all later."

"Bye, Amberly," Kaos said, shooting her a comforting smile before he left the room.

"See, you, babe," Trace said, walking to her bedside and kissing her cheek before walking out.

"Feel better soon," Kire told her.

"Bye," Rose said, then she walked out alongside Kire.

Now that she was alone, Amberly could finally be herself again. And all she would want to do is cry. So that's exactly what she did. She cried and cried until the pain meds she had been given took over, and suddenly, it became impossible for her to stay awake.

Amberly found herself outside of her house again. It looked just as it had when she first pulled up to it and her aunt's car earlier that morning. It was still daylight outside. From where the sun was positioned, Amberly could tell that it was bright and early in the morning. And all around her, the neighborhood was still. Everything felt quiet. Maybe even a little *too* quiet.

But Amberly noticed she was standing in a different spot than she had been when she first pulled up in her aunt's car. This time, she was standing across the street, in front of another house, on the sidewalk. The sun nearly blinded her as she squinted at her own house. Everything felt the same. Her mother's house was in the same state it always had been. The overgrown front lawn. The sense of abandonment. A fiery explosion had never happened here at all.

Everything was just as it should have been.

The only thing Amberly noticed that was different was the fact that she remembered it being incredibly cold out. But as she stood there on the sidewalk, she felt perfectly neutral. Not too cold, not too hot. It was as if the temperature suddenly didn't even exist. She couldn't feel it at all.

That's odd, she thought. And she wasn't exactly sure why she was standing across the street looking at her house. But then she realized there was also something else that was different. Her aunt's car wasn't there. She hadn't driven there. She had gotten to her mom's house some other way. She tried to think how, but nothing came to her. One minute, she was back at the hospital. Then the next thing she knew, she was here. Maybe her lack of sleep was making her begin to lose entire chunks of time. *What is happening?*

She turned about herself, unsure what to do. Then, a car pulled up that looked just like her aunt's car. It turned into her driveway and parked itself. Then the car turned off, and Amberly stood there dumbfounded, expecting her aunt to get out of it. She felt even more confused when she watched a young blonde girl climb out of the driver's seat and shut the door.

"Seriously, *what* is happening?" she asked herself out loud this time, squinting to get a better look at the person who had just gotten out of her aunt's car. It looked a lot like.... "Is that *me*?"

She couldn't believe her own eyes. Across the street, there she was. But yet, she was right here, too. *How is this even possible?*

"Hello!" she called, but the person didn't seem to have heard her, for she didn't turn around. Amberly watched in utter bewilderment as the other Amberly slowly walked inside the house. The real Amberly, or at least, she thought she was the real one. Stood there on the sidewalk, too freaked out to even move.

Am I having a dream? she wondered. That thought worried her. Because if she was having a dream, then that meant...

She stared at the house, wondering what was going to happen next. Wondering how any of this was even possible. What was real and what wasn't?

"I was late with the explosion," a voice suddenly said right next to her. She looked to her right, but there was no one there. She turned around and looked all about herself. Still, she saw no one. But their voice sounded like they were right next to her.

It had sounded familiar, too.

"Rezin," she said, knowing immediately who was speaking to her. Suddenly, it made much more sense. She was in a dream, after all. One that Rezin was controlling. She must've fallen asleep. She hadn't meant to. She had been doing such a good job so far keeping herself awake so that this wouldn't happen. Now, she was stuck and couldn't get herself to wake up.

"You were supposed to stay inside of that house," his voice continued. "Just a little bit longer. I had it all planned out."

Amberly looked back over at the house. This was from earlier today? This was the scene from when she had come here to start going through her mom's stuff.

"Is this some sort of... memory?" Amberly asked, starting to feel the fear inside of her. No wonder the house didn't look as if some fiery explosion had occurred.

It was because the explosion hadn't happened yet.

She didn't want this to happen. She was leaving Rezin to toy with her again. And the last time he toyed with her... he killed her mother.

What was going to happen this time?

"One by one," Rezin's deep, terrifying voice said. "I am learning about you Quintets, that you're better off alone. Separated from each other. You're much easier to take down that way."

"No," Amberly tried.

"You were supposed to die first. Then I would've moved on to the next one." His voice was sinister and menacing. "Then the next one. And the next one. Until you were all gone."

Amberly was shaking, but she forced herself to look and sound brave. "You won't win," she told him. "You couldn't even kill your first pick." She wanted Rezin to feel pain. Pain like he had made her feel. She wanted to get payback for what he had done. He had killed her mother and she was certain of it, regardless of if anyone else believed her or not.

She looked around, wondering why Rezin wasn't saying anything. She wondered where he was. What he looked like. What he was thinking. Why had he suddenly fallen silent?

She looked across the street again. The other Amberly had come outside to snap a picture of the house, and then she retreated back in again. It was going to be a while before she came back outside to put the box in her car. A little while before the explosion.

Amberly was about to ask where Rezin went and why he wasn't answering her, but then all of a sudden, she felt something around her neck. It was tight, choking her. And she knew it was Rezin's invisible grasp. Rezin was doing this to her.

"I can kill you now, though!" he bellowed, louder than any of his other sentences had been. It vibrated through her body as she tried to fight against his hold. As she squirmed and tried to get rid of him, she struggled to breathe as well. It was true; he was able to kill her now. He was easily able to overtake them in their dreams when they were powerless to do anything to stop him.

As she was being choked, she felt herself being lifted off the ground. All around her, it started to get windy, and she realized it was the feeling of the memory speeding up around her. When she side-glanced to her left, she could see the other Amberly coming outside with the box in her hands. But it was moving at triple the speed. And all the while, Amberly kept choking.

She tried to pry invisible fingers off of her neck, but it was useless. As she floated there in the air, she tried to yell out for the other Amberly to watch out. But the other Amberly didn't even seem to notice she was there. So the real Amberly was forced to float there in the sky and watch as her house exploded and her body from the memory flew back through the air.

"All asleep... alone in your hospital bed..." Rezin was whispering to her, chuckling darkly. "You're mine, Amberly McHenry..."

Amberly stared at her unmoving body on the sidewalk and her

house that was engulfed in flames. Everything was starting to get hazy around her. She knew that Rezin was right. She knew that she was going to die soon.

Her eyes snapped open, and suddenly, she was back in the real world. She had just awakened from the dream, and it was because that nurse was back, shaking her shoulders.

Amberly gasped and choked and sputtered, and the feeling of Rezin's fingers gripping her throat was now gone. She could breathe again, but she still felt like her windpipe had just been crushed.

"Are you okay?" the nurse asked, her forehead crinkled with concern. "I just came back to give you some more meds and saw you looking like you couldn't breathe."

Amberly rubbed her neck and tried to get her breath back. She wanted to hug this lady. She wanted to thank her for saving her life. She had woken Amberly from her dream, and now, Rezin wasn't able to continue choking the life out of her.

She decided not to say anything to the nurse because she knew the nurse would think she was crazy.

"I'm fine," she decided to say instead. "I was just having a nightmare. That's all."

"Some nightmare…"

When Amberly was left all alone again, she looked out the window and saw how dark it was outside. On the whiteboard across from her bed on the wall, she saw that Saturday's date was still written, which meant it was sometimes late at night. She wondered how long she even slept. How long it took for Rezin to take over her dream and torture her.?

As she lay in her bed, she thought about what Rezin had said to her in the dream, how he had nearly killed her because she had been able to finally sleep. But then she wondered, maybe he had just made her *think* he was killing her. Maybe she needed to get control of her dream somehow. She needed to try and remember that she *could* breathe, even when he was trying to make her feel like she couldn't. Maybe he was just toying with her thoughts. Making her think things that weren't true. Maybe there was a way that she could regain control.

But she didn't know the first way to go about it. It left her feeling hopeless. And afraid. Afraid because Rezin was beginning to figure out how the Quintets worked. He had outright just told her his plans on how he was going to defeat them when they least expected it. It made her worry, not only about herself but about the rest of the Quintets as well. Even Rose.

If they couldn't even defeat Rezin, what were they going to do about Yash?

The hopelessness she was feeling deepened. Everything she had ever loved was being taken from her. First, her mother. Then her home. Her friends were going to be taken next. What was the point of her even trying to stop it all?

Yash would come. It was inevitable. He would come, and he would defeat all of them. Amberly felt that her life was meaningless. That it was useless to keep trying to fight against it all.

Maybe she would feel differently if she wasn't lying in this hospital bed all alone. Maybe if Trace had stayed behind to comfort her, she would have had a little more confidence. Maybe if he had been there, she wouldn't have been tortured in her dream at all.

But nobody was there to save her.

And Amberly certainly didn't feel like trying to save herself.

Not anymore.

19

The next morning, Amberly was walking out of the bathroom in her cold, poorly decorated hospital room when she saw, much to her surprise, Kire standing there awkwardly looking around the place. Amberly had been in the bathroom staring at her poorly lit reflection in the mirror, trying to make herself look presentable even though she didn't have makeup or even something as simple as a hairbrush. She felt disgusting, but other than some slight soreness, she could tell she was nearly completely healed from the incident already. It amazed her that she had the capability to heal quickly like this, even when she didn't have her gauntlet on. It was as if the first time she ever put it on, it left its mark deep inside of her.

Amberly looked at Kire, wondering why it was him she was seeing, and not Trace or Kaos first thing in the morning. It had to be incredibly early still. Even though Amberly had been given more medication after her dream with Rezin last night, she had refused to sleep. She guessed that it had only turned to daylight a little bit ago.

Standing on the other side of the room, Kire had his backpack on and looked tired. There were circles under his eyes and he still had a bit of bedhead. Amberly wondered if he had even looked at himself in the mirror before leaving his house that morning. But then again, she was one to talk. She looked horrible herself.

"Oh, Kire," she said, her voice tight. "Uh, hi."

He stopped observing the room around her and met her eyes. "Hey. Uh, how are you today?"

This is so weird.

"I'm... fine," she forced herself to say. It wasn't the slightest bit true, but she didn't need Kire to know that. At least in the physical sense, she was fine. And maybe that's what Kire had been referring to anyway.

"Are you sure?" he asked. One of his thick brown brows was raised high.

She rolled her eyes and waved a hand at him. "Super healing abilities, remember?"

He offered a small smile. "Yeah. Kaos told the whole floor before we left last night that you didn't need to be given anything other than something to help you sleep. He had them all under his weird little crown spell. It was crazy to see. Crazy and awesome."

Amberly's stomach dipped. She knew Kaos had good intentions, but his little mind games with the other people on the floor meant it was his fault that Amberly had fallen into that horrific nightmare with Rezin who had nearly killed her last night. If she had never been given the meds, she wouldn't have fallen asleep. She wouldn't have nearly choked to death.

She tried to brush it off. "Huh," she said to Kire. "Now it makes sense. I was wondering why no one wanted to do any other tests or bandage changes on me. I wish he would have just manipulated them into letting me go back to my home... my aunt's house... instead. Now that I would have been appreciative of."

It would have also been great if Kaos could have used his powers on Trace to make him want to stay with Amberly. But Amberly knew they couldn't use their gifts on each other. It really bummed her out sometimes. How nice it would have been to simply just pick up Rose with her gauntlet in the lunch room and physically remove her from their lunch table.

"Yeah," Kire agreed to what Amberly had told him. "For as smart as he is, he doesn't always get it right, huh?"

"I bet you think you do, though," she teased.

Kire quickly shook his head. "Not at all," he argued. "In fact, I constantly find myself wondering if I am saying and doing the right things. In every aspect of my life. Home, school, Rose, Rezin…"

"You're doing your best," she told him, rolling her eyes and sitting down on the edge of her bed. She vaguely wondered when they would be bringing her breakfast and how gross and fattening it was likely to be. "We all are."

"I guess," Kire replied. Then they fell silent.

Did Kire really just swing by to check on her and make sure she was doing okay? Why was Kire being the nicest one out of her best friends when she had been treating him and his girlfriend like garbage?

Feeling a little bit guilty, Amberly was about to bring up how she appreciated him coming and how she was sorry for how she had been acting, but then Kire pulled his backpack off of one of his shoulders and took out a brown paper bag from the largest pouch.

"Well," he told her as he held it in his hand. "I just swung by to give this to you. It's another delivery. Maybe hide it under your pillow or something until you get back to your aunt's house. I would hate for one of the nurses to steal it or something."

Amberly stared at the bag.

Oh.

So he didn't come just to check on her. He was just dropping off money from their dad. The money she was likely going to have to spend on hospital bills. And it reminded her that now that the house was gone, she didn't think she was going to get any money from the sale after all. This raised worry inside of her. She had been so close to having a nice little fund waiting for her when she turned into an adult. Now it was all gone, and she was back to relying on her stupid deadbeat dad to give her his little paychecks.

Suddenly, her good mood was gone again. In the blink of an eye, Amberly's mood changed frequently. She knew she needed to get a better handle on her emotions, but what she didn't know was how.

"Cool." She snatched the bag from Kire. "Well, you can go. I should be getting let out of here soon anyway."

"Okay," Kire said awkwardly. He put his backpack on and then turned as if he were about to leave.

And Amberly was ready to let him go, too. She wanted him to get out of there. He wasn't actually there to check on her. To see if she was okay. To see if she needed anything. To see if she was dealing with the loss she had just suffered all right. He didn't care. He just was doing his duty and dropping off what belonged to her.

As she sat there on her bed, she knew the truth. She didn't really want Kire to go. She wanted him to know what had happened to her. She wanted him to know the danger that they were in. She felt it was her duty, as part of the Quintets, to relay all of the information to another member about what was happening with her. About the things that Rezin had told her in her dream last night. As much as she didn't want to. As much as she wanted to pretend as if it had never happened. As much as she just felt like Yash should just come and end the world and get it over with already.

Kire had stepped completely outside of the door and was about to be out of her sight.

"Kire, wait," she said to him at the last minute. She jumped off her bed and rushed over to him. She grabbed his wrist and yanked him back inside her room and then closed the door, not caring if she wasn't supposed to. "Rezin created the explosion," she explained. "He's... he's messing with me."

"What are you talking about?" Kire asked, looking alert.

"Last night... I had a dream..." Quickly, she explained everything that had happened to her.

When she finished, she couldn't ignore the plainly worried expression on Kire's face.

"What are we supposed to do?" Kire asked, suddenly pacing around the hospital room as Amberly sat back down on the bed, feeling exhausted. "It's not like we can spend every waking second with each other, binding ourselves together so that we are harder to fight. Who knows which one of us he is going to come after next?" He ran a hand through his hair, appearing very stressed out.

"Kire," Amberly said, thinking quickly. "You have to use Halo to try and summon Albus. He can help."

Kire stopped pacing and turned back to Amberly.

"But, Amberly," he said, looking doubtful, "the last time we talked to Albus, he said he wasn't going to be able to help us anymore. Remember? He's got a lot that he's dealing with over in the magical realm. That... and we don't even know if he's still even alive."

"I know that," Amberly said, her voice full of attitude. "But, Kire, come on. You have to try. You have to."

"There's no point."

"Yes, there is! Things are going downhill and fast. Who knows how much time we have? You have that stupid backpack with you. Which means I know that you brought Halo with you. So just. Try." She glowered at him as if daring him to do otherwise.

He held his head a little higher. "I take her with me everywhere," he explained. He didn't even seem embarrassed about it. "Just like you should be taking your gauntlet with you everywhere, too."

She rolled her eyes and waved her hand dismissively. "Whatever," she said quickly. "Hurry up before a doctor comes in here and interrupts us."

Kire sighed and dropped down to his knees. He pulled Halo out and opened the book up. He wrote something down in ink, and then he sat back, and the two of them waited.

Nothing happened.

"Is Halo even saying anything?" Amberly asked, feeling hopeless. Why couldn't it just work? Why can't, why couldn't Albus come, just for a moment? Just to tell them what to do.

"Hang on," Kire said, leaning closer to the book to read some words that were writing themselves out in a language that only Kire could read.

"What is happening?" Amberly asked impatiently.

"It's just Halo. She says that Albus cannot come."

"Why not?" she demanded.

"She's not telling me why," he said.

"Ask her if it's because he's dead," she said.

Kire shot her a look that was slightly horrified.

"We have to know, Kire."

Sighing, he did as Amberly instructed.

"She's not answering me. She doesn't want to say."

Amberly's stomach dipped. She could tell, based on the look on Kire's face, that they both felt the exact same way. Worried about the fate of Albus.

"Oh." Amberly felt disheartened.

Kire closed the book. "I told you it won't work."

Suddenly, she was over him being there. She stood up. "Ugh," she complained. "Just get out now, will you?!"

He shoved the book quickly back into his backpack and got to his feet. "Gladly," he said in a dark voice. He shot her a glare, and then Kire turned and finally left the room.

20

All Sunday morning long, Amberly was continuously torn between feeling impatient about wanting to leave the hospital and wondering what was taking so long for her to get discharged, but also wishing she could stay in the hospital. She didn't like being there initially, but she realized that she felt a little bit safer there. With people watching her so often and waking her up to change her meds and whatnot, she was more protected. She was safer from being attacked in her dreams by Rezin. Back at her aunt's house, if she were to fall asleep, the only person that would be around to save her was her aunt. And herself, if she could. But Amberly had no idea how to save herself in a dream where Rezin was controlling it. Not yet, anyway.

Finally, Amberly was released from the hospital sometime around the beginning of the afternoon. When she stepped out into the cold air through the automatic hospital doors, she saw that it was an overcast, dreary day. It was slightly misty, too, and she instantly shivered and pulled her jacket tighter over herself.

"Are you feeling okay?" her aunt asked her as they both got into her small silver car. Somehow, it miraculously had been unaffected by the explosion from Amberly's former house. The firemen had been able to save it. This also meant that, thankfully, the pictures Amberly had wanted to keep of her and her mother were safe.

If nothing else in the fire made it, Amberly was grateful she at least had those.

"Aunt Lydia, you don't have to keep checking on me," Amberly said to her aunt, "I promise you, I'm fine. I'm feeling practically one hundred percent recovered. There's really nothing to worry about."

"Okay." Her aunt started driving. "I just worry about you, that's all. The stove exploded. That's what the firefighters said. But how does a stove just explode like that? Apparently, they're still searching for answers. I can't believe how quickly those flames engulfed that whole house, too. It's all over the news."

"I can," Amberly said, shrugging. "Everything was so old. And there was lots of furniture made from wood. And tons of thick curtains."

"It's horrible," Aunt Lydia said. "I'm so sorry again, Amberly. I feel just terrible that you lost so much. Was there a lot that you had been wanting to keep?"

Amberly felt a little bit guilty. She had marked that there was a lot she wanted to keep, but only because she wanted to annoy her aunt with how much stuff they were going to have to put in a storage unit that her aunt had to pay for.

"Not a whole lot," she decided to say.

"Well, here's the deal." They were stopped at a red light, and her aunt was turned in her seat to face Amberly. She pulled her wallet out of her back pocket and then took out a chunk of change. "I want you to have this."

Amberly stared at the cash, not taking it. "What?" she asked, confused. She already had the giant bag of cash from her father tucked away in the bag with her burned clothes that the hospital had given her when she was discharged.

Her aunt smiled at her encouragingly, bringing her hand closer toward Amberly so that Amberly would take the money. "Go on. It's yours."

Amberly leaned away so that her back was against the passenger door. "Aunt Lydia…"

"I want you to go on a shopping spree. It's a perfect day to spend indoors. Like at the mall. If you're feeling up for it, of course. I am sure you might also feel like just going home and resting."

"I definitely don't feel like resting," Amberly said, shaking her head a little more dramatically than she needed to as she accepted the money from her aunt. "I, um…thank you."

"Don't mention it. It's the least I can do to make up for the fact that I made you go over to that house in the first place. I feel responsible for all of this."

"It's not your fault," Amberly said, wishing she could explain to her aunt just how true that statement was.

The rest of the drive back to her aunt's house was silent. When she hopped out of the car, they headed to the front door together, and that was when her aunt decided to speak again.

"So, when you go on the shopping spree, feel free to take my car again. And… you should invite someone if you'd like."

"Invite someone?" Amberly was surprised that her aunt wasn't inviting *herself* to tag along. For whatever reason, Amberly was finding that she wouldn't have minded if her aunt had asked to come with her. In fact, she might've even said *yes*.

"Yeah," Aunt Lydia said. "If you want. You can pick them up in the car or whatever. I trust you, Amberly."

"I'll probably just go alone," she said.

"Why?" Aunt Lydia asked as they went inside.

Amberly shrugged.

Her aunt wasn't satisfied with the answer. "Do you have any girlfriends to go shopping with? It was, like, my *favorite* thing to do when I was in high school."

"Well, that was a long time ago," Amberly snapped, realizing a little too late how rude it sounded.

"Right," her aunt agreed. "Well, in any case, have fun."

"I'll just go freshen up and then take off, then," Amberly said.

She and her aunt went their separate ways and Amberly got ready to go on the shopping spree. She wasn't exactly certain whether she felt like shopping, but it would at least get her out of the house. It would at least be something to distract her from all of the horrible thoughts she had been having lately.

As she was finishing up her makeup a little while later, she decided to give Trace a call.

"Are you out of the hospital?" he asked right when he answered.

"I am," Amberly replied. "Finally."

"I'm glad. And I'm guessing you're fully healed, too."

"You know it."

"Did they ever figure out what caused the fire?"

"Um... not yet," she said. She didn't want to tell Trace about Rezin and how it had been all his fault. She would just leave that for Kire to fill him in on it. "But anyway," she continued before he could say anything else about it. "That's not why I called. I'm headed to the mall. I need to buy a whole bunch of new stuff since so much was destroyed in the fire. Want to come with?" She tried her best to sound as casual as possible. Like she didn't have a care in the world if Trace was to say no. But deep down, she was hoping and praying that he was going to say yes.

"Oh, shoot," he said instead. "I'm sorry, Amber. I'm sort of busy with the guys. We're doing an extra soccer practice out at the park. We really need the extra training. We've all been slacking a lot lately."

The rejection stung a lot. But naturally, Amberly couldn't let Trace know of this.

"Of course," she said. "Have fun."

"Babe?"

"I'll talk to you later." Amberly ended the call without even saying goodbye. She realized right away that she probably didn't do the best job of hiding the fact that her feelings were hurt by Trace. She had been snappy on the phone and clearly sounded offended.

Whatever.

Amberly finished getting ready, forced herself to put on a happy face, and made her way to the mall in her aunt's car. Just as she had done during the drive over to her mom's house before everything went bad, She rolled the windows down and blasted loud pop music. She didn't even care that it was still freezing outside and that it looked like it was going to start raining at any second. She welcomed the cold.

It took her a few tries to park the car. She wasn't that used to driving, and then she entered the mall through the food court. Instantly, her nose was filled with the scents of cinnamon rolls, French fries, and Kung pow chicken. Normally, Amberly would've craved a cinnamon roll to snack on while she walked around the mall, but today, she didn't have the appetite for one.

It was a busy day at the mall. Kids ran around screaming. Teenagers grouped together, talking and gossiping and loitering. Rich suburban moms went into the expensive stores. Men walked out of the barbershop with fresh, clean haircuts.

Amberly went into a couple of stores and bought anything that made her happy. Even after she blew through her aunt's money, she still continued spending the money she had received so far from her dad. Not all of it, of course. Just enough to where her mood was finally boosted when she saw how many shopping bags she had accumulated.

After she left the shoe store, she walked through the corridors of the mall and couldn't help but observe other happy couples spending their Sundays together. There was one by the fountain, sitting together and sharing an ice cream cone. There was another one, holding hands and sliding past her as they giggled about something together. Another couple took pictures of each other as they stood on the escalator as it was going down to the bottom level. Everywhere Amberly looked, she seemed to be finding these happy couples.

Seeing them made her unable to help but wonder...

What was even the point of being with Trace anymore?

It hurt her stomach just to think about it. They had been together for so long. They had gone through a lot together. They had always been the perfect pair. But lately... it seemed as if Trace didn't want anything to do with her. It seemed as if he wasn't interested in being around her anymore. And Amberly hadn't exactly been the greatest girlfriend to him lately, either. In fact, it seemed as if they hardly even liked each other anymore so what was the point? Why were they still together? Why were they trying to force this thing to continue to work?

Amberly was so overcome with her own emotions and questions about her relationship with Trace that she sat down by the fountain, far from the cute couple with the ice cream cone. What was she doing with Trace? Possibly one explanation made the most sense, but she really hated that she was even wondering about it.

Were she and Trace together just because they were popular? Just because they made sense together? Or was Amberly still hoping for them to have the relationship she always wanted them to? Did she see something more in Trace than everybody else saw? Did she truly believe that they could be a good couple?

As she sat there in that mall with her millions of shopping bags around her, Amberly realized she had absolutely no idea.

<h1 style="text-align:center">21</h1>

When Amberly walked through the door of her new home, her arms full to the brim with her shopping bags, she had been hoping that her aunt wasn't anywhere near her so that she could get to her room with the bags in secret. She didn't want her aunt to see how much stuff she had bought at the mall.

But of course, to Amberly's dismay, her aunt was at her usual spot at the dining table in front of her laptop. Aunt Lydia's eyes widened when she saw Amberly and all of the bags she was holding in her hands.

"Um, hi, Aunt Lydia," Amberly said with a slight smile. She was embarrassed, and she hoped that her aunt didn't notice it.

"Wow," Aunt Lydia said to her. "That's *some* shopping spree you went on. You were really able to get that much stuff from the money *I* gave you?"

Amberly managed to close the door behind her with all of the bags still in her arms. She dropped them to the ground, giving up on trying to get to her room with them discreetly. Flustered, she pushed some hair behind her ear. "Oh... yeah," she lied. "There were some insane sales this weekend. Turns out, it was the perfect time to go. Like you said."

"That's impressive," she said. "But something also tells me with your great style that you know how to shop."

Amberly *definitely* knew how to shop. But when she shopped today, she didn't even check for sales. In fact, she didn't even read any of the price tags on anything she picked out.

"I go shopping every once in a while," she said. "To be honest, we've never really had a lot of money. I used to have a job where I'd work on the weekends to make money so I could go shopping. But even then, I didn't do it often because most of my money had to go to paying bills. Mom was too sick to work."

Aunt Lydia's face fell. Amberly could tell that she felt sorry for her. Usually, Amberly hated when people felt sorry for her. For some reason, staring at her aunt inside her new home, Amberly realized that she didn't mind the look her aunt was giving her. She shrugged it off. "It is what it is," she said.

"That doesn't sound like a very fun teenage life," Aunt Lydia commented. She got up from the table and walked over to all of the bags. "Let me help you take these to your room."

Amberly didn't say no to the offer to help, and the two retreated into her room, where they dropped the bags onto the floor. Amberly would just go through them later. She felt almost as if she had blacked out while she was shopping. She couldn't even recall half of the stuff she had purchased. And still, she had plenty of money left over from what her dad had given her so far.

I really need to open a bank account and start saving some of this.

"Well..." Aunt Lydia stood in the doorway, hovering. It was well after dinner. Amberly had spent practically the entire day at the mall. "I was going to pop some popcorn and watch some cheesy chick flick on the TV in the living room. Did you maybe... want to join?"

Amberly stared at her aunt.

"You totally don't have to," Aunt Lydia said, blushing slightly. It was as if her aunt thought the last thing Amberly would want to do was hang out with her when she could be chatting with her boyfriend or hanging out with friends from school.

"Oh, no, I'll totally join." Amberly felt the need to prove her aunt wrong. She didn't mind spending some time with her. In fact, Amberly felt that she had grown a little bit closer to her aunt since the incident with the explosion of her house, where she had seen her aunt so worried about her... It had struck something inside of Amberly. A new sort of fondness.

Aunt Lydia smiled. "Great! I'll get to popping, then. Why don't you change into some comfy jammies and I'll meet you out there?" She went out of Amberly's room and then practically skipped down the hall.

Amberly chuckled and did exactly as her aunt suggested. She had the perfect pajamas to wear: ones she had bought at the mall earlier that day. She slipped them on and brushed out her hair and removed her makeup. When she walked out into the living room, she could smell the fresh popcorn. Her stomach growled. She finally had a bit of an appetite.

Aunt Lydia split the popcorn into two bowls, handed her one, and then they made themselves comfortable on the couch. Aunt Lydia insisted they watch *Gone with the Wind*, a classic that Amberly apparently just *had* to see. Amberly didn't argue about it. Black-and-white movies weren't typically her thing, but even her mother had talked about wanting her to watch this one. And if her mother had wanted her to see it, then Amberly definitely wanted to give it a try.

"Did you and my mom ever watch this together?" Amberly found herself asking as they munched on the popcorn while the movie started.

"Maybe once," Aunt Lydia said, "when we were really little."

"So, you guys used to get along at some point," Amberly pointed out.

"Oh, yeah," Aunt Lydia agreed. "We were the *best* of friends,

Amberly. You don't even know. Having a sister can be amazing. Like a built-in best friend. But it can also... it can be really hard. There can be a lot of jealousy. Resentment. Cattiness. And it was just your mother, me, and our mom, your grandma. All of us females live under one roof. It was practically inevitable for us to stop getting along. There were no males around to break up some of the... overwhelming estrogens everywhere." She chuckled like it was all a big joke to her. But it wasn't a joke to Amberly that she and her mother weren't close anymore.

"You don't seem that bad to me," Amberly pointed out. "I don't know what issue you and my mom had with each other, but I sort of wish you could've figured it out so that I could have seen you more often growing up."

Her aunt squeezed her knee. "I so wish that, too," she said. "It sucks that we stopped getting along."

"It does," Amberly agreed. She would've loved to have a movie night with her mom and her aunt when she was little. She could have seen movies like *Gone with the Wind* ten times over by now. But when it was just her and her mother, these movie nights hardly even happened. Either one of them was working, or her mom was sleeping, or Amberly was doing homework.

"Your mom was the one who got me into black-and-white movies," Aunt Lydia explained. "I always thought they seemed so boring since they didn't have color. But I was so, so wrong."

"I'm beginning to see that," Amberly replied as they continued watching the movie. It was still some time into the beginning, but Amberly found herself enjoying it. She couldn't recall if she had even watched a black-and-white movie before this.

After some time of silence, Aunt Lydia turned to look at her.

"What?" Amberly asked, a little annoyed that her aunt was staring at her because she had been fully invested in the movie and wanted to know what was going to happen next.

"You can be so much stronger than her; you know that, right?"

"Stronger than Scarlett O'Hara?" Amberly asked, confused.

"No, your mother."

"What do you mean?" Amberly didn't understand. It wasn't like she was sick like her mother had been. Of course, Amberly could be stronger than her. She had a much better immune system.

"Your mom... she sort of... and I *really* don't mean to speak badly about her since she passed, but... she let people walk all over her, Amberly. Part of me thinks it's the reason you two ended up in the situation that you did."

"Our situation..."

"You know, in that small, old house. You having to work even though you're just a teenager and should be out living your life. Your mom falling depressed and then getting ill."

"You think all of that happened because she was a pushover?" Amberly asked.

"Maybe not *just* because of that. But I think it is a big contributing factor. Your... your father..."

"You know who my father is?" Amberly was surprised by this. Since she and her mother never talked, she assumed that Aunt Lydia would know nothing about her mother's romantic life.

"I just know *of* him," Aunt Lydia explained. "And from what I heard, it wasn't good. He had always been a horrible person. I couldn't understand why your mother was with him, Amberly. It was infuriating. And there was no getting through to her, either. He would mess up over and over again, and she would forgive him. Ugh, how I hated it."

Amberly's stomach dipped. "I never knew what it was like for them to be together. So I never got to see what you're talking about."

"I know," she said, shaking her head sadly. "I know that you had to spend your life without him in it. And it makes me sad for you."

"Don't feel sad for me," Amberly said, clashing her eyebrows. "I'm serious." Amberly sat up straighter. "I don't need it. I am a strong, independent, capable woman. I'm not like my mother. I don't put up with anyone's bull."

"I'm impressed," Aunt Lydia said, putting a hand to her chest. "And I'm glad." She moved closer to Amberly and grabbed both of her hands. "Listen to me, Amberly. You are indeed a strong, independent, capable woman. Don't let anyone tell you otherwise. Don't let anyone ever make you think otherwise. And... do the opposite of what your mother did. Do not let anyone ever take anything away from you."

"I won't," Amberly said.

"And... just please, promise me you won't live the life that she did."

"Sitting in the same chair every single day coughing up a lung? Not a chance."

Amberly and her aunt smiled at each other.

"Good," Aunt Lydia said. "It's important. I want you to have the best life possible. And for that to happen, you need to be bold. You need to be daring. You need to be a fighter. And from the Amberly that I've come to know, I know that you have all three of these qualities inside of you."

Amberly was so flattered by the compliment that she didn't even know what to say or do. She instead rolled her eyes and turned away from her aunt. "Yeah, yeah," she said, waving her aunt off. "Now, pay attention to the movie already, will ya?"

22

All through watching the movie with her aunt, Amberly couldn't stop thinking about the words Aunt Lydia had told her. *Bold, Daring, Fighter*. Aunt Lydia knew that Amberly had all of those qualities inside her, so Amberly had to believe that she did, too.

I can be bold, daring, and a fighter, she thought to herself. *Haven't I been these things already? I'd say saving the world has proved that at least a little bit.*

She thought about it some more.

What about when it comes to Rezin? What about when it comes to me trying to get any sleep?

The thoughts that were all swirling through Amberly's head distracted her during the majority of the movie, and before she knew it, her aunt was turning off the TV and turning to her and saying, "Well, I'm beating. I am going to hit the hay. How about you?"

"Oh..." Amberly looked around, not even realizing that the movie had ended. "Yeah." She yawned, and it wasn't even a fake one. She was exhausted, of course. "Yeah, I should get to bed as well."

They got off the couch together, and then Lydia went to go put the popcorn bowls back in the kitchen. They both walked to the hallway together, but then they got to a point where Amberly had to turn left to go to her room, and Aunt Lydia had to take a right.

"I had a really good time with you tonight; you know that?" Aunt Lydia asked Amberly with a hopeful smile on her face.

"I had a good time, too." And the craziest thing was that Amberly meant it. She was actually enjoying spending time with her aunt. She was actually coming to like this lady more and more. Amberly hadn't thought that would ever happen, seeing as her mother had never liked her aunt. And it made Amberly almost feel guilty that she liked Aunt Lydia. But whatever issues her mom had with Aunt Lydia, that was between them. Amberly just told herself that she was allowed to have her own separate relationship and opinions of Aunt Lydia. So far, the woman hadn't done anything to make her feel as if she wasn't likable. After all, what kind of woman would travel across the country, move into town, and take care of a moody teenager after a sibling they didn't even like passed away?

They said their goodnights to each other, and then Amberly wandered to her bedroom and closed the door. But she didn't go over to her bed. Because she wasn't prepared to go to sleep. It didn't matter how tired she was.

Now, what do I do to keep myself awake? she wondered as she paced around her room as soundlessly as possible. She didn't want to do anything that would wake her aunt after she fell asleep. She didn't want her aunt to know that she wasn't sleeping well. That she was too afraid of her own dreams. She would come off as a baby to Aunt Lydia, and after the conversation they just had, she couldn't let her think anything like that.

But, was not going to sleep making Amberly unable to fit the criteria her aunt Lydia said she had inside of her? Did being afraid of going to sleep mean she wasn't brave, daring, or a fighter?

I don't want to fight Rezin alone in my dreams, she thought to herself as she looked at her reflection in her floor-length mirror.

"I'm not sleeping," she whispered to herself. She looked strong when she said it. She looked like she was a fighter. A fighter of sleep.

So she continued pacing around her room. She braided her hair. She unbraided her hair. She got on her phone and checked social media. She played with the jewelry in her jewelry box.

She looked through the photos of the only box she had saved from her mom's house before the explosion happened. She yawned over and over again, and she squeezed her eyeballs shut tightly and opened them as wide as she could, hoping that would help. She even smacked herself on the cheek a couple of times, wondering if *that* would help. Part of her thought maybe she needed to go dump a bucket of ice water on top of her head. That would keep someone awake, right?

She stared at her bed, longing to be on top of it. Longing to be inside of the covers, her head resting on the extra fluffy-looking pillow.

Don't do it, Amberly, she thought to herself. If she laid down, she knew she was a goner. She couldn't sleep. No matter how much sleep was fighting to consume her.

I'm not going to sleep.

I'm not going to sleep.

I'm not going to...

All of a sudden, Amberly had been transported somewhere else. Somewhere dark and scary, with bushes rustling and branches snapping around her.

Amberly's stomach dropped violently. *How did I get here?*

She turned about herself in a slow, slow circle. She was in a forest of sorts. And after a couple of seconds, she realized that it was the White Forest.

How had she gotten there? The last thing she remembered was being in her bedroom. Standing, on two feet. She hadn't gone to sleep. So what did that mean? Did she black out and walk over here somehow?

"Amberly," a voice choked out, like it was trying to yell but was being held back because of something. Something painful.

Amberly turned again. This time, she found that she was only a few feet away from Kaos. Kaos, who had vines wrapped around his ankles, wrists, and throat. He was suspended in the air, the vines pulling tighter and tighter on his skin with every step Amberly took toward him.

"Kaos?!" Amberly called. Terror raced through her veins.

How is this happening?

She tried to use her powers to get the vines off of him. But when she looked down at her arm, she realized she didn't have Gomora, her gauntlet, on her.

She was powerless to help Kaos.

"Help," Kaos tried anyway. It just seemed to be the two of them in the forest. No one else was around to hear them or help them. But why *would* there be anyone else around? It was the middle of the night, and people generally avoided the White Forest anyway.

Amberly was afraid to move any closer because she didn't want the vines to go around him any tighter. But Kaos was starting to turn blue. He was in pain. He was going to be killed from this torture by the great Rezin...

"How?" Amberly cried, falling to her knees. How could she help him? What could she do without Gomora? She wasn't strong without her gauntlet. She couldn't help without her gauntlet.

If only the other Quintets were there with their gifts. They would know what to do. They would know how to help.

This has to be a dream... This has to be a dream... This has to be a dream.

Somehow, Amberly figured she must have fallen asleep, even though she couldn't remember doing so. This had to be a dream. This could not be real life. She had tried her hardest to stay awake, and it hadn't been enough. Right?

But as she watched Kaos so clearly, in the White Forest that was so familiar, she felt uncertain. She could not differentiate between reality and dreams. It was probably partially to do with the fact that she was just so, so tired. Was it possible that she had fallen asleep while standing, sleepwalked over there, and woken up to find herself in this situation?

Or was this all in her head? What if it was just a normal nightmare, one not controlled by Rezin? What if she was in her bed, simply making this all up on her own?

Kaos struggled against the vines in front of her. He wanted out of their grasp, but he was only making things worse.

"Don't...don't fight it, Kaos!" Amberly tried. She thought it was only going to hurt him more the more he fought. The vines seemed to be tightening their grip around him with every pull and thrash he did.

She looked around herself for something she could use to help. She also searched for any signs of Rezin so that she could try and stop him. It was horrible watching Kaos being tortured like that. And it was horrible how powerless she felt to stop it.

There's nothing I can do to help him! she thought, *Not without Gomora!*

It was even more horrible to consider the fact that maybe even though this was possibly a dream, this could be Rezin showing her what he was doing in the White Forest with Kaos at this very moment.

She could be dreaming.

Or she could be actually in the White Forest, and this could be actually happening right in front of her right now.

Or, she could be dreaming about the reality that was happening in the White Forest. She could be in her bed right now while Kaos was tied up by vines in the forest, calling out for her, hoping she would come and save him.

She needed to figure out what the truth was.

It's a dream, right?

She felt, somewhere deep inside of her, that even though she had no recollection of getting into bed and going to sleep, she was in the middle of a dream. One created by Rezin.

There was only one thing she needed to do.

She needed to wake up.

"I don't think so," a voice surrounded her and enveloped her. It was Rezin's.

Suddenly, Amberly was choked. Choked and lifted off the ground by an invisible, strong hand.

She pried at the fingers she couldn't see or feel around her neck. And still, she was being choked. Rezin was attacking her. Rezin was furious that she had figured it out. That she knew it couldn't be real.

It couldn't be.

So he was retaliating. He was doing whatever he could to prevent her from going back to the present. And if Amberly stayed here in this dream with him, then she was surely going to die.

Wake up, Amberly, she told herself. "Wake up!"

Amberly awoke on the floor of her bedroom, right beside her bed, in front of her closet. She coughed and sputtered and clawed at her throat, which was still in pain as she gasped for air. It hurt a lot, but she found she could finally breathe again. Rezin couldn't get to her here, like this, while she was awake.

She had been dreaming, after all. She had passed out on the floor beside her bed.

Still coughing, she crawled over to her full-length mirror and used her dresser to help herself get to her feet. She checked out her reflection, specifically her neck, and saw the red fingerprints. The bruises that were already forming from how tightly Rezin had squeezed her throat. She had been right. If she had stayed there in that dream Rezin was causing her to have, he would have killed her.

Rezin didn't want Amberly to realize that she had been in a dream after all.

He didn't want Amberly to come in time to make it to the White Forest to be able to save Kaos.

Rezin had choked her to try and stop her.

And if, in the dream, the choking had been real, then the torture of Kaos must have been real, too.

The decision was easy.

Amberly grabbed Gomora and put it on her arm. She shoved her feet into some shoes as quickly as she could.

There wasn't even time for her to tell the others. Kaos was being tortured by those vines in the White Forest *right now*.

So, without letting anybody know where she was going, Amberly snuck out of the front door and just started running.

23

Amberly ran in the dead of night through her neighborhood as quickly as she could to get to the White Forest. She didn't know where inside the White Forest Kaos even was; all she knew was that she had to get to him. She had to do whatever it took to stop Rezin from killing him.

She pumped her arms quickly. Her feet pounded the pavement harder than they ever had before. Then finally, she reached the edge of the forest and practically dove inside it. She didn't feel any fear. She hardly felt anything at all other than just plain adrenaline. It coursed through her veins, making her move quicker. Making her see clearer. Gomora on her arm felt as if it was a part of her. And as she ran through the forest, she used her powers to move anything out of her pathway so that she wouldn't trip or risk it taking any longer than it needed to finally reach Kaos.

With the tunnel vision she had, she didn't even realize that someone was coming diagonally but forward in the same direction as her, and suddenly a body slammed into her, and both people fell back on their butts on the damp forest ground.

"Amberly!"

Amberly looked to her right at the figure she had plowed into, and while she hoped it was Kaos, who had freed himself from the vines and was running away, she found that it was not him. Instead, Rose looked at her with giant eyes. Amberly could see the whites of them even in the darkness of the forest.

Amberly crawled to her as Rose crawled over to her, and they quickly helped each other up to their feet.

"What are you doing?!" Amberly shrieked.

"I... my dream led me here!" Rose cried.

"So did my dream," Amberly said, out of breath. "The dream Rezin made me have. We... we have to get to Kaos, Rose, now!"

"Kaos?"

But Amberly didn't even stop to think why Rose is questioning it. She didn't answer her. Instead, she grabbed Rose's hand and took off with her again. Together, they would at least be able to have a better chance of getting Kaos freed from those vines.

Amberly and Rose ran through the White Forest. Amberly was determined to find Kaos. She knew the forest was large and wide, but she also knew she would get to him and that she had to be going in the right direction. It was as if she could sense him. She wondered if Rose could, too.

After another minute or so, Amberly heard more rustling in the bushes and quick feet on the forest ground. Feet from multiple people. Then suddenly, she was in front of all of the other Quintets.

All of the Quintets formed together in a huddle, touching each other's arms and staring around at each other with the wildest expressions on their faces.

"Wait a second," Amberly said, feeling very confused. Feeling trapped. Feeling played. "You're all... you're all okay..." She looked at Kaos, who seemed like he hadn't ever been tied up by vines at all.

"What's happening?" Trace asked, looking angered. "How are you all here right now?"

"We were led here," Kire said with a sigh, figuring it out.

"Lead here by a dream that Rezin caused us all to have," Kaos added, figuring it out as well.

Amberly looked around at the forest surrounding them. At the darkness of it. How quiet it felt. There weren't even any bushes rustling or tree branches swaying anymore. It was still.

Maybe even *too* still.

"What does that mean?" Rose asked with chattering teeth. "If Rezin led us all here..."

The answer was obvious. "It means that he led us straight into a trap," Amberly breathed out.

And the moment the words left her mouth, the forest was full of wind. A powerful, gushing wind threatened to knock them over.

"What's happening?!" Kire yelled.

"He's attacking!" Kaos shouted.

The wind was so loud that they all had to shout. Suddenly, thunder rumbled overhead. And when Amberly looked up, the sky peeking through the canopy of leaves showed lightning. Lots of it. And the thunder was loud as if the lightning was only feet away from them. It was loud enough to make Amberly want to cover her ears.

Next came the rain. But the rain quickly turned to hail. Large, golf ball-sized pieces of ice started falling through the trees in the forest and landing right on top of their heads.

"Aargh!" Trace bellowed, covering his head for protection. Everyone followed suit as the golf ball-sized ice kept pelting down on them harder and more powerfully. Then around them, the branches of the tree started moving as well. Vines, just like the ones Amberly had seen in her dream, started weaving their way, as if by magic, as if Rezin w manipulating them, going toward the Quintets.

"What do we do?!" Rose asked.

"We need to fight back!" Amberly shouted. She used her gauntlet to fight off the branches and vines coming toward them. Rose clutched her pendant and closed her eyes to focus on manipulating the trees to do the opposite of what Rezin was trying to make them do. Two magical forces fighting to make the plants do opposite things, which just made them freak out even more.

"It's not working!" Kaos cried. He had his crown on his head and looked as if he was trying to focus intently on figuring out where Rezin was and how to stop him. But he also looked hopeless. It was impossible to control Rezin.

A vine swung toward Amberly violently before she could even see that it was coming in time to move it away with her powers. Thankfully, though, Kire pushed her aside, and the vine missed her. Instead, it wrapped around Kire's ankle. But Amberly was quick to get the vine off of him.

"Thanks," she muttered to Kire.

"No problem."

"Guys, I don't think we can beat this," Trace said as he used his sword to try to cut the vines and branches away from him. The hail was still pelting down violently. Lightning and thunder grew louder and louder, and Amberly knew they were in danger of being struck by it at any moment.

"I think he's right," Amberly said.

"So then what?" Kire asked.

"We need to run! Now!" Kaos instructed.

And they all followed his lead.

Sprinting, they all went in the direction of the caves. At least inside there, they wouldn't be able to be struck by the lightning. They dove inside it, stopping for a moment and wondering if they were safe in there. If they were better protected. If maybe Rezin had lost track of where they had run off to. If maybe the attack would be over.

But then, the wind burst through the cave opening, creating a loud enough whistle to sound like a train as it nearly knocked them over again.

"Keep moving!" Amberly instructed, running ahead of everyone. When she looked over her shoulder, luckily, she saw that all of the Quintets were following her. But not as luckily, she saw that behind them, the vines of the trees and the branches had started swarming their way through the cave's opening as well and were chasing them.

"Faster!" Amberly bellowed, noticing that Rose was starting to fall behind.

"I'm trying!" Rose cried. No doubt, Rose was probably feeling weak after working her magic. She always was.

We just have to keep going, Amberly thought to herself as she pumped her arms harder. She had exerted a lot of energy just getting to the forest at all, but yet, as she ran through the cave, she felt as if she hadn't run in days and that she had endless energy inside of her.

"What are we supposed to do? They're going to keep coming after us!" Kire shouted. "How do we get away?!"

Amberly didn't have the answer to that. And as they kept running and nobody said anything, she realized nobody else did, either.

But she also knew the direction in which all the Quintets were running anyway. It seemed as if they all were secretly thinking the same thing, even if nobody wanted to say it. They were all running in the direction of the lake. The lake that Amberly had drained.

Amberly had forgotten until they approached the caved-in wall, that she had drained the lake and hidden it from everyone.

"How could this have happened?!" Kaos yelled angrily as he saw the caved-in wall in front of the lake where they were hoping they could run to in order to escape.

"It caved in?!" Trace called, his eyebrows furrowed together.

"We need to think of something, and fast!" Kire shouted. When Amberly looked over at him, she followed his gaze and saw that the vines were getting closer and closer. The howling wind was growing nearer and louder.

Quickly, Amberly strategically moved the pieces of rock that she needed to so that they could crawl through and get to the lake on the other side.

"Go through here!" she shouted at the others. She let them all go in first until it got to Trace. Trace stalled and motioned toward the opening.

"Go!" he demanded of Amberly. He didn't want her to be the last one in there. Amberly gave him an appreciative glance and then dove into the other side. At the very last second, a branch snaked itself around Trace as he dove into the hole. But Amberly and Rose were there quickly to get it off of him. Then, using her telekinesis, Amberly resealed the hole with other rocks and finally, it seemed as if they were no longer under Rezin's attack.

"Finally," Amberly said, her chest heaving as she lowered her arm and found that she could now relax for a moment.

The others were silent.

Amberly slowly turned around and saw that they all had their backs to her because they were walking toward the now-drained lake. They could see the portal, glowing blue, at the bottom of it.

"What is this?" Trace breathed.

"Oh... that..." Amberly hadn't told them that she had drained the lake. This was their first time seeing it like this. "I did it," she said.

They all turned and looked at her. No one said anything. They just waited for her to continue explaining herself.

Amberly was somewhat embarrassed, but she decided to come clean about what she had done anyway. "I just wanted to see if I could do something like this, something that would require a lot of my powers and a lot of my strength, without needing the help of you guys being here with me," she said. "So I came here one night and I... I drained the lake. And then I made it look like this area of the cave had caved in so that nobody could discover the portal that everyone can clearly see now at the bottom."

"When did you do this?" Rose asked, her voice almost sounding as if it was in awe. She was probably jealous because there was no way she would be able to do anything like this without the others around. Not without her nose bleeding and her fainting.

"I don't know. The other day. It's not a big deal," Amberly replied.

"Well... it's seriously... impressive," Trace said. "But I don't like the idea of you being here all alone without any of us, Amber."

"I was fine," she snapped quickly.

"Apparently," Kaos said, whistling as he looked at what Amberly had done again.

Suddenly, there was a rumbling behind them. A rumbling against the wall that Amberly had put together to make it look like this part of the cave had crumbled.

"He's still trying!" Kire pointed out. "How well do you think that wall is going to hold, Amberly?"

"I... I have no idea," she said honestly.

"We need to come up with a plan!" Trace said. "We need to figure out a way to fight back!"

"Fighting isn't working!" Kaos said. "I don't think we have any other option."

"Any other option than what?" Rose and Amberly asked at the same time. But then Amberly saw that Kaos and Kire and Trace were all looking at the portal down at the bottom of the drained lake.

"Rezin can't reach us over there!" Kaos said.

The rocks began crumbling. It was only a matter of seconds.

"Fine!" Amberly shouted. "Then hurry up and run!"

At once, they all ran down to the bottom of the lake. They reached the glowing blue portal and practically shoved each other inside of it.

They were going back into the Albus realm.

24

Since all of the Quintets had jumped through the portal around the same time, when they tumbled out the other side, they all rolled a little and landed on their hands and knees.

There, Amberly thought as she stood up and dusted herself off. *Rezin can't get to us now*. They were safe. Safe until they went back over to the other side.

"That was close," Kire said as he got up and helped Rose to her feet. Trace and Kaos got to theirs as well. Amberly didn't quite understand the reasoning why, but Trace stood next to her with an angered look on his face.

"Too close," Kaos said.

"Why hadn't we been able to fight back?" Trace bit out.

"What do you mean?" Rose asked.

"Back there!" He was yelling now. "Against Rezin! We were all there together. We were all using our powers together. And yet, we ran from him! I'm sick of running from him, you guys! I want to defeat him already! Why haven't we been able to do it?"

"I was wondering the same thing," Kaos said bitterly. He didn't sound as angry as Trace did, nor was he as worked up, but he did have a distinct bitterness in his voice. One that Amberly was much used to hearing. Kaos was often a bitter person. "We should have just been able to take him. Instead, we ran like a bunch of cowards."

"I just don't think... I don't think we were prepared enough," Kire replied, trying to make excuses for the group. But Amberly didn't even want to hear his excuses. Quickly, she realized she was on Trace and Kaos's side.

"We are brave, capable beings with our powers," she said. "And, the last time we were in this realm, we had been unstoppable fighters. Remember? What on earth happened?"

"Yeah. And if we can't even protect ourselves against Rezin, who is still one of Yash's minions despite how powerful he is, then what the heck are we supposed to do when Yash gets here? We can't take on Rezin, so I feel that there's no chance we're going to be able to fight back against Yash. We're all doomed!" Trace was still very much worked up. He even walked away from the group a little, into the cornfield surrounding them, as if he were trying to collect himself.

"We'll figure something out," Kire said. "We were just off our game. We were distracted. Caught off-guard. It's hard to fight someone when they're not physically right in front of you."

"We need to do better," Kaos said. "I don't wanna hear those stupid excuses, Kire. We need to own up to the fact that we're not doing enough. We're just..." Kaos stopped speaking, for Trace had quickly returned to the circle and smacked him with the back of his hand against his chest. Kaos had turned and looked angrily at Trace, but then saw that Trace was staring up toward the sky, over in the distance behind them all.

Amberly followed his gaze next.

In the direction of where they saw the castle the last time they were there, it was impossible to see anything now. The Albus realm was in bad shape. That much she knew for sure just from looking ahead. The sky... she couldn't even see the sky. It was under cover of clouds and dark, thick, black smoke.

It seemed as if the entire realm was on fire. As if the only spot they were standing in was the only safe space. The only untouched part of the entire world.

Amberly couldn't stop herself from moving toward it. From carefully stepping forward, one foot in front of the other, slowly. She just couldn't believe her eyes. She couldn't believe how much worse it had gotten since they were last there. The beings of this realm had been fighting this battle without the Quintets. Without Amberly and the others able to help.

We should have been here, she thought. She felt horrible. Guilt swelled up inside of her. They should have fought more. They should have come back here. Why had it taken them so long to come back?

After a few moments, Amberly felt it as the others joined her in the slow walk through the cornfield. The cornfield then turned into a forest. Even the forest seemed to be in ruin. Like a giant wildfire had spread through it. Gone was anything green. It was all black. Charred. Burned to a crisp.

"I don't even see signs of life at all," Rose breathed. "I can't sense any animals or creatures or anything."

Just because Amberly was mad at the situation already in general, hearing Rose's voice irritated her. She knew she shouldn't direct her anger at her but didn't stop herself as words tumbled out of her mouth. "You're probably relieved. You'd be terrified of them anyway."

"Whatever," was Rose's lame comeback.

They kept walking.

"It's horrible," Kire whispered.

"Where do you guys think Albus is?" Kaos asked. "His family? The other Albuses? Do we think any survived? Is this world... Has it officially been taken over by Yash's minions? Did Yash's army win?"

"We can't think like that," Kire tried. "We don't know anything for sure." Then he took his backpack off of his shoulders and got Halo out of it.

"What are you doing?" Amberly asked, noticing that he had stopped walking to do so.

"I just need to ask her..." Kire trailed off, mumbling to himself. He pulled out his pen and started writing in her.

Halo didn't write back.

Kire shook the book a little bit. "Why won't you answer me?!"

"What did you ask it?" Rose asked, tenderly touching Kire's shoulder even though he had seemed to develop a sudden temper.

"I wanna know why she didn't tell us!" he snapped. "Why didn't she have us come back here sooner? I want to know why she's not answering me now!"

He wrote again. And still, Halo didn't reply.

"You should've shown me!" Kire continued to cry. "You should've had us come back!"

The book lay lifeless.

Rose carefully took it from him and closed it. "Just let it go. Let it go for now. We don't even know for sure what the situation is yet."

Kire turned away from her, his face red.

For a while, they all walked in silence, with no specific direction in mind. They were all just walking to continue checking out the destruction of the world. Maybe they were hoping to come across another area other than around the portal that had been untouched by Yash and his minions.

"What led you guys to the White Forest anyway?" Kaos asked after a while. "Like, how did we all know to go there?"

"I... I saw Kire," Rose said softly. "He was in trouble. Rezin was torturing him. And when I woke up from the dream, I thought... I don't know. I thought it was real. And I couldn't just go back to sleep, not knowing the truth or not."

"I saw *you*," Kire replied to Rose. "The same thing. You were... you were hurt. Rezin was hurting you. I had to make sure you were okay."

"And I saw you, Amberly," Trace said. "You were tied up to a tree trunk, and Rezin was moving a thorn all on its own, and it was cutting your arms and legs up. You were screaming so loudly... It was like I couldn't get there soon enough after I woke up. I mean, like you guys, part of me wondered if maybe it was a dream and if I was being a psychopath for running into the forest in the dead of night to make sure, but it just felt...so real."

"So... we all saw our significant others then? Or... the people we care about?" Kire asked curiously.

Amberly's stomach dipped immediately. She hadn't seen *her* significant other...

"I don't have a significant other," Kaos said. "I saw my parents, though. They were tied up by vines. They were screaming my name and asking for help. I was so out of it when I woke up that I ran right to the forest without even going upstairs to check if they were in their bed first. It feels stupid looking back at it. But I had been so certain... I don't know why. Rezin has a way of getting to me I guess."

Amberly could feel everybody's eyes go to her next. They all wanted to know who she saw. Kire saw his girlfriend. Rose saw her boyfriend. Trace saw his girlfriend.

But Amberly had seen Kaos.

Her mouth felt dry, and her throat raspy. And not just because Rezin had nearly taken the life out of her in her dream earlier. "I, um, yeah," she said. "I saw you Trace." She couldn't bring herself to look at him, though. Instead, she just focused her gaze on her gauntlet still wrapped around her arm.

They all continued walking. They seem satisfied with her answer.

But Amberly remembered what she had said in the forest when she first ran into Rose before they met up with the others. She said they had to get to Kaos. So it meant that Rose had to know. She had to know that Amberly was lying. And yet, Rose stayed silent about it.

She better, Amberly thought to herself. Rose wouldn't like what came to her otherwise.

The others started talking to each other and trying to think of their next course of action. But as they all chatted, Amberly fell to the back of the group, questioning herself. Questioning Rezin. She was still so stuck on the fact that the others had seen their boyfriend or girlfriend if they had one, and yet, *she* had seen Kaos. And Rezin had shown her Kaos. It had been his choice to show her Kaos instead of Trace.

What does that mean? Why had he chosen Kaos instead of Trace to show her?

She should've dreamed about Trace. He was her boyfriend. He was who she cared most about in the world, wasn't he? Why was Rezin playing mind games with her? Tricking her and making her feel more confused than she already was? How was it that Rezin seemed to be able to get inside her head and figure out things that she didn't even know about herself?

But maybe Rezin didn't know anything. Maybe this was all just part of his plan to mess with her. To make her think that somewhere deep in her mind, she did prefer Kaos over Trace.

It's not true, she thought to herself.

Trace was her boyfriend.

Trace was the one she cared about most.

What exactly was Rezin trying to do to her?

25

At some point, it must've become a little more obvious that nobody in the group knew exactly where it was they were walking to inside of the Albus realm. Eventually, Kire was the one who said something about it.

"Guys, let's just stop walking for a second and think about this," he said loudly, pausing in his step and allowing Amberly, who had still been in the back of the group mulling over the fact that her dream had been about Kaos, to nearly slam right into him. She stopped walking in time and let out an annoyed huff. The rest of the group stopped walking as well.

"What do you mean?" Kaos asked, standing at the head of the group. He had been leading the way. He was the leader of the group, after all. That was how Amberly saw it, anyway.

"I mean, *where* are we even going?" Kire continued. "What is our next plan? How are we going to get back home? What are we doing about Rezin? Why are we just walking aimlessly through this burned-up world?" He looked skeptical, fidgety, and uneasy in his spot in the middle of them all.

"I thought it was obvious what we were doing," Kaos said to him. "We're going to go find the castle first."

When Amberly tried to look into the distance, she couldn't even see the castle because of how thick the smoke was. She didn't even know if it was still standing.

"It's our best bet as a place to start," Kaos continued. "Once we get there, we'll see what's going on and what the state of everything is. Then we'll figure it out from there."

"It *didn't* seem obvious, actually," Kire argued. "I don't see why we would have to go back there. We didn't find anything useful last time. Albus wasn't there. We need to figure out something else."

"Actually," Trace interrupted, stepping closer to Kire. "It *had* been useful last time. You found a book, remember? A book with contents you once wanted to show us but then suddenly changed your mind about. We still don't know what's in that book, Kire. And I think you don't want us to go to the castle because you don't want us to find it out. I just don't know why."

"Guys, come on." Kire didn't deny the allegations.

"He's right," Kaos said. "There was something in that book, Kire. Something useful. Something we all need to see. I think we should go to the castle first."

"It's pointless to go there. What was in the book was pointless. Let's just move on from that."

"Not a chance," Trace said, shaking his head confidently.

"We're not going to drop it," Kaos said. "We're not going to find another way. We need to know what was in that book, Kire. You can't just keep this information to yourself. You're probably already keeping endless bounds of information to yourself already with Halo. Who knows what other stuff she tells you that you don't tell us?"

"They're right, Kire," Amberly decided to say with a stern voice. She didn't want to come across as a brat, because Kire *had* done a nice thing and saved her from being attacked by some vines earlier in the White Forest back in their world, but she also needed him to know that she wasn't on his side about this. That she wanted to also know what was inside that book that he no longer wanted them to know about.

"Look. It was stupid. Okay?" Kire tried. "It just had information on how to close the portal. But it wasn't anything that we would ever be able to do. I promise you. We're going to have to find a different way to steal off the portal. And we're not going to find the answer in that library."

"So, that's what was in the book?" Amberly asked. "It tells us how to seal off the portal? You've known, all of this time?"

"You guys don't understand,"

Kire and Trace started closing in on him. "You've known all along. We could've closed the portal forever ago. And yet you've kept it to yourself." Trace looked worked up all over again.

"We're never going to be able to do what the book said to do, okay?! Just trust me on this. We have to find another way! And there were no other books in there that would've told us a different way! That's why we need to not go to the castle. We need to find Albus. *Any* others. We need to figure this out!"

Kaos was the one who got closest to Kire's face first. "You know what? I'm sick and tired of you thinking you're somehow the leader of the group. Everybody here knows that it's me. That *I'm* the one who ultimately makes the decisions. And *I'm* the one who has decided that we're going to the castle. And then we're going to see what is inside of that book, and then we're going to do whatever it takes to make sure that we get that portal sealed off. That's the whole point of everything. Don't you get that? We need to seal the portal, Kire. We need to keep the bad guys out of our world. And that includes Yash. Or else everyone will die. *Everyone.*"

Kire repeatedly shook his head. "We can't do it. We won't be able to do it. It's literally impossible. Just trust me." Then his eyes darkened. He seemed to be processing some other words Kaos had just said to him. "And what do you *mean* everybody here thinks you're the leader? Because you know what I think? I think that *I* am more of a leader than you have ever been. I think I'm the one who'd come up with all of the ideas. Who made all of the ultimate decisions, who had got a better handle on my gift. I don't think you're the leader of this group at all, Kaos. It's me. It should be me."

"Are you kidding me?" Kaos's face twisted into a scowl.

"You don't just get to make yourself a leader," Rose joined in, clearly on Kire's side about it.

"And neither does Kire," Amberly chided.

"You're not a leader, Kire," Trace said. "You're a follower. I mean, look at yourself. Look at how you behave in school. You're a sheep. Kaos has always been a leader. He has that leadership quality in him. We're doing what he said, okay?!"

"No, we're not!" Kire yelled back.

"Stop fighting it, Kire!" Amberly shouted.

"Don't yell at him!" Rose shouted back. "I'm sick of you always being such a brat to him. To all of us!"

"Excuse me?" Amberly hissed at Rose, taking an angry step toward her. Amberly was taller than Rose. She overpowered her. She was more confident and secure in herself than Rose was. Rose had no idea who she was talking to.

"You heard me!" Rose shouted, not backing down. In fact, she didn't even seem the slightest bit threatened by Amberly getting closer to her. She looked around at everyone. Not just at Amberly. Then she spoke some more. "You guys want to know the reason why we were horrible and miserable back there trying to fight against Rezin? It wasn't because we couldn't see him. It's because we haven't been acting like a team. We acted like a team the last time we were here in this realm, and we crushed it, even with me being unwell. But then, we got back to Earth, and everything changed! Don't you guys see it?!"

"That's ridiculous," Kaos said, shaking his head. "We've been getting stronger as a team. We've been doing what it takes to put the work in to be better with our gifts and therefore be better together."

This made Rose let out a high-pitched, sarcastic, incredulous laugh. It made everyone look at her like she was the slightest bit crazy. "Are you out of your *mind*? So what if we sit together at lunch? You've seen the way Amberly treats me! The way she treats Kire! And you're not really much better, Kaos. There is still this division between us. There always has been!"

"She's right," Kire agreed.

"We don't have to be best friends for us to work well as a team," Amberly complained. "What you're saying is stupid, Rose."

"It's not," Kire snapped. "Because of you, Amberly, we did a horrible job back there! If you would just let Rose in. If you would just be more accepting of who she is and who I am instead of being miserable all the time about every little thing, then we could have overpowered him in an instant!"

"Don't put this all on Amberly," Trace said quickly. "How the heck are we supposed to fight somebody we can't see?!"

"Our powers would have worked better!" Rose yelled. "We would have been able to at least get those leaves and vines and branches to stop attacking us! We could have figured out a way to put our heads together to locate where Rezin was. We don't have to see him before we defeat him. Not if we have each other and if we have trust in our powers. But we don't have either of those things."

"Come on, Rose," Trace said. "We've been letting you sit at our table. We've been trying to let you in."

"You know what?" Amberly snapped suddenly, turning her body toward Trace. "Speaking of 'not feeling like we're all on the same team,' it really hasn't felt much like *you're* on *my* team lately, Trace."

"What are you talking about?" Trace asked Amberly, looking completely bewildered.

"You heard me," Amberly said. Her blood was bubbling with anger inside her veins. Trace had not been acting like a good boyfriend for weeks now. He had been acting like he wanted nothing to do with her, in fact. Or at least, that was how Amberly had been taking it.

Trace scratched the top of his head. He looked more hurt than angry. More confused than defensive. "Amberly, I've done nothing but try to be a good boyfriend to you. I've done nothing but everything I can think of to do and say the right thing for you."

"Yeah, right!" Amberly threw back.

"Ha! If even the world's cutest couple can't agree on if they're a team or not, then I think that pretty much proves it," Kire said. "We're not a team. Maybe we never were. Maybe we came close, but it still nearly killed Rose the last time we were at that point. I know I was thinking that we need to stick together, to get along and whatever in order to be our most powerful best selves in order to defeat Yash, but it doesn't seem like it's going to be possible! But I, for one, am not going to let the world just die. So whether we're a team or not, I will figure out how to fix this. I will figure out how to save the universe even if I do it completely by myself."

"I am on your side," Rose said to Kire, firmly grasping his hand.

"Fine," Kaos said. "We're not a team. We're three against two here. Whatever. We don't need you guys anyway. What we do need, though, is that stone. So hand it over, Kire."

"The stone? I don't even have it," Kire said.

"It's in that stupid backpack of yours. Don't even try to lie," Kaos snapped.

"I don't have it," Kire tried again. But there was something in his eyes that told Amberly otherwise. She didn't believe him for a second.

What a bad liar, she thought.

"Just hand over the stone, Hunter," Trace snapped.

"No," Kire said, not even bothering to deny it anymore.

"I'll give you one more chance!" Kaos yelled, slamming a fist into his hand. "Give me the stone!"

Kire looked at Rose. "Come on, let's just get out of here."

But before they could get anywhere, Kaos suddenly lunged at Kire.

Amberly watched in slight horror, slight amusement, as Kire and Koas went at it with each other. They were both fairly strong, so they were somewhat equally matched, neither of them able to quite bring the other one down to the ground.

"Guys!" Rose shouted, making Amberly feel like she was making this fight about her. Like she thought guys were fighting over her, which she knew was absurd. But Rose had a look of shock and worry on her face as if this was all her fault. "Please stop! Now!"

"Listen to her!" Trace called as well. He wasn't joining in the fight, and it honestly surprised Amberly to see that he wasn't. He stood back, one of his fists balled while the other hand was on the handle of his sword in its scabbard. "Knock it off, will ya?"

Amberly said nothing as Kire and Kaos continued to attack each other. Fists flew, spit flew. Curse words soared through the air, echoing through the burned forest around them. Neither teenager seemed like they had the slightest desire to stop fighting each other. It was as if they had been waiting months for it, maybe even years, to finally be able to get their hands on each other like this.

"That's enough!" Trace demanded in a loud commanding tone

that reminded Amberly why she had gotten a crush on him in the first place what felt like forever and ever ago. "Kire!"

Trace took a step toward the fighting boys.

"Don't gang up on him!" Rose shouted behind Trace, and then suddenly, she was running to him, her face twisted in rage, her arms extended as if she were going to use all the strength she had in her to push him away from Kire.

"I don't think so," Amberly said to herself. "What do you think you're doing?!" she yelled at Rose as the plant girl made her way to Trace. Amberly knew she had to defend her boyfriend. She couldn't let anybody scrawny girl attack her man!

So the next thing she knew, Amberly was running at Rose as Rose slammed into Trace, who had been trying to get himself between Kaos and Kire.

Now everyone seemed to be in one huge group fight.

"Aargh!" Kaos yelled, seemingly the most in the middle of it all. "Just give me the stone, Hunter!"

"No!" Kire yelled back. "Amberly, leave Rose alone!" he added when he seemed to realize that Amberly had Rose by one of her stupid braids.

"Get the heck away from my boyfriend!" Amberly shouted at Rose, ignoring Kire.

"CAN'T YOU ALL JUST STOP?!" Trace shouted as he tried to get Rose off of his back and the other boys away from the fists they were throwing at each other.

It was complete and total chaos. Amberly knew this was all wrong. The gang shouldn't be fighting like this. They were pulling even farther and farther away from being a team with every hit and push and punch and pull that any of them threw at each other.

"We're—not—supposed—to be—doing this—to ourselves!" Trace yelled, seeming to read Amberly's thoughts.

Finally, Amberly tugged on Rose's hair hard enough that she was able to get her away from Trace, who no longer had to worry about keeping Rose off him while he tried to separate the other boys.

"You're such an idiot, Rose!" Amberly yelled to the other female in the group. "Don't you see he's just trying to get Kire and Kaos to stop fighting!?"

"I... Ouch!" Rose screeched as Amberly still had a hold of her hair. "Let me go!"

Now that they were far enough away from the boys, Amberly finally did.

So then, not attempting to run back at Trace again, Rose answered her. "I thought he was going to attack Kire, too. And two against one didn't seem fair!"

"None of this is fair!" Amberly complained.

Trace was still trying to break up Kaos and Kire. It seemed like the last thing they wanted to do was to stop fighting with each other. As Trace tried to get more and more in the middle of it, hands began flying in his direction when they weren't meant to. Kaos even ended up shoving Trace back a little bit so he could continue trying to throw punches at Kire.

"All right, I am seriously getting real sick of this!" Trace whined. Amberly knew it was probably a good idea for the boys to stop fighting, but she couldn't exactly tell herself she wanted it to stop or that it wasn't amusing her slightly. Trace had always been the best fighter out of the three of them, and that fact was being made clear now by how lamely the other boys were fighting. Their hair was messy. They were getting dirt all over themselves. Their clothes were getting torn. Their faces were red and bloody. It was quite a sight. And Amberly sort of wanted them to ride it out because this was clearly something they had been wanting to get out of their systems with each other for a while.

Suddenly, before anyone could predict what was about to happen, Trace barreled toward both of them, looking like a linebacker in football ready to tackle. Trace totally had the build for a football player. It made Amberly wonder why he didn't do that sport over soccer.

Trace slammed into both of the other boys, but upon doing so, one of them got hit a lot harder by Trace's bulging shoulders.

And that person was none other than Kire, naturally. Amberly wondered whether or not Trace planned it that way. Whether or not he wanted to make sure he hurt his own friend the least when it came to getting the both of them off each other.

Kire flew to the ground, crying out in pain.

"Kire!" Rose screamed, racing to his side to help him up. Kire shrugged her off and glared at Trace and Kaos from his spot on the ground.

"That's it!" he shouted at them. "I'm done with you!"

"Fine by me!" Kaos yelled back.

Even though it seemed as if Kire didn't exactly want Rose's help, she stayed there crouched on the ground next to him, looking up at the others with tear-stricken eyes. "How could you guys behave this way?!" she demanded.

"Oh, come on, Rose," Trace tried, looking apologetic like he hadn't meant to make her cry. On the other hand, Amberly was proud of her boyfriend for making Rose do so.

Kaos ignored Rose and walked over to Kire's backpack, which had fallen off of him during the fight, and unzipped it. He was retrieving the stone, and finally, Kire was doing nothing to prevent him from doing so.

"I wasn't trying to attack Kire," Trace continued. Then his eyes went to Kire. "I'm sorry, man; I was just trying to get you two to stop acting like a couple of idiots. We have bigger problems right now than what you two think of each other and your leadership capabilities."

Kire didn't look at anyone. He just stayed there, down on the ground, seething.

"*We?*" Rose asked, apparently doing he speaking for him. "*We*, Trace? There is no 'we.' Look at us! We're farther away from being a united team than we will ever be! We are not a team! It's you three against us! And you know what, it's always been that way. And it will probably *always* be that way, too. We would have never ended up together if you three hadn't chased Kire through the White Forest to attack him. Mind you, all that time ago! Even back then, you were ganged up on him. When you finally accepted him, accepted us, it wasn't even true! That much is obvious! That's why I still get the nosebleeds and why I am still so weak!"

Kaos dropped Kire's backpack to the ground. Amberly looked over at him, wondering why, but then she saw it was because he had found that blue, shimmering stone. He held it in his palm, looking accomplished, his eye swollen and his lip bleeding. Amberly was slightly concerned about his injuries, but not too much because she knew he would recover quickly because of his rapid healing capabilities.

"Hey," Amberly piped up, her arms crossed as she stood a little away from the group. "Don't blame us for your inability to be a better fighter. It's no one's fault but your own. You heard Albus. You're the one who is all closed off and alone all the time. Like you prefer it that way. You're not being able to open up and let people in is what got you where you are now. I mean, look at you! Even with Kire, who adores you, you're still a closed door with him when all he wants to do is literally give you the world."

"Just... Amberly, leave it alone, Kire said, finally getting himself to his feet, allowing Rose to help him up this time. It seemed as if, finally, everyone was beginning to calm down.

"I'm just saying," Amberly retorted, throwing some of her hair behind her shoulder as if to say, *Whatever.*

"Well, we have the stone now," Kaos said. "Trace, Amberly. Since it's as Kire says, and it's us against them, we should let them be on their own then. Let them do whatever it is they want to do. And in the meantime, the three of us can head to the castle, like the plan was supposed to be all along."

"That's how we're really going to do this?" Trace asked, shaking his head disappointedly. "You guys really want to split the group apart? No longer be a team?"

"I don't want to go anywhere you guys are going," Kire spit out as Rose ignored everyone and inspected Kire's injuries with worried eyes.

He'll be fine, Amberly thought with an eye roll. *Rapid healing, remember?* She wanted to say something spiteful but decided to just keep her mouth shut instead.

"They don't belong with our group anyway," Kaos said darkly, adjusting the crown on his head with his free hand. "They never did."

"I can agree with that," Amberly called. Although, if she was being honest with herself, she could admit that she had started not to mind having Kire around. After all, she *was* his sister. They were related by blood. And he had finally told their father that he knew of her existence, and he was bringing her all that hush money from him...

Whatever, Amberly forced herself to think instead. *Wherever Kire goes, Rose goes. And she's the one I don't want around our group.*

"Fine." Trace shook his head. "Let's use that rock and get back to the castle then."

"Yeah," Amberly agreed. "And we can leave these two to go back to Earth with their tails between their legs, or whatever it is they want to do other than be brave and figure out how to save both this realm and the Earth one."

"You don't even know what you're talking about," Rose said.

"And you do?" Amberly asked, jutting a hip out. "Tell me, Rose. Do you know what was in that book that Kire doesn't want us to know about? Or is he keeping it a secret from you, too?"

At this, Rose fell silent and looked at her feet. It answered Amberly's question. Kire wanted to keep it a secret. One all for himself.

What a selfish jerk.

"Let's go," Kaos said. He turned and started walking away, not even bothering to glance back for one last look at Kire and Rose.

"Coming," Trace called, glaring at the other two before taking Amberly's hand and walking behind Kaos.

So, it was settled, then. The group was officially split into two. Kaos, Trace, and Amberly would go to the castle, find that book, and figure out how to close off the portal to the bad ones. Rose and Kire would... do whatever it was they wanted to do. They were the Quintets no longer.

27

S o, uh..." Trace trailed off as he, Kaos, and Amberly made their journey toward the castle together. Every so often, one of them would cough or wipe their watering eyes from all of the smoke that was around them. "Why exactly are we walking if we can just use that stone to teleport right back to the castle?"

"I just..." Kaos trailed off next. "I just needed some time to cool off before we get to the castle in case we're bombarded with people. Yash's minions waiting to attack. Some time to cool off before we figure out what state the castle is in. What state the rest of this realm is in."

Trace nodded understandingly beside his best friend. Apparently, Kaos was still a little bit heated from his fight with Kire.

"You know, the fight didn't have to happen," Trace said. "It wasn't necessary. We could've gotten the stone from Kire eventually."

"Dude, who are you?" Kaos asked. "The Trace I know would *always* be game for a fight."

"Not for a fight when we're supposed to be a team," he said. "I don't really know how you guys expect us to be able to do anything without them if I'm being honest."

"Are you seriously saying that you didn't want to split up?" Amberly asked, infuriated. "After how they behaved? How they treated us? What they said to us?"

To make her even more annoyed, instead of giving her a direct answer using his words, Trace simply shrugged and didn't even look at Amberly. It felt as if she didn't matter at all. And it made her feel incredibly crummy.

They continued walking for a little bit. Amberly was ready to just teleport to the castle, but she didn't want to push Kaos to do anything he wasn't ready to do. She didn't want him to lose his temper yet again. To turn around and decide he wanted to fight his own best friend next.

"You guys notice..." Trace looked around them all as he spoke. "How quiet everything seems? How... deserted it all is?"

Amberly noticed it, too. "Or maybe Yash's minions just want us to *think* that it's deserted," she wondered. "Maybe they're going to pop out around the tree or behind the bush at any moment, and we're going to be completely caught off guard."

"We should be prepared for anything, just in case," Kaos said, still walking in front of them, not even bothering to turn his head to look at them behind.

They walked for a little while longer until Kaos had finally relaxed his shoulders from underneath his ears and his fists had unclenched.

"Okay," he said, finally turning to face them. They all stopped walking in the middle of the pathway through the forest. "I'm ready. Let's just go to the castle and get this over with."

The three of them stood in a triangle as Kaos held the blue stone in his hand. "Hurry up and grab onto me," he instructed. Amberly and Trace both grabbed one of his arms and squeezed tightly. Amberly wasn't the biggest fan of the way it felt to be teleported, but it also beat the three-day journey it would take them to get to the castle otherwise.

Kaos closed his eyes and looked to be in deep concentration.

Then, too afraid to keep her eyes open, Amberly closed hers as well.

Suddenly, her feet lifted off the ground and she was soaring, soaring, soaring...

They all landed, not on their feet, in front of the castle. They had picked up a lot of dust along the way and compared with the smoke, it made them all break into a coughing fit as they helped each other get up from the ground.

"I hate that thing," Trace muttered as he dusted Amberly off in a way that felt almost affectionate, and it made Amberly feel a burst of feelings toward him.

"Same," she agreed.

Kaos wasn't saying anything to them. And when Amberly turned to see what it was he was looking at, she figured out why he wasn't responding.

The castle. It was in even worse shape than it had been when they had found it the last time they were here. It was more decayed. More crumbled than ever. Smoke was coming out of some of its windows, thick and black as if fires were still going on inside of it. The whole thing looked unstable, like it could break off from the side of the mountain at any moment.

"Do we even really want to go in there?" Amberly asked, feeling afraid. She thought that if they took one step inside, the whole thing might come crumbling down on top of them. That was not the way she wanted to go out. It also got her wondering... which way *did* she want to go? If she had to?

"Well, we're here," Kaos said, even though his voice wavered a little.

Great, Amberly thought. His uncertainty didn't make her feel any better.

This time, Trace proved to be the brave one as he led the way inside the falling-apart castle.

"I think we should look for that prophet guy again," Trace said.

"Good idea," Kaos and Amberly agreed at the same time. They

walked to where they had found the creepy old bald man the last time. However, it was more difficult to get to it because of all of the ruin; all of the rocks and broken stones they had to climb over. Eventually, when they got to where they had first seen the man, he was no longer there.

"I don't know what we expected," Kaos said. "I mean, *look* at this place. There's no way he survived another attack in here."

"I wonder why there *was* another attack in here," Amberly said. "If he was the only one here... Why have another battle in here? Why make the castle in worse shape than it already was?" Surely one prophet wasn't much of a threat to all of Yash's minions he had sent down. Yes, The Unlikely Defenders had gotten rid of most of them, or at least a good chunk of them. But surely it hadn't been enough to make them worried that maybe they were going to be defeated here in this magical realm before they could get to the earth realm.

"Who knows?" Trace said. "What do we do now, then? Keep searching the castle for him?"

"I think what we should do next is obvious," Kaos said. "I think we need to go to the library."

THE LAST TIME the gang had been to the library, other than a thin layer of dust coating everything, the entire room looked untouched.

That was not the case any longer.

It looked to be just us falling apart and broken and destroyed as the rest of the castle. Shelves were on their sides. Books were burned to a crisp. Armchairs were turned over. Lingering smoke wafted through the open window.

"This is horrible," Amberly breathed. It had been so beautiful the last time she was there. The bookcases were taller than most walls. The comfortable-looking red armchairs in front of the beautiful stone fireplaces. The shiny wooden tables lined up in neat rows. Even the paintings of old men in French wigs that lined the walls were gone, for the walls that held them were also no longer standing. Not even the one that contained the picture of the Albus they all knew and cherished.

"Great," Trace grumbled. "I don't know how the heck we're supposed to find that what Kire found now."

"If it wasn't destroyed with most of the other books," Kaos added.

"Let's try to have some optimism, gentlemen," Amberly tried. "Instead of standing here and complaining about it all, let's just start looking."

Without waiting for them to agree with her or do what she said, Amberly stepped forward and started her search. While it hurt her a little to see the beautiful library so destroyed, she had to tell herself that it didn't even matter. She didn't care about books or libraries. She didn't care about architecture. She wasn't into that kind of stuff. It shouldn't bother her.

She tried to remember what it was the book looked like that Kire had held in his hand the last time they were here. She was pretty certain it had a green binding. Emerald green. Leather bound, maybe. She remembered some wrinkles on the cover. Some stitching on the spine that was... black?

She sifted through books and books. Burned ones and ones that had managed to survive. She looked up and found that Kaos and Trace had disappeared to other parts of the library, and she was glad that they had decided to listen to her and look for the book even if it seemed hopeless for their chances of finding it.

However, it wasn't hopeless. Not when Amberly turned the corner around a partially knocked-over bookcase and found there, on top of a pile of books, an emerald green one with black stitching.

"Is this the one?" she asked aloud as she bent over and picked it up. She opened it and started flipping through it. As she read through, she began to feel more and more certain that she was correct. This was the book that Kire had been reading.

So what was it that he didn't want them to see?

Finally, her eyes landed on a page, and she didn't turn it any further.

She read the contents of it. Then she read them again.

And then she read them again.

She got a squeezing, horrible, disgusting feeling inside of her stomach.

No, she thought to herself. She said the words over and over again in her head. Or maybe they were out loud. She couldn't even tell at this point. *No, no, no, no.*

She didn't even know how long she stood there, her eyes glued to the page, her feet glued to the floor. She couldn't move. She couldn't think. She could hardly even breathe. This couldn't be right. This couldn't be what Kire had wanted to show them and then changed his mind about.

But suddenly, it made sense as to *why* Kire might wanted to have changed his mind.

She wondered to herself, *Do I tell the others? Do I bring them over here to read what I'm reading? Or maybe I should just pretend I never found it. I should hide it under some burned books so that the others don't find it, either. There's no point in them reading this. This can't be the way. This can't be how we close the portal off to the bad guys.*

If she hid this book from Kaos and Trace, she knew she would be a hypocrite. She knew it wasn't the right thing to do. They had spent so much time wondering what was inside the book and why Kire had changed his mind about wanting them to see it. Amberly couldn't hide it from them, too. She didn't want to be just as bad as he was.

So eventually, not knowing how long it took before she finally decided to do it, she called out. "Guys, I think I found it!"

She had to instruct them to follow her voice so that they could find her hidden in the wrecked stacks, but when they eventually came to her, they froze upon seeing the look on her face.

"You don't look so good, Amber," Trace said.

"Are you okay?" Kaos asked, reaching a hand out like he wanted to touch hers. But he didn't. He held back and refrained.

Amberly said nothing. Instead, she just handed the book over to them, open to the page that she needed them to read.

Now, they would *all* know why Kire hadn't wanted them to see it.

After they finished reading, they looked up at Amberly in horror.

"So..." Trace trailed off. He had no idea what to say about it. No idea what they should do next. That was clear all over the expression on his face.

"There's just no way we can." Kaos had been about to dive into the conversation about what they had just read, but he fell silent because somewhere in the distance, somewhere inside of the tumbling castle, they all had heard a noise.

"What was that?" Amberly asked, jumping. "Who's here?"

"Maybe it's the prophet?" Trace asked hopefully.

"I highly doubt that," Kaos replied. "I'll bet it, somebody from Yash's ship. I'll bet, finally, more of his minions have found us, and they are looking for a fight."

Whether Amberly liked it or not, it was time for them to prepare.

Time to prepare for their first big fight without the others.

28

Everyone, I would hurry up and get prepared for the fight," Kaos instructed immediately.

Amberly already had her gauntlet on. She was ready to go. Trace pulled his sword out of his scabbard. He held it like a valiant knight, ready to risk it all and do what he had to do in order to protect this realm and anyone that he could.

Kaos straightened his crown and tried to focus. "I'm trying to figure out who it is we heard out there. But I'm not getting a good read."

Amberly's stomach dipped. Already, that wasn't a good sign. Already, their powers weren't going to work as well without the other two. *Don't think like that,* she told herself. It was all of this negativity they were feeding each other that was what was not making their powers right. It wasn't the fact that Kire and Rose weren't with them. It couldn't be. They didn't need them. They could fight Yash's minions without them.

"Are you guys ready?" Kaos asked.

"Are *you*?" Trace asked, fear clear in his eyes. It was a strange sight to see because Trace was never one to seem scared. But yet, there he was.

"It'll be fine," Kaos said. "I probably can't get a good read because of all the smoke. And because I'm not on Earth. Earth is where I got the best at handling my gift. Things are just different here."

"That makes sense," Amberly said, but even as she said it, she wasn't certain she believed that. And based on the look on Kaos and Trace's faces, she wasn't sure they believed it, either.

Still, they all stood next to each other as they walked toward the exit of the library. Toward where they were still hearing noises coming from somewhere else inside the castle. They were going to fight the intruders, and they were just going to have to give it their all and see what happened.

Trace was in the middle of them. It made it easy for Amberly to reach out and take his hand. They clasped each other tightly and continued walking. Just holding his hand, she felt a little bit stronger, even if things had been weird between them lately. Her heart was racing. She could feel Trace's pulse through their hand-holding, too. He was moving quickly as well. They were nervous. They were afraid. But they were doing it anyway. And that made Amberly feel pretty dang brave.

They tiptoed, wanting to be able to take their intruders by surprise. And the further they got inside the castle, the quieter it seemed to become. As if there weren't intruders inside at all. As if they had all made up hearing any noise.

Amberly was about to ask if there was even anyone there, but then suddenly, she heard the sound of a rock falling, and somebody else making a slight gasp of surprise.

"That... that doesn't exactly sound like an intruder..." Kaos whispered. They peered straight ahead, and then, sure enough, three figures rounded the corner. Three figures that Amberly immediately recognized were *not* a threat. In fact, she knew who one of them was.

Albus.

The Albus.

And with him was a woman. A woman who looked just as old, just as wise as Albus did.

The third was a man who looked really similar to Albus. He had completely white eyes, a long and narrow nose, large pointed ears, and lots of white hair that was curly and ran down to his waist.

The main difference was that the other Albus had harsher facial expressions. His resting face was angrier. More threatening. More intimidating.

Their Albus looked friendly and harmless.

But all three of them looked to be in bad shape. That much Amberly could tell straight away.

"Albus!" Trace cried out. "Is… is it really you?"

Unlike the last time they had been around Albus Bridge before, he no longer floated in front of them. He was no longer a foggy figure of half of a humanoid. He was whole. And he was right in front of them. It was real.

Albus wasn't dead.

"Right as rain," Albus replied. But even his voice was weaker and raspier than Amberly remembered it being.

She couldn't believe her eyes.

He had survived!

She didn't know whether she wanted to hug him or hit him. Why hadn't he projected himself to them before? Why had he spent so much time ignoring them when they needed him most? Sure, he had his own stuff he was dealing with over here, but he could've at least summoned himself to their world to tell the Quintets that they needed help. That The Unlikely Defenders of Earth were needed in another realm. They would have come. They would've come in an instant if Albus had just asked them to.

"I can't believe you're okay," Kaos said.

"Barely okay," Albus said. Behind him, the other guy who looked just like him, who was undoubtedly named Albus as well, because they *all* were, grunted.

"What… what happened to you?" Amberly asked.

"I should say the same to you," Albus replied. "But I'm being rude. This here is my wife, Gertrude. And this here is my dear friend, Albus."

No one moved to shake each other's hands. They all just stared back and forth at each other, keeping a safe distance between them all for some reason. Amberly knew that the people in front of them weren't a threat. But she still felt like she didn't want to get too close.

"I can't believe you're actually here," Trace said. "What... what happened?"

"How did you get here?" Amberly joined in. "And when?"

"Well, actually, we arrived by magical carriage." Albus was looking over his shoulder. "And we didn't come alone."

Two more people rounded the corner.

It was Kire and Rose.

Instantly, Amberly glared at them. What were they doing here? Kire didn't want to go to the castle. So why did he come?

"Oh," Kaos said, his tone full of distaste.

"I know you may not be super happy to see them, but it is important that they are here. I found them first, and I collected them in our magical carriage, and I brought them here. Where they said you guys were."

"And why is that?" Kaos asked. "We don't need them here. We don't want them here. They didn't want to come."

"Wait," Trace said, looking at Kire and Rose. "You guys got to take a ride in a magical flying carriage? How crazy is that?"

Kire couldn't conceal his smile. Rose looked rather serious, still.

"It was incredible!" Kire cried.

Amberly rolled her eyes. She looked at Rose and saw that she was rolling her eyes, too, as if Kire was being entirely too immature about the whole thing. As if taking a ride in a magical flying carriage wasn't a big deal. But inside, she knew that Rose had to be screaming.

"Great," Kaos said, not sounding thrilled at all. "But why did you guys come here? Why did you have to bring them back to us, Albus?"

"I didn't say anything to Kire and Rose yet because I wanted to have you all together before I dove into yet another lecture," Albus said.

"Albus really does love his lectures," Gertrude said. She looked frail and tired, and Trace, who seemed to notice it at the same time Amberly did, quickly found a chair that was knocked over on its side, picked it up, and pushed it behind her so that she could take a seat. Amberly couldn't help but beam at him with pride. Trace was always so kind to those who deserved the kindness.

She liked to think that if Trace had gotten to know her mother better, they would have become really close. But of course, Amberly refused to let that happen because she didn't want anyone to know the state that her mother was in. Not until it was too late.

Amberly was suddenly overcome with how much she missed her mother, and tears quickly welled up in her eyes. She turned away from everyone so that they wouldn't see. Then she composed herself as Albus began talking.

"As you can see, our realm isn't in the greatest shape," he started. "In fact, this portion of it is completely in ruin. There's no life left here. And it's not that everyone died, of course. Although there was a great number of deaths. But they all fled. They're in different parts of the realm. Parts you guys have not been to yet. But here, where the portal is, I don't know if it'll ever be habitable again."

"That much is clear just looking at the state of everything," Kaos said.

"Exactly. We are becoming fewer and fewer in number. We have been fighting back to the best of our abilities. "

"I still wish you would've told us we were needed here," Kire said.

"You have other things to focus on," Albus argued. "Like on how you needed to work on being better as a group. So that you could all be at your strongest."

"I don't need them," Kaos said. He was talking about Kire and Rose.

"Oh, but my dear boy, you do," Albus said. Kaos snapped his jaw shut. He clearly knew it was pointless to argue with Albus.

"There is nobody left here," Albus sighed. "The fight has moved on to other parts of the realm. And the battle is still huge. All of us are exhausted."

"Do you think there's a chance that anybody followed you back here?" Amberly asked, wondering if some of Yash's minions would show up at any moment.

"I suppose there's always a chance," Albus said.

"We got out of there undetected," the other Albus said in a little bit harsher voice.

"If he says it, it must be true," Albus replied, looking like he was fighting back an urge to roll his eyes. It appeared as if he and the other Albus were old friends. Friends that had been friends for so long that they mainly got on each other's nerves more than anything else nowadays.

"I've told you, kids, time and time again that it is impossible to defeat Rezin if you are not all together. And if you cannot even defeat Rezin, what makes you think you're going to be able to defeat Yash?"

"We can do it," Kaos said. "We've all been getting better at our gifts. We know how to use them. At least the three of *us* do. Even if we have to take on Rezin and Yash alone. We don't need Kire and Rose. They've done nothing but hold us back the entire time anyway."

"That is not true," Albus said, shaking his head slowly. "You need them. And don't try to fight me on it either, Kaos. I can feel it in your mind that you want to. But if you are not a team, you must understand this. What I'm about to tell you is absolutely certain: you will all be killed."

None of the Quintets looked at each other, despite what they all were thinking. They had doomed themselves.

"And let me also say this," Albus added. "There is not much time left before Yash comes. Not much time at all."

29

"But, when you say there isn't much time..." Kire trailed off, clearly wanting Albus to give them a more specific answer.

Albus, however, simply shook his old, slightly injured, tired-looking head. "There is no way to be one hundred percent certain about the future," he said. "You all must know this. And Kire, I would expect *you* to understand this better than anyone."

"Why?" Kaos asked like he was offended because Albus was perhaps insinuating Kire was the smarter being out of the two of them.

Albus gave Kaos a quick, pointed look. "Because he has Halo. Halo, who writes the future. But what happens when she does this for you, Kire?"

Kire looked down at the ground. "It changes. The book rewrites itself all the time. Depending on the choices and decisions that are made."

Albus nodded encouragingly. "Exactly. You see, minds change all the time. Sometimes every other minute. So there is no certain way of knowing exactly when Yash will finally find that it is time for him to come down to the Albus realm and to make his way to the portal so that he can get to Earth. I do suspect he knows that the

Unlikely Defenders are not decided on how they are going to close the portal, and there are still a decent number of us left here for his minions to fight, so he is taking his time. What... we could use it as an element of surprise here. Close the portal straight away, let him not even see it coming so suddenly."

"But if we close the portal and he can't get to Earth," Rose said, "what if he... gets angry and retaliates?"

"What do you mean, dear Rose?" Albus asked.

She looked saddened. "What if he comes here himself anyway out of anger that he can no longer get to the Earth realm, and he destroys *this* place? And you all no longer have a way to escape to somewhere else where you can be saved?"

"If we close the portal to everyone, then it feels like we're dooming you all," Koas added.

"What other choice do you have?" Albus asked. Behind him, his wife looked saddened. It made Amberly feel saddened, too.

"There has to be another way to close the portal to just the bad ones," she said. She wanted to be right about it so badly.

"You all now know the contents of that book," Albus retorted, nodding his head in the direction of where they had found the book that told them the truth about the portal. That had told them the reason why Kire didn't want them to find out about what was inside of it. "You know what needs to be done. The portal needs to be destroyed. Closed off. From both sides. It is the best way, the *only* way to protect your people in the Earth realm."

"Can't we... can't we at least *try* to find another way to keep it open?" Kire asked, his eyes desperate.

"Maybe there's a way to seal it off, but not permanently, or something," Trace added. "It's not right, closing off the connection you've had to the Earth realm all this time. Closing it off to so many beings just because of *one* single person."

Albus shrugged as if he agreed with Trace but there was nothing that could be done about it. "Yash isn't just a person, as you understand, Trace. He is so much more than that. It leaves there to be no other choice."

"But there *is* another choice," Amberly muttered.

"What was that?" Albus asked, unable to hear her, likely because of his old, old age.

"There is a way we can seal it off to just the bad ones," she said, a little louder this time, her jaw a little less stiff.

Grumpy about the situation, Trace turned around and kicked some rubble on the ground.

"Still working on controlling our temper, I see," Albus pointed out. Trace turned around, his face slightly pink and twisted.

"It's not fair!" he bellowed. "Why weren't we just told this at the beginning? And Why does it have to be up to us? Why did *we* have to be the ones who stumbled upon those stupid gifts in the first place? If we had never gone in that stupid cave, we would have never even known any of this was happening. We would be just like every other ignorant person back in the Earth realm who has no idea their lives might be ending soon!"

Albus stared at him for a long, slow while. It seemed to Amberly as if he was just giving Trace some time to cool down. Some time to collect himself.

Then, he finally spoke, all of the Quintet's eyes on him. "Be that as it may," he said in a grave, but still strong and echoing voice, "We are all so eternally grateful that it was you five that found the gifts. As you'll recall, you five have gone further than any other group of defenders has. You five defeated Jago, and Heno. And I can feel that you're more than capable of defeating Rezin as a team as well."

"Yeah right," Kaos said, barking out a sarcastic laugh. "Every time we have encountered him, we've all run away with our tails caught between our legs."

Yeah, Amberly agreed inside of her head, to herself. *We've all been too scared to try and fight back, and because of that, my mother is dead. Rezin killed her.*

"With all of your gifts, you have what it takes to end him," Albus said. "I am certain of it. And you all need to carry that same sort of confidence with you."

Even so, Amberly was growing exhausted from all the fighting. With all of the running. How much longer was she going to have to keep doing this? What if it never ended? What if they sealed off the portal forever and defeated Rezin, but somehow, it still wasn't over, and they remained the Earth's defenders until the end of time because there was always some other threat to their realm? Could Amberly really do that forever?

"Is that truly it, then, Albus?" Kaos asked, crossing his arms as he stared at the old man.

"Is what it?" Albus asked.

"The only way to seal off the portal to the bad guys. Is the way we all discovered in that book truly the only way?"

"It can't be," Kire's voice barked out confidentially. Maybe a little *too* confidentially. How could he be sure? How could he know? Had Halo said something to him? Probably not. As far as Amberly knew, Halo hadn't been helpful to Kire at all lately.

Albus lowered his head, seeming as if he didn't want to be the one who had to say this to them. "I am afraid it is," he finally said. Then he looked at each one of the Quintets in turn. "The only way to close off the portal to just the bad ones, leaving it so the rest of the beings in the Earth realm and the Albus realm can still move freely in and out of the portal, would be to sacrifice one of the good ones."

Even though Amberly had just read that in the book not long ago, it hurt her stomach to hear it be said out loud. To seal off the portal to the bad guys, one of them had to die. How would they ever find someone they were okay with sacrificing, even if someone were to waltz up to them right now and tell them they wanted to be the one to do it? Amberly would have someone's death, *another* person's death, on her conscience for the rest of her life. She knew she couldn't handle that. She knew she didn't want to endure that. And as she looked around at the other people standing in that room with her, she considered them as well. What if one of them tried to take one for the team? What if one of them was willing to be the sacrifice?

No. It could never happen. It didn't matter how much Amberly didn't get along with Kire or Rose. She could never let one of them kill themselves. It was a sacrifice that was just much, much too big for one of them to make. They were all still so young. They all still had so much life to live. So many things to experience. So much growing up to do. None of them could die, even if it *were* to save the universe.

So, did that mean that was that, then? They had no other option but to close off the portal to everyone and just hope for the best for the Albus realm. Would they ever even have a way of knowing what became of it afterward? Would Albus still be able to project himself to their realm so that he could keep them updated on everything that was happening? Would their world be okay, able to rebuild after so much destruction from Yash's minions? Or would it be like Rose mentioned, and Yash would come down anyway, just to get his revenge on Albus and his realm for helping the Quintets figure out how to do it?

Amberly's head physically hurt from thinking so hard about it.

"No." Kire's voice rang out suddenly and firmly. It made everyone's eyes snap at him. He looked defiant. There was a certain fire in his eyes as he stared what seemed to be straight into Albus's soul. "I'm sorry, but no. Are you all-knowing, Albus?"

Albus just stared at him.

So Kire tried again. "Do you know everything there is to know about everything in this realm? In our realm?"

"I... no... but I do consider myself to be quite more knowledgeable than most."

"Then you can't tell us you are one-hundred-percent, *absolutely* certain that there is no other way to close off the portal to Yash and his minions," Trace jumped in, a new look on his face replacing the angry one he had just been wearing. This one had some hope. Some excitement, maybe even, too.

Amberly couldn't believe what the boys, suddenly united with each other, were saying to Albus. That they were just outwardly telling him he was wrong. Amberly wouldn't have even thought to question *anything* Albus told her. She saw him as the smartest being in perhaps all the realms that ever were to exist. Something about his presence just made it seem as such.

"Now, listen here, boys," Albus tried, looking back at his wife as if he were hoping she would be able to somehow jump in and go to his defense. But before he could continue with what he had been about to say, Kire interrupted him again.

"Look, I am sorry, Albus, but until Yash is on his way here, we are going to search for another way. There has to be another way. There is always more than one solution to a problem."

"But Kire, my boy," Albus tried. Again, he was interrupted, this time by Trace.

"And you know what else?" Trace asked the wise old man. "Maybe I don't want to just be an Earth defender, ya know? I like fighting. I like protecting people. And I want to protect you, your wife, and everyone else in this realm, too. I want to be a defender of *realms*. Not just of one of them."

At this, Albus finally snapped his jaw shut. He looked as if he knew there was nothing else he could say to these boys to get them to listen to him and change their minds.

But Amberly was hardly even listening to any of them anymore. All she could think about was what she had learned in that book. About the way to close it off to the bad guys. About the human sacrifice. For some reason, thoughts of it just simply would not leave her mind.

30

Eventually, Albus told the Quintets he had nothing more to tell them. He suggested they go back home to the Earth realm and destroy both sides of the portal immediately. He gave them all grave stares, almost seeming as if he weren't certain he was ever going to see the five of them again, and then he and his wife went on their way, leaving the five teenagers alone inside the crumbling, dark castle.

"That went well,"

Rose said with a huge sigh, being overly sarcastic. She walked over to the chair Gertrude had been sitting in and collapsed into it.

"So well," Kire agreed just as sarcastically, sitting down on the armrest of her chair.

"What is our next move then, wise guys?" Kaos asked, looking back and forth between Kire and Trace. "Since you two want to keep on this search for a way to keep the portal open for us and for Albuses and their people?"

"I don't know," Trace said. He looked at Kire. Amberly wondered why he hadn't made eye contact with her in quite some time now. It made her stomach dip. Meanwhile, when she curiously glanced in Kaos's direction, she saw him staring straight at her. Quickly, she looked away from him and didn't stare at anyone. She didn't want any of them to ask her what she thought. She didn't want any of them to try and get her opinion. She didn't know what was running through her head right then. She was confused and tired and stressed and scared.

"I..." Kire trailed off, looking deep in thought. "I suppose we keep searching for another way," he said. "But for now, we should get back to our realm, before we get attacked by some of Yash's minions here. I have a feeling that since the five of us aren't really feeling too united right now, we wouldn't perform well in a fight against anyone."

"I agree," Rose said. She got to her feet. "Let's see that rock then, Kaos. And let's go back to Earth."

Once more, the five teens stood around the blue stone. They gripped each other's hands. Amberly squeezed her eyes shut. Her feet lifted off the ground. When she opened them again, she was in front of the portal. The one that they had to close. And soon. Yash was coming in no time at all. They had to move fast with whatever it was they were going to do.

Normally, Amberly would say something about how they needed to come to an agreement straight away about what the plan was. But right now, she was too exhausted to do anything other than cross through the portal and hope to get home without another attack from Rezin.

Trace went first. Then Amberly followed him. So, for just a moment before another teen came through to the Earth side, they were alone.

"Are we good, Amberly?" Trace asked.

"I don't know," she whispered, crossing her arms. Trace sighed. Even if they were fighting, he didn't let it stop him from gently pressing his lips to her forehead in a small kiss. Even though they weren't getting along, he made it clear to Amberly that he still cared about her. And it meant a lot to her.

IT HAD BEEN A WEEK. A week of Kire and Trace teaming up and trying to find another way to close the portal to Yash and his minions. It had been agreed upon by the rest of the Quintets that since Kire and Trace were the ones who still wanted the most to try and figure out another solution instead of what Albus told them. That it should be them that searched for the answer. And they set a time limit, too. By the end of that current week, if they hadn't found the solution, the gang had no other choice but to listen to what Albus had told them and close off the portal entirely.

While the boys were off on their journey doing just that, between school and soccer practice, Amberly was more lenient about letting Rose and Kire be at their lunch table. She was more accepting of the possibility that Albus was probably right. They did need to do a better job of sticking together so that they could fight stronger.

But more had changed within Amberly over the last week than just that.

On top of letting Rose sit at her table and bring down her coolness factor, she had stopped having any interest in being popular and cheerleading. And when her fellow teammates came up to her to confront her about her issue, she had no desire to be her usual sassy self and fight with them. In fact, she almost pitied them. They had no idea that much bigger problems were happening outside of their precious school status or their stupid little cheerleading squad. Their universe was on the brink of devastation, and they didn't even know it! Sometimes, Amberly wanted to scream it at them, but she knew if she did, they would think she had turned fully psychotic. She had to keep the secret to herself and the Quintets.

And at home, Amberly didn't feel much happier, despite the fact that she was getting closer to her Aunt Lydia. She liked the woman and the privacy she allowed her, and how she seemed like she wanted to be friends with Amberly more than she wanted to act as a motherly figure, but Amberly sort of missed having a mother figure in her life. In fact, she missed it a lot. She missed her mother more and more with each passing day, and she hated it. Wasn't it supposed to get easier? Wasn't she supposed to start getting more used to not having her mother around? Why did it still have to hurt her so, so much?

One day that week, when Amberly arrived at school, she found she was the first one out of their group to get there for a change. Kaos and Trace had stopped asking her if she wanted a ride to school in the mornings in Kaos's car because Amberly had made it clear she now preferred to walk. She liked the alone time. The time to clear her mind. Or the time to think about things. Very, very carefully.

When Kaos rolled up in his shiny car, Trace in the passenger seat, they pulled into his parking spot, music blasting, and got out. Lately, Kaos had also been picking up Kire and Rose in the mornings since they had been acting more like a close group these days, but today, Rose and Kire didn't get out of the backseat with them.

Amberly gave the guys questioning looks as they approached her. She didn't even have to use words for them to immediately know what she was asking.

Kaos was the first to shrug. "Kire just texted me a bit ago and said he and Rose would not be needing a ride today. I don't know. Beats me."

Then Trace hugged Amberly. But it was only with one arm, and he barely smiled at her. Every day, it seemed as if Trace was drifting further and further away from her. And Amberly knew it wasn't just a one-way street. She was responsible for some of that drifting, too.

"That's weird," Amberly said after the awkward hug with her boyfriend. "I wonder what they're doing instead."

"I think maybe they went to..." Trace paused to look around him to make sure the coast was clear before he continued in a whisper. "The other realm for a bit to do more research."

"Then why aren't you there with him?" Amberly asked. "Besides, Rose told me at lunch yesterday that she didn't want to go back to the other realm unless we were *all* going. She thinks it's too dangerous for her health."

"I don't know then," Trace said, scratching the back of his thick neck. "All I know is Kire and I still haven't found another answer."

"Time is ticking," Koas said.

THE SCHOOL DAY ROLLED BY, and Amberly, Trace, and Kaos grew increasingly aware that it seemed as if Kire and Rose were avoiding them altogether. They didn't talk to them in classes or acknowledge them in the hallway, and when lunch rolled around, Kire and Rose didn't join them at the table.

"But they're not even in the cafeteria at all," Trace tried, looking around the place to be certain as he sat next to Amberly with his lunch tray. "Maybe they're just... busy working on a project or something."

"I really hope they're not avoiding us," Kaos said. "But that's what it seems like. And we're supposed to be a team here." He looked back and forth between Trace and Amberly. "Did one of you maybe say or do something to them I don't know about?"

"Did *you*?" Amberly fired back, immediately getting on the defensive. Before, it would likely be the case that Amberly had said or done something to get them to stay away from their lunch table. But she had given in and accepted them, and Trace and Kaos knew that.

"No," Kaos snapped, looking grumpy. "I just don't know what their issue is."

"They won't even respond to the group chat," Trace said. "They're definitely avoiding us."

"Maybe Halo told them something," Amberly suggested. "Or told Kire something that he only wanted to tell Rose and that he doesn't want to tell us. Just like he did with the whole sacrifice thing."

Trace looked ready to fight someone. "That better not be the case."

"Then what is it?" Kaos asked, furrowing his brow. "*Man*, I wish my powers worked on Kire's brain."

Suddenly, a realization swept over Amberly. One she couldn't tell Trace or Kaos about. But maybe it was *her* fault after all that Kire and Rose were suddenly avoiding them. She thought maybe it was Kire who wanted to do the avoiding and that Rose was just being a dutiful girlfriend and avowing them, too, because of it.

As Amberly sat there at the lunch table with her favorite people, she realized that the money had stopped coming. That it had been over a week, and Kire hadn't shown up with any more brown paper bags for her full of cash.

It made her feel suddenly sick to her stomach. She had gone on a major shopping spree. She was using shopping as retail therapy. She had done so because she had been under the impression that plenty more money would be coming her way. But now it wasn't, and she hadn't been doing a good job storing away the money she *had* received.

That had to be it, though, the reason why Kire wasn't around. The reason why he had just decided it was better to avoid them all. Because he had no money to give Amberly anymore, and he didn't know how to break the news to her.

But why had it stopped? How had this happened? What had Kire said to make it so? Had he still been so angry about the way things went down when they got into their fight in the Albus realm that he had told his dad he no longer wanted Amberly to get any money? Was he keeping all the money to himself instead?

Amberly felt a new sort of low, but she tried to fake a smile so the guys didn't see it.

Kire, who was generally a pretty caring dude, must really not care about Amberly and what happened to her at all.

31

Amberly wasn't in the mood to see or talk to anyone the next day when she arrived at St. Bernard High. She had taken time to dress in a devilish, overly confident outfit that consisted of red boots, black leather, and even redder lipstick. Her hair was in a sleek, high ponytail. She walked with her eyes narrowed. They were narrowed because they were focused on one goal for the day. And one goal only.

"Amberly!" Trace called from where he and Kaos were standing at their usual spot in the morning before the bell rang for them to get to their first class of the day. Amberly shivered at the sound of Trace's voice, or was it just freakishly cold that morning? She kept walking, pretending like she hadn't heard him. She marched right in through the school's doors, her heels clacking on the linoleum tile as she went. She would explain herself to Trace later, maybe. There wasn't time to talk to him or Kaos, not when Kire was purposely ignoring and avowing her.

No one got away with avoiding Amberly if she didn't want them to.

And Amberly certainly didn't want to put up with Kire avoiding her. Kire not wanting to give her the reason why the money had stopped coming, the money that Amberly needed. The money that she deserved. It was for her future, after all. Without the house that Rezin destroyed, she had nothing for when she graduated and started a life of her own. Nothing. She and Kire's shared father was her only hope of setting something up for herself. So she needed that money, and she needed Kire to make sure it kept being brought to her, even if that meant she had to shake it from him a little bit.

Amberly walked taller than she had in days through the halls of her school. She ignored everyone who waved to her and tried to talk to her. She ignored the other cheerleaders and the dirty looks they gave her when they saw that she didn't want to talk to them—again. She didn't care about any of that, not when there were so many more important things going on at the current moment.

When she saw a friend of Kire's, she pushed him up against his locker and yelled out fiercely, "*Where* is Kire Hunter?" inches from his face.

"I-I don't know! Why should I?" his friend asked in return, his eyes wide in fear.

Amberly slammed him into the locker once more and then stormed away from him, growling.

Dang, it! she thought to herself. Had Kire resorted to just completely not coming to school at all to avoid this confrontation? Had Halo predicted the future and told him this was coming? Was Halo telling Kire exactly where Amberly was at all times so that Kire could stay hidden? *What a coward!*

She didn't find him before the bell to get to their first class rung. Somehow, in their physics class, Kire managed to sneak in at the last second, slipping into his desk when the teacher, Mr. Loch, had already begun his lecture. And then, when the bell rang, signaling that the period was over, Kire dashed out the door before Amberly could reach him.

"Kire!" she called as she stormed out of the room after him. "I need to talk to you!" She looked around herself and saw her peers staring. "Which direction did he go?!" she yelled at everyone.

"Babe," Trace said, coming up behind her. "Why do you need to talk to him so badly?"

Amberly whirled around to him angrily. "None of your business!" Then she stormed off in the direction a scared sophomore boy was pointing out to her.

"Amberly, wait!" Trace called. But just like Kire was ignoring Amberly, Amberly was ignoring her boyfriend.

She kept catching glimpses of Kire's jacket turning corner after corner as he practically ran from her. And before she knew it, the bell signaling the start of their next class had rung, and Amberly was still chasing Kire down through the hallways of their school, not caring that she was missing class.

Maybe I will just have to be a little dramatic about this, she thought. It was risky, what she was thinking of doing, but Kire was leaving her with little to no other options if she wanted to get him to stop running from her and finally face her.

Determined to corner him, and seeing that no one was around now except for her—and Kire, somewhere—she unzipped her bag, pulled out her gauntlet, and put it on. She loved the feeling of it fitting to her arm and spreading itself to be a part of her. She loved the way it glistened. She loved how strong it made her feel every time she put it on. She already felt fearless in this outfit and hairstyle she had decided to wear for the day, but with the gauntlet on, she felt simply unstoppable.

She watched Kire turn yet another corner, so she zipped after him, the slightest hint of a smirk on her face because she knew she had him now. She knew she couldn't use her powers on Kire, but she could use them to help her get him to stop running from her, at least.

When she rounded the same corner, she saw Kire heading toward some doors that led outside.

She had to think quickly, which she did. The first thing she did was use her telekinesis to break the camera aimed at them so that there was no evidence of her using magical abilities. The sound of it crashing and breaking to the ground made Kire spin around to her right in front of the door, his eyes wide and alert; then she moved the trophy case from its spot against the wall to in front of the exit so that Kire had nowhere else to run. When he noticed what she had done, he had that "trapped animal" look on his face. It made Amberly smile wickedly.

"Finally," Amberly snapped, her voice echoing down the long hall as she approached him, taking her gauntlet off and putting it away to hide the evidence in case a teacher or student was to come walking out of a nearby classroom. "You've got nowhere else to run to, Kire."

"Amberly, come on," Kire tried, looking desperate as he stood in front of the trophy case.

"No, *you* come on!" she snapped, finally reaching him. "Why are you continuously avoiding me, Kire? Huh? What's happened?"

You told your dad—our dad—to stop helping me, didn't you?! she thought loudly in her head, needing to hear him tell her the truth out loud. She wanted answers; she wanted Kire to come clean to her, to stop being so afraid all the time, to man up and tell others the truth, regardless of what the consequences were once he did. He needed to take responsibility for his actions. He couldn't just keep running from everything for the rest of his life.

"I just... it's really complicated, okay?" Kire tried.

"What's complicated?" she asked. "Say it. Tell me the reason you're avoiding me. You and I both know the reason. But I need to hear the words out of your mouth, Kire Hunter."

"All right!" he cried out exasperatedly. "All right. I don't have any more money for you. Okay?"

And there it was. Amberly almost had been expecting Kire to lie and tell her he had money coming and that he just needed a little more time to get it or something along those lines.

But no.

There really was no more.

"But you have no idea how complicated things have been for me," Kire continued to say, backing up so that he was pressed against the trophy case. He almost looked like he was worried Amberly was going to try and attack him. She was honestly sort of considering it.

"I don't know if I feel like hearing your excuses," Amberly told him. "I needed that money, Kire." She hated that she was admitting it and appearing vulnerable in front of him. "How could you do this to me?"

"I know," Kire said. "And I really wanted to make sure you got it, okay? I did. Amberly, please just hear me out."

"What other choice do I have?" Amberly asked, crossing her arms. She wanted to hear his lame, pathetic excuse.

He nodded and shoved his hands in his pockets. "I told my— *our*—dad about you, just like you asked me to. And... Amberly, I'm not telling you this to get your pity, because that's the last thing I want from you, okay? But he... he hit me. He was furious at me. For what? Knowing? I don't know. All I know was that he got drunk and attacked me. And at first, I was afraid. But then I thought—who cares if I am afraid? How is being afraid going to help Amberly? I knew how much you needed the help, Amberly. I did. So I was determined to get it for you."

"He... he hit you?" Amberly asked.

"I told you he wasn't a father worth having in your life," Kire said.

She pursed her lips and waited for him to continue instead of saying anything else back to that.

He sighed. "So I slept on it while I thought of how I could make this work. Then I thought of the one person who didn't know anything about any of this—my mom. And suddenly, it clicked. I could blackmail my dad into giving you the money you have deserved all of these years from the child support your mother never made him pay. So I told him he had to give you money or

I'd... I'd tell my mother about you. And that's what made him agree. He was mad as all get out, Amberly, but he still agreed, and he started fishing out the cash."

Amberly wasn't sure she had realized how things were at home for Kire. She hadn't stopped to consider that even though he had a dad in his life, it didn't necessarily mean he had a *good* life. Their dad drank and got rowdy? Their dad hurt Kire? Their dad was keeping it a secret from his own wife that he had another kid with another woman?

Amberly struggled to find the right words to say. She felt bad for him, but she wasn't good at expressing that to people. She wasn't good at showing pity. And besides, it wasn't like she hadn't had it hard her whole life, too. But it also made her wonder— would it have been better to not have a dad in her life at all than a dad who drank all the time and hurt her?

She wasn't sure. All she knew was that for her whole life, she had wanted Gerald to accept her.

"Okay..." Amberly finally trailed off. "So, since the money stopped, I'm guessing it's because you told your mom I existed, didn't you?"

"What?" Kire asked.

Anger slowly began to build inside Amberly as she forgot that she was even feeling pity for him in the first place. She was back to thinking about how the money wasn't coming anymore, and there was a likely reason why.

"How could you do that to me?" she asked. "You were mad about the fight we got into back in the Albus realm, and you went home and told your mom I existed so that our father could stop giving me the handouts."

"Amberly, no, that's not at all—"

"Don't try and lie to me, Kire! I am so sick of all the lying all the time!"

"But, you're not understanding—"

"Just shut up!" Amberly was so close to throwing her gauntlet back on and making a destructive mess of the entire hallway. So much so that it would cost thousands to repair, and then she'd pin it all on Kire and get him expelled, and maybe his parents would send him so far away she would never have to see him again.

"She found out!" Kire yelled. "I don't know how!"

But Amberly was far, *far* past believing another word out of his mouth. She glowered darkly at him. "I hate you, Kire Hunter."

Then she turned sharply on her heel and started running away from him. Tears were streaming down her cheeks, but she was hopeful she had turned from him in time so that he didn't see any of them.

She ran for the girls' room and then hid away in a stall. There was no way she would even bother trying to return to class after that. All she could think about was her hatred for Kire and Gerald Hunter and how unfair the world was. How hard her life was, and how nothing ever went the way she wanted it to.

Amberly was getting really sick of it all.

32

———

Amberly battled with herself for the rest of the day and all evening long, but eventually, she knew she had a world to save and that there was no way she could avoid it. Kaos had told everyone in the group chat on their cell phones that they all needed to sneak out of their houses late at night and meet up to practice training to defeat Rezin together. Koas had also said they all had to be there and that he wouldn't take no for an answer. He mentioned how he didn't care who was mad at who and who wasn't talking to who. Bigger things were going on in the world—the galaxy, really—than the five of them having their little repeated quarrels with each other. Amberly had a duty to fulfill, whether she liked it or not.

So, she met up with the others in the dead of night. They trained hard and long. None of them hardly got an ounce of sleep —but Amberly was plenty used to that now. And she didn't feel like sleeping anyway, despite how badly she desperately needed to. At the end of it, when they were all exhausted and ready for the training to be over for the night, Amberly chalked up the fact that they hadn't done that great to everyone just probably being too tired.

"These middle of the night sessions aren't that great of an idea because none of us are that well rested," she had explained. "We're better off meeting super early in the morning before school or hiding out in the White Forest somewhere after school when we have more energy."

Kaos shrugged, and Amberly could tell that he didn't agree with her. She could tell that everyone knew they weren't working as well as they could be together because they still weren't getting along, despite what Albus had warned them back in his realm. He had warned them that if they didn't work together as a team and overcome their differences and disagreements, they were doomed to die.

To *die*.

The words replayed in Amberly's head over and over all night, especially when she tried out a new move with her gauntlet, and it failed. But she just couldn't help her anger toward Kire. It was his fault she was feeling the way she did about him! He was the one who ratted her out to his mother. He was the reason her entire future was probably ruined! How could she not be mad at him?

Amberly was still thinking the night over when she got to school the next day. She wouldn't have minded hanging out with just Kaos before the first bell rang for the day—he was the only one out of the other four that she didn't have some sort of issue with—but wherever Kaos was, Trace was usually with him or not far behind. And naturally, when she arrived at school, Trace and Kaos were already there, having arrived via Kaos's car, where they undoubtedly gave Kire and Rose a ride as well.

"Amberly, are you going to hang out with us this morning?" Kaos asked in a friendly tone as Amberly approached them, sulking. Next to him, Trace was yawning from the long night of fighting with his sword. Amberly remembered watching him fondly, amazed at how strong he was and how well he carried it. But she didn't want to compliment him about it because things felt too strained between them.

"Why wouldn't I?" Amberly asked, even though just yesterday, she had walked straight past them. They both looked at each other before looking back at her. And luckily, neither of them decided to mention how she had ditched them yesterday.

"Uh, I don't know," Kaos said, quickly shaking his head.

"Hey, Amber. Is it okay if I talk to you about something real fast before the bell rings?" Trace asked, looking hopeful as he stared deep into Amberly's eyes. How was she supposed to tell him no with a look like that on his face?

"Um, okay, I guess," Amberly replied.

"I'll just see you guys in class, then," Kaos said slowly, looking like he wanted one of them to tell him he didn't need to go anywhere. But Trace and Amberly both nodded their heads at him. So with one last look at Amberly, an expression on his face that Amberly couldn't read, Kaos turned and walked away, leaving Trace and Amberly alone with each other.

"What's up?" Amberly asked, trying to avoid his serious gaze. Her stomach dipped in anticipation over what he wanted to discuss with her.

"I talked to Kire on the phone this morning before I picked him up," Trace said, "which was weird because I didn't see myself as someone who would ever have a phone conversation with Kire Hunter. Especially about the sort of thing we uh... talked about."

Amberly already wasn't liking this. "And what exactly was it you talked about?" she asked her boyfriend as she crossed her arms and put on a snooty expression.

"He wanted to see if I could talk to you for him. Because when he tried to explain himself to you... in the hallway that you apparently trapped him in yesterday... you didn't want to hear what he had to say."

"So, you're telling me you're on *his* side about what happened, then?"

"No, I'm not saying that. I mean—you don't even know the full story, because he learned something new when he woke up this morning that he wants me to tell you because he doesn't think you'll listen to him, but—"

"I won't listen to him because he's full of lies, Trace!"

"Just hear me out, okay?" Trace's voice was stern, like he was sick of Amberly interrupting him and not just letting him explain himself to her.

She snapped her jaw shut and pursed her lips. But she wasn't happy about doing so. She didn't want to hear the excuses. She didn't want to hear whatever lie Kire had probably stayed awake all night thinking up to get her to not be mad at him anymore. Amberly was still very much angry over yesterday. She still very much felt like she hated Kire Hunter. Hated him for hating her. For not caring about her and what happened to her. For being a secret bad guy—trying to make everyone else think he was purely good. At least Amberly owned up to her evil ways. At least she didn't try to be someone she wasn't.

"He told me about your dad and how he's been giving you money and how Kire was blackmailing him into doing it and threatening to tell his mother about you," Trace explained. "And he told me about how his mom found out about you. And how he had no idea how."

"Hah, yeah, right," Amberly muttered. Trace gave her a pointed look, so she shut her mouth again.

He continued. "His dad was furious when he found out his mom knew. He went ballistically mad and nearly destroyed their entire house. Kire had no idea how his mom knew because he hadn't told her a word, Amberly. He swore he didn't."

Amberly opened her mouth to interrupt and say something nasty, but then she remembered how she was supposed to stay quiet and just let Trace finish whatever it was he had to tell her. It was getting increasingly hard to stay silent, though.

"Kire got the chance to talk to his mom last night before we all met up to train," Trace explained. "And, Amberly. She told Kire she had the strangest dream. That she had a dream that you were her husband's secret daughter, and when she woke from the dream, she just had the strangest feeling it was true. She called it her 'motherly intuition.' She tried to just keep it to herself, but eventually, she couldn't any longer, and she decided to ask him about it. She claimed to know, with one-hundred-percent certainty, in her mind, that the dream had been telling her the truth. As if it was by magic somehow."

"Magic?" Amberly rolled her eyes.

"Why are you rolling your eyes?" Trace asked. "You and I both know magic exists. Think about it. What would have caused Kire's mother to have a 'magical dream'?"

That was when Amberly's stomach took a sudden, sharp turn downward.

Rezin, the monster who was out to ruin their lives, to torture and destroy them. It made total and complete sense. Of course, Rezin would pull something like this. He would try and ruin Amberly and Kire's and everyone else's chance at happiness. He wanted to weaken each of them as much as he could—whether mentally or physically—so that they were much easier to take down when the time came.

It all made sense. The reason why Amberly wasn't getting the money anymore wasn't Kire's fault after all. That meant Amberly didn't have to hate him. She didn't have to feel pinned against him like Rezin wanted her to be.

Finally, Amberly let out a long, slow, sigh. She didn't have to keep hating Kire Hunter after all. And because of this, they could now work stronger as a team. Because of this, they had a better chance and protecting their world.

"So, yeah," Trace finished, shrugging. "That's what he wanted to make sure I explained to you."

But as Amberly stood there and looked over at Trace, she realized there was still something holding her back from being able to work with the team as well as she could. And it was right in front of her. It was Trace she still had major issues with. Ones she kept trying to ignore because there had been so much else going on around them.

"I don't get you," she said to him suddenly.

He furrowed his brows. "What do you mean?"

"You don't treat me like other guys treat their girlfriends. You hardly act like a boyfriend to me at all."

"Are you serious?" he asked. "All I do is try and make you happy, Amberly."

"How? Show me how you've made me happy lately."

"I-I've been trying to do everything right! I've been trying to give you space and not smother you since your mom's passing! Every time you've gotten mad at me, I've thought it's been because you just need more space, more alone time to process what happened to your mother."

"*More* space?" Amberly thought the idea was ridiculous. "Why would I want that, Trace? What I *want* is someone who will be there for me. Someone who will pick me up in the mornings over their other friends. Someone who wants to be on my side at all times instead of trying to get me to agree with what other people think and want!"

"Jeez, Amberly, I have no idea how to please you!" Trace was suddenly yelling. "You know that? *No* idea! None! It's impossible! I try, and I try, and I try, and to you, it's like I am not even trying at all! But I don't know what else I can do!"

"You don't know what else you can do?" Amberly was hurt by this. "Then what are we even doing, Trace?"

He opened his mouth to reply but was interrupted by the bell ringing. Instead of saying anything, he just shook his head and walked away.

33

How was Amberly supposed to make it through the school day feeling the way she was feeling? She was certain that her and Trace's relationship was on the brink of being nonexistent. What had it been that he had been about to say before the bell had rung? Was he about to break up with her? It certainly had felt that way. The last person Amberly had that she was close to in her life... gone in the blink of an eye. And if Trace broke up with her, then Kaos surely would stick by Trace's side, and she would never get to see him, either. Only when they were doing Unlikely Defender stuff.

Amberly missed her mother, she missed how she would have been able to give her a call in between classes or vent to her about her rough day when she got home. She had no one she could do that with now. Sure, she had her Aunt Lydia, but it wasn't quite the same. Aunt Lydia would never be her mother. They would never share the same amount of closeness. And It was very difficult for Amberly to be vulnerable in front of people. To open up to them. It took a long, long time for her walls to come down. A long, long time before she was ever ready to show her true self to others. Even with Trace, whom she had been dating for a while now, she still didn't feel like she was ever her true, authentic self around him because she was always so afraid that he wouldn't like what he saw and that he would leave her. Could this all be because of the abandonment issues she felt she had dealt with her whole life, knowing who her father was, knowing her father knew she existed, and knowing her father wanted nothing to do with her? It was very much possible. But how could Amberly ever undo years of that trauma?

For the entire day, Amberly floated through her classes. She felt like she wasn't really there, like she hardly even existed. Like for once, no one noticed that she wasn't around. Like all of her hiding and avoiding everyone was finally starting to work, and no one remembered who the ruler of their school was anymore. Amberly didn't even feel like she was the leader of St. Bernard High anymore. Like she had probably been replaced by someone like Angela. And the weird thing to Amberly was that she was finding out that she didn't care. It was so strange to her how much of herself had changed since she became an Unlikely Defender and lost her mom. She had no sense of identity at all anymore.

Who was Amberly McHenry? And who even cared, anyway?

The sadness built up more and more as the day went on. And it made her angry when she had to see other couples looking cute and happy together. Among those couples included Kire and Rose. They walked together in the hallway past Amberly, not evening seeing her because they were too busy giggling at each other, Rose bright red from whatever sweet thing it was that Kire had just whispered in her ear as they held hands.

It wasn't fair. Things might not have been going well in Kire's home life, but at least he was in a happy relationship. Nothing about Amberly's life felt happy. And she was bitter about it. Angry. She was annoyed that Kire was happy when he was supposed to be struggling over the fact that his dad hated him and that Amberly was angry at him. But no. There he was, acting like he didn't have a care in the world. Like it truly didn't bother him that he could no longer give Amberly money for her future from their father.

It made Amberly's sadness turn into anger, and it was an anger that was white hot. Uncontrollable. All Amberly knew was that when the bell rang, signaling the end of the day, she had to unleash her anger. She had to get it out of her. She had to retaliate.

And what better way to retaliate than by going after Kire's significant other? What better way than to try and make him feel as miserable as she was feeling? *It's only fair, right?* Amberly thought to herself as she left her last class of the day. She wasn't going to head into the locker room to change for cheer practice. No. She had another destination in mind.

Amberly walked out of the high school, but not before making a pit stop in one of her teacher's classes first. Then, carrying the slightly heavy, slightly moving box in her arms, she made her way down the path to the seemingly empty greenhouse. But Amberly knew it wouldn't be entirely empty. In fact, she was certain she knew the exact person who would still be inside of it, tending to the plants and probably using her powers when no one else was looking.

Charlie Rose.

Amberly snickered evilly as she stood outside the greenhouse. She could see Rose inside, singing to herself, in her own little world as she took notes on a pointy-looking plant. Then, Amberly looked around at her peers that were lingering nearby, and she summoned them to come to her to see what she was about to do. She motioned for them to come closer but not to make a sound. Then, with her slightly moving box in her hand, she opened the door to the greenhouse and then emptied out the contents of the box inside of it before she closed the door again and held it shut, so Rose, nor the massive, slimy, green class snake Amberly had just let loose inside of the classroom, could make their escape.

Around her, Amberly's peers giggled, and the giggles grew

louder when Rose let out a loud, terrifying squeal from inside the greenhouse.

Take that, Kire's stupid girlfriend, Amberly thought to herself as she laughed and watched Rose climb up on a stool as the snake slithered in her direction.

"Help!" Rose screamed. Kids continued to laugh at her and take pictures and videos of her through the window. Amberly watched Rose clutch the pendant in her hand that hung from her neck, but then she seemed to notice all the kids outside who were watching her. It was the main reason Amberly had told them to gather around—this way; Rose couldn't get herself out of this situation with her magic. Not without exposing herself to everyone.

"What's going on over here?" a voice angrily yelled behind Amberly. She turned and saw the new soccer coach, followed by the soccer and cheerleading team—who had been having their practice outside approaching the greenhouse upon having heard Rose's terrified screams.

Amberly was quick to let go of the door handle. "I was just about to go in and try and save her!" she quickly lied.

"Yeah, right!" Kire yelled, pushing his way to the front of the crowd so that he could speak to Amberly directly. "*You* did this, didn't you? You did this to get back at me!"

He pushed Amberly aside and dove into the greenhouse to rescue Rose from the snake. The second the door opened, the other kids scrambled backward and squealed, not wanting the snake to get out and come for them instead.

"Is that true?" Coach Fletcher asked before running into the greenhouse after Kire, not even giving Amberly time to answer him.

The crowd watched as the soccer coach and Kire wrestled with the snake and got it back inside its box while Rose stayed standing on top of the stool, tears streaming down her cheeks. Then, the three of them walked out of the greenhouse to join everyone, Coach Fletcher holding the green snake in its box in his arms.

"What is wrong with you?" Kire bellowed at Amberly, his arm

around Rose. "You're cruel, Amberly, you know that? Just plain cruel!"

"Oh, please," Amberly said, rolling her eyes and standing tall. There were too many eyes on her for her to act less than her usual, confident self.

"No, I'm serious!" Kire shouted. Next to him, Rose looked at the ground and stayed silent. "You have no heart. I don't know why anyone lets you get away with the things you pull—you're not just acting out because your mother died, Amberly. This is who you really are! It's who you've always been! You're an evil, evil person!"

The words equally shocked Amberly, cut her deep, and shut her up too. She had no idea what to say to that. Suddenly, it weighed heavily on her what she had just done. Out of pure jealousy over how Kire's life was going, she sought to hurt his girlfriend.

What's wrong with me? she wondered to herself.

"All right, everyone, break it up," Coach Fletcher said. The crowd started dispersing, including Kire and Rose. The ones who stayed were the soccer and cheer coach, Miss Cooper. Right away, Amberly knew she had really done it this time. Her cheer coach had caught her ditching practice. And the reason she had been ditching practice was not for a good reason.

"You are in huge trouble, missy," Coach Fletcher said to Amberly, pointing a finger at her, his face red.

"I can handle it from here," Miss Cooper said, tossing her red hair over her shoulder and squinting at Amberly in a way that worried her slightly.

The soccer coach shook his head, gave Amberly one last glare, and then went to return the snake to its rightful home.

That left Amberly alone with her cheer coach.

"Is this why you didn't come to practice?" she asked Amberly in an angry, grumbly tone.

"Um..." Amberly couldn't even think of a good enough excuse. Kire's mean words—mean but *true*—kept replaying over and over again in her mind. All she could think was, *Maybe I am cruel. Maybe that is why I have found myself so alone.*

"What has been going on with you lately, Amberly McHenry?" Miss Cooper asked. "Seriously."

"I mean... my mom died... and..." Amberly couldn't think straight. She felt horrible.

"I'm sorry," Miss Cooper replied. "You can't keep using that as your excuse. You're supposed to be the head cheerleader, Amberly. And you hardly ever even show up to practice anymore. What kind of head cheerleader doesn't show up for her own team?"

"I know," Amberly replied, hanging her head shamefully.

"I have no other choice but to take that title away from you."

Amberly wasn't even surprised. She knew that had been coming. "I understand," she mumbled miserably.

"The girls don't even want you to be on the team at all anymore," Miss Cooper continued, "You know that?"

"I... I didn't," Amberly said, sinking even lower. She wished the earth would just open up and swallow her.

"But you're a good cheerleader," Miss Cooper told her. "And I know you've been through a lot. So, I'm not kicking you off. Not yet."

A slight bit of hope swam through Amberly's veins. At least she still had cheerleading, she just had to take it more seriously and show she was dedicated. She bet she could even get her spot as captain back.

"But you're on probation," Miss Cooper said, making Amberly's heart fall yet again. "One wrong move and you're off the team for good, am I clear?"

"Yes, Miss Cooper," she muttered.

"Good. And as for your little stunt today. Detention after school for a week."

Amberly nodded dutifully. Then when Miss Cooper walked away, Amberly sank down on the bench outside the greenhouse.

Probation. Detention. And a whole world—possibly *multiple*—to save? There was no way Amberly could handle it all. She felt like she was on the brink of losing everything.

34

There was a world out there that needed saving. A portal that needed closing before the inevitable Yash came to Earth and destroyed everything inside of it. And yet, there Amberly McHenry was, sitting in her new home in her room on her bed, feeling lousy and sorry for herself and the way she had been behaving. In the back of her mind, she knew there were other things she needed to be thinking about. She knew the week was coming to a close and that they were going to have to make the tough choice to close the portal off to not just the bad ones, but to all the Albuses and everyone in the Albus realm, too, even though the two realms had been connected for a long, long time. Amberly knew it was highly unlikely that Trace and Kire had figured out another solution. Albus had told them himself that he didn't believe there was any other way than to sacrifice someone good. So, it made zero sense to her as to why Kire and Trace wanted to challenge him on it. Albus was a genius. Albus knew the truth—he knew what had to be done.

Amberly threw herself backward on the bed so that she was staring up at her unmoving ceiling fan. She hadn't bothered to turn her bedroom light on, and it was already getting dark in the room because the sun was already setting. She wanted to get herself out of bed and do something productive. Maybe something like training with Gomora some more so that she would be nice and distracted from the day's events.

Soon, there was a knock on her bedroom door, and Amberly wondered how long she had been lying on her bed doing absolutely nothing but wallowing.

"Yes?" Amberly called, not in the mood to be disturbed by anyone. Even her aunt.

"Oh, you *are* in there," Aunt Lydia said through the door. "I didn't see any light shining through the bottom of the door like there usually is so I wasn't sure if you were even home. Are you napping?"

Amberly tried her best to sound exhausted. "Something like that," she lied. *Please don't ask to come in and chit-chat*, she thought to herself.

"All right..." Aunt Lydia sing-songed, making Amberly wonder if her aunt believed her about the napping thing. Would her aunt be able to guess that Amberly had been just lying in her bed like a person battling a deep depression would? *Was* Amberly battling some sort of depression? Or was this just what being a teenager was like?

"I'll get up soon," Amberly called in her fake-groggy voice.

"Okay. I don't feel like cooking so I'm ordering Chinese for dinner!" Aunt Lydia called.

Amberly listened for the sound of her footsteps retreating down the hallway, and then she finally sat herself up.

"I can't just sit around like this," she whispered to herself. "This is exactly the sort of thing my mom would have spent the day doing if she were still around." And Amberly had told herself she wouldn't be anything like her mother. She would be brave. She would be strong. She would be daring.

She forced herself off of her bed. She turned on her bedroom light. She put on Gomora, and she practiced with it as soundlessly in her bedroom as she could without drawing any attention from her aunt. She did some homework, too. She put on some music to try and lighten her mood. But all the while, as she worked and did what she could to distract herself, she found that it was nearly impossible to get herself fully away from thoughts of what had been going on. More specifically, she couldn't stop thinking about her father and how he no longer wanted to give her any money for her future even though she definitely deserved it. She hadn't *asked* to be born, after all. Her father needed to own up to his responsibilities.

Eventually, Amberly left her bedroom and joined her aunt at the dining table, where they ate through cartons of Chinese food. Amberly hadn't realized until she took her first bite of Kung Pao Chicken that she had been starving. She had a mindless small talk with her aunt, but then, toward the end of the meal, she put her fork down, wiped her face with her napkin, and looked Aunt Lydia in the eye while she told her the lie.

"If it's all right with you," she started, forming the words carefully and trying to sound as believable as possible, "I was going to hang out with Trace after this. We have some homework we can work on and... I haven't really gotten to spend much time with him lately, and I've been feeling really bad about it because he keeps asking to and I keep saying no." It was a big lie. Amberly only *wished* Trace would keep bugging her to spend time with him. But apparently, Trace hardly even wanted anything to do with his own girlfriend.

"Go for it," Aunt Lydia said, giving Amberly an encouraging smile. "But it *is* a school night, so just don't stay out too late, okay?"

"Sure."

"I don't see myself going anywhere for the rest of my night, so feel free to take the car, too, if you'd like."

Where Amberly was actually going to be short enough that she didn't need to take a car. And besides, she figured walking there would help her clear her mind before she reached her destination.

"Thanks!" she said anyway.

She didn't want her aunt to question anything, so after they finished eating, they cleared the table, and Amberly put on her coat and took the car keys while Aunt Lydia replaced the Chinese food cartons on the table with her laptop once again.

"Okay, I won't get home too late!" Amberly told her aunt cheerily.

"Be safe!" her aunt called back.

Amberly gave her one last smile and then started her walk.

Her walk was to the Hunter residence.

She wasn't actually going to go see her boyfriend, nor was she going to the Hunter residence so that she could talk to Kire again. No, this time, she had made up her mind, and her mind had told her she wanted answers, that she deserved answers, and she wanted to get those answers straight from the source.

"I'm being brave," she said to herself as she walked through the frigid air, able to see her own breath in the cold. "I'm being strong and determined. I am going after what I want." The idea of facing Gerald Hunter in person terrified her, but she still wanted to do it. She still felt deep down that it had to be done and that sooner or later, she needed to come face-to-face with the man who was her father.

But what will I say to him when I see him? she wondered to herself. *Or what if when I get there, Kire's mother opens the door and doesn't let me talk to Gerald?*

These horrible what-if scenarios kept replaying through Amberly's head as she walked in the direction of Kire's house, and eventually, they were overwhelming her enough to get her to stop walking.

"This is ridiculous," she told herself. *I can't just show up on the doorstep of my father's house and demand he gives me money!*

She immediately turned on her heel and started walking back in the direction of her aunt's. But as she did so, she felt a sinking feeling in her stomach. She felt disappointment swimming through her veins, and she felt the opposite of brave, she was being a coward.

Again, she stopped walking.

I am a Quintet! she told herself. *If I can fight off aliens and mythical creatures, then I can talk to a stupid old dad!*

Once more, she turned back in the direction of Kire's house and resumed her walk with the original destination in mind.

Amberly did this stop-and-go thing over and over again as she pondered what she would say to Gerald Hunter when she saw him and how he would react to seeing her on his doorstep. Over and over, she turned around to go back home, feeling stupid and pathetic, and then she would remind herself she wasn't either of those things, and she would turn back to go to the Hunter household.

And by some miracle, Amberly finally found herself standing there outside of Kire's house. She stood there, gasping at the old, red brick, four-bedroom house, almost shocked she had actually made it there. The tall old maple trees swayed slightly in the cold breeze. There were some lights on in the home, seen through the closed curtains on the windows, signaling to Amberly that there were still people awake inside.

She was here. She was finally going to confront her father.

She swallowed audibly, walked up the sidewalk to the front door, and forced herself to ring the doorbell, ready for whoever it was who answered.

The sound of the door unlocking made stones drop in Amberly's stomach, but she stood tall. There was a creaking noise, and then in the entryway, looking down at her with red, bloodshot eyes, was Gerald Hunter.

Her father.

"Whaddaya want?" he asked, his voice sounding slightly slurred as he wavered where he stood. It alarmed Amberly at first how big and tall the blonde-headed man was. She had seen him from afar, but never this close-up. As he squinted down at her, his face was scrunched up.

"Um, hi, Mr. Hunter," Amberly said, feeling awkward. Did he really not recognize her or know who he was standing in front of? Off put by him, she took a step back.

"You here for Kire or something, girly?" Gerald grumbled. "Well, I hate to break it to you, but that boy already has a little girl toy over."

"N-no," Amberly stuttered. *Come on, you can be braver than this!* she thought to herself. "I'm here to see you."

He froze for a moment. Then he stared at her harder, and suddenly, it was as if he finally could make out who she was.

"Amberly McHenry." He didn't say the words like a question. He knew very well who she was.

"Um, yes," Amberly said, then she tossed some of her silky blonde hair over her shoulder in an attempt to look more poised and confident in front of him, "Your daughter."

He barked out a short, sarcastic laugh. "I think you hardly qualify to be able to call yourself that, sweetheart."

It hurt, but it also powered the venom inside Amberly. If he wanted to be nasty toward her, she could be nasty right back at him. He deserved it after all the years of treating her so poorly. "Okay, and whose fault is that?" she asked icily.

He just stared at her. He had the slightest hint of a smirk on his face. It made Amberly curious if he was thinking something along the lines of, *She must have got her attitude from me.*

Amberly crossed her arms and jutted out one hip—her signature move, "Anyway."

"Yes. Please tell me why you have come to interrupt my evening," he replied, looking almost bored and still slurring his words. That's when it hit Amberly—she was pretty certain her "father" was drunk.

Amberly opened her mouth to confront him about all the years he should have been around and about all the money he still needed to give her to make up for it, but noise and something moving in the corner of her eye drew her attention elsewhere. She looked to her left and saw Kire and Rose leaving the backyard from the side of the house. Were they sneaking out?

"I... I came to confront you," Amberly said, now feeling slightly like she was being used as a distraction by Kire and Rose so that they could leave the house undetected. Did they even know she was on their porch right now?

"Confront me?" Gerald asked, "And just what do you think you're here to confront me about, young lady, at my own house?"

Amberly was distracted now though; Kire and Rose crossed the street and put hoods over their heads. In the doorway, Kire's father didn't even seem to notice them. Amberly could tell Kire had his black backpack on. She knew that meant he had Halo with him. Where would he and Rose be going if they needed to bring Halo with them? And why did it look as if they were headed in the direction of the White Forest?

35

"Amberly," Gerald Hunter said in a commanding tone when she didn't answer him right away because she had been too busy watching Rose and Kire take off toward the forest. Why hadn't they told her they were going there? Had they told Kaos and Trace at least? Amberly felt completely out of the loop, and she was so concerned about it that she could no longer focus clearly on what she had come to say to her father.

Still, Amberly forced herself to look back at Gerald and cleared her throat. "Yes, you see, I—you—the money you've been giving me—"

None of the words were coming out like she had wanted them to. She looked over her shoulder again to make sure it still appeared as if Kire and Rose were headed to the forest, and they were. She felt certain of it. Did that mean they were going to the portal? And if so, why? Who did they think they were, going without them? Had Kire found an answer to closing off the portal to just the bad ones after all? Why was she so in the dark about it?

"Did you really come here to ask me about money?" Gerald asked Amberly, hiccupping.

This was stupid. Pointless. "You know what?" she suddenly said to him. "I shouldn't have come here. This was a huge mistake."

"Now, what makes you say that?" Gerald asked in a bemused tone.

"You're drunk!" Amberly spat out, "You're probably not even going to remember anything I say to you! In the morning, you'll probably have forgotten I was even here at all! And it took me a lot to come here, ya know."

His smile finally fell. Amberly was surprised by it. "Now, let me tell you—" Gerald started, but Amberly didn't want to hear it. She just wanted to leave.

"Save it," she told him.

"No," he told her right back. "You obviously came here to see me because something has been weighing heavily on your mind, Amberly McHenry. So why don't you tell me what it is you came here to say to me?"

"Do you even care that my mother died?" Amberly blurted out. "That a woman you once had feelings for, that you once had a child with, died, and that the offspring you got from her is standing right here on your doorstep? Do you even feel bad? Do you feel remorse? Do you feel anything at all?"

Amberly expected the man to get angry and belligerent. Instead, he seemed to stop in his tracks. He opened and closed his mouth several times as he if were trying to figure out what he should say back. Or what he *could* say back. It made Amberly wonder if she had finally talked some sense into him if she had finally made him see just how horrible he was.

Gerald leaned his large body on the wooden door frame for support. Amberly could smell that inside their house; Kire's mother had recently cooked dinner. It smelled like delicious chicken and maybe something cheesy like homemade Mac. Amberly never got any homemade meals growing up.

"Look, kiddo," Gerald finally said as Amberly looked over her shoulder again in the direction Kire and Rose had taken off. "I am sorry about your mom. I really am."

Amberly couldn't see the two members of the Quintets anymore. They had gotten out of her sight, and Amberly didn't like it one bit. She had an overwhelming need to know what they were doing. It was like an alarm was going off inside of her head, and it made her wonder if all the Quintets were somehow magically connected like they could sense whenever another member was doing something important without the others.

She looked back at Gerald, trying to pay attention to his pathetic attempt at an apology. The strange thing was that he seemed to mean it. She could tell by the sudden serious expression on his face and the sadness in his light blue eyes.

"Your mother was a good woman, once upon a time," Gerald explained. "But when I met Kire's mom..."

"I don't need to hear the details about how you were a traitor," Amberly bitterly spat out.

"Fair enough," Gerald said.

Amberly took a step back. "I'm just going to go. I shouldn't have come here."

"Wait a second," Gerald said, trying to stop her as she kept backing up. Amberly didn't want to wait; she wanted to get to Kire and Rose and see what they were up to. "Just... did you come here for more money?" Gerald continued. "Is that it?"

"I... it doesn't matter right now," Amberly said distractedly.

"Just hang on, kid. Yes, clearly, it does matter to you. Do you have anyone who takes care of you now? Or are you living in a foster home or something?"

"I stay with my aunt."

"Your mom had a sister?"

"You hardly knew her at all. And why did you hit Kire when your wife found out that I existed?"

His face turned red and splotchy at her question. "Look, I—"

"No," Amberly interrupted. "I'm done here. Enjoy your drunken night, Mr. Hunter. You don't get to do that to Kire, and you don't get to act like you care now. If I find out that you've done something like that again, your wife finding out will be the least of your worries." Then she spun on her heel and took off at a run away from him.

"Wait!" he called after her. Amberly couldn't understand why he didn't want her to leave all of a sudden. But it didn't matter; she had more important things she needed to attend to.

As she ran away from the house, she didn't look over her shoulder to check if her biological father was staring after her. Instead, she whipped out her cell phone and quickly gave Trace a call as she sped in the direction of the White Forest.

"Hey, Amberly," Trace answered in a voice that sounded a little distracted. In the background of wherever he was, Amberly was pretty sure she could hear the tinny noises of a video game on a TV.

"Trace, have you heard anything from Kire today?" she asked quickly. Then she threw in a, "Or Rose?" even though she desperately hoped Rose hadn't been talking to her boyfriend one-on-one.

"No," Trace said, making Amberly sigh a small sigh of relief. "Why? What's up?"

"It's just that—"

"Hang on, I'm with Kaos. I'm putting you on speaker!" Trace called, and seconds later, Kaos's voice called out, "Hey, Amberly!"

"Hi," she said quickly, *Great.* So Trace and Kaos were hanging out together. "Where are you guys?" Had Kaos invited Trace, or had Trace asked Kaos if he was free? It mattered because if Trace had been the one doing the asking, Amberly's feelings were going to be hurt that he hadn't asked *her* if she could hang. After all, they still hadn't finished their discussion from earlier... the one that left Amberly wondering if she and Trace still even had a relationship at all.

"We're just hanging at my house," Kaos said. "Everything good? You sound all out of breath and weird."

"I..." Amberly wasn't sure how to explain why she had been at

Kire's house and what she had just seen. She squeezed her eyes shut as she walked and just hoped they wouldn't ask any further questions once she told them. "I just saw Kire and Rose head toward the White Forest together, I have a feeling they are going to the portal, and they didn't say anything to any of us about it."

Kaos grumbled. "Why are they always doing this?"

"You're sure that's where they're headed?" Trace asked.

"I guess not one hundred percent, but I'm sort of... following them now, and that's the direction they're headed."

"You're following them?" Kaos asked.

"What are you doing out alone at night with Rezin still on the loose?" Trace snapped.

"It's a long story," Amberly said, rolling her eyes even though she appreciated that Trace seemed to be worried about her. That meant he definitely still cared about her, right?

"Well, where are you now?" Kaos asked. "We'll come to get you, and we'll confront the two of them and see what they're up to together."

"Kire and I have been trying to find another solution to the portal, but as far as I know, neither of us has come up with anything. He would have told me if he had, I don't know why he'd keep it a secret," Trace said.

"I'm... I'm in Kire's neighborhood," Amberly explained.

There was silence on the other end.

"Again, long story," she said.

"Okay," Kaos replied, "We're getting in the car, and we'll be right there. Be careful, Amberly; it's dangerous out there."

"Make sure you have your gauntlet on," Trace instructed.

"Okay." Amberly nodded and pulled her gauntlet out of her shoulder bag. She had become much better at remembering to never leave the house without it.

In no time at all, Amberly could hear the sound of Kaos's loud red car squealing down the street, and it pulled to a sharp stop right beside her. Trace hopped out of the passenger seat, looking as handsome as ever in a way that was really annoying to Amberly, who was supposed to be mad at him, and he gave her a quick hug and then let her have the passenger seat while he climbed into the back.

"Hey," Kaos said to her, giving her a flash of a smile and squeezing her forearm quickly before he resumed driving. "Thanks for calling us this time and not trying to figure it out on your own."

"What are you talking about?" Amberly asked as she buckled her seatbelt.

"Just... you know... we're supposed to be a team and you keep trying to do things alone. You keep isolating yourself, and so do Kire and Rose. This is a step in the right direction; all three of us are going to confront them together, they need to learn that we can't keep doing this if we want to defeat Yash, let alone if we want to *live*."

"Amen to that!" Trace said in the back seat. "They definitely need to be spoken to, maybe a little pounding, too, eh, babe? I take Kire and you pull Rose's hair?"

"No," Amberly and Kaos said at the same time. Then they grinned at each other and rolled their eyes at Trace, who always liked to resort to violence.

Kaos sped to the White Forest, parked the car on the side of the empty, quiet road where people usually parked to use the hiking trails, and then they all filed out, and Amberly shivered again at the cold.

"I should have brought my jacket to give it to you," Trace said, frowning as they entered the dense greenery of the forest together. He was wearing a long sleeve shirt, but that was apparently all he needed. He had enough bulging muscles to keep him warm and his flaming sword.

"Here," Kaos said, appearing on the other side of Amberly as he pulled off his black hoodie. "Take mine."

Flattered, Amberly accepted the hoodie and pulled it on over her outfit. It was big on her, and it was warmed up from Kaos's body heat; Amberly was very appreciative of it.

"I can hear them up ahead," Kaos announced as he put his crown on.

"Let's hurry," Amberly said, taking off at a jog. The boys quickly followed her, and before they knew it, they had sight of Kire and Rose just up ahead.

"Hey!" Trace yelled out to them, making them stop, jump, and turn to face the rest of their gang.

"What are you guys doing here?" Rose asked.

"I saw you guys," Amberly said. She still couldn't believe they hadn't even noticed she had been at Kire's house, talking to Gerald.

"When?" Kire asked.

"Does it matter?" Kaos snapped, "What the heck are you two doing out here?"

"And where do you think you're going?" Trace added.

"Without telling us about it," Amberly joined in.

She was beginning to get very sick of having to be in a group with the pair of them.

36

Kire and Rose stood in the White Forest, facing Amberly, Trace, and Kaos. Kire exchanged a look with Rose as if the two of them were having some sort of silent conversation with each other. Amberly didn't like this one bit.

"Why did you guys come here without telling us?" she asked. "What are you doing here? What happened?" She was certain *something* had happened.

Rose only looked at Kire as if it were up to him to answer the question because it had been he who wanted to come here in the first place.

Kire looked at his feet for a second, then he adjusted the straps on his backpack and eyed the others down. "Fine, I was with Rose when Halo finally reached out to me again," he explained.

"And you didn't think to call or text us right away when it happened?" Kaos asked. He had a dark look in his eyes, he was angry at Kire, and Amberly was right there with him. It seemed Kire and Rose were always doing things privately. They were supposed to be acting like a team.

"I didn't have the slightest clue what I was supposed to do, actually," Kire blurted, a bit of snippiness evident in his voice. "You guys haven't made this exactly easy for us; we're always divided. It seems like we always will be divided. After the stunt Amberly pulled back at school, neither one of us really wanted to fill you guys in on what Halo told me."

Trace took a step toward the both of them and said, "It doesn't matter what stupid little feud you two have going on with Amberly."

Ouch, rude, Amberly thought, crossing her arms sternly as she listened to Trace continue.

"Don't you get that us being a team to protect the world and the Albus realm is so much more important than whatever stupid fight you're in? How immature can you be?" Trace continued.

"Yeah," Kaos joined in as he motioned to Amberly, "She came here as soon as she saw you guys headed here because she knew we all should be here together, despite whatever it is that happened. At least *she* is mature enough to know how important it is that we all stay together!"

Thanks, Kaos, Amberly thought to herself. She was flattered that he was talking her up like this. It made her feel brave and a little less childish, even though she still did have deep regrets about what she had done at school earlier that day. It had definitely been the opposite of mature to set a snake on Rose.

"Sorry," Kire said defensively. "I didn't think Amberly wanted anything to do with either of us after what happened today."

"I don't have a choice. We're the Quintets," Amberly said.

Rose sighed. "Well, do we have to keep fighting about it right *now*?" she asked. "Or since we're all here, should we just get over to the portal and get to business?"

"Why are we going to the portal?" Kaos demanded. He looked sharp and brave with the crown on. He looked like the true leader of the group, and Amberly wanted to do whatever Kaos wanted them to do.

"Halo had a vision," Kire said. "Yash's minions, there are a ton of them were headed to the portal in the Albus realm right now. Rose and I were going to try and fight them off."

"We're about to head into a battle?" Trace asked, sounding excited as he whipped out his sword.

"You two were about to take on multiple minions of Yash without us?" Kaos asked skeptically. "Come on." Immediately, he started speed-walking past Kire and Rose, leading the way of the group and nodding his head that the others needed to follow him. "We shouldn't be wasting any more time."

And that's why he's in charge, Amberly thought smugly. Kire would never be the leader of the Quintets, no matter how much he wanted to be.

"We all need to keep our eyes, ears, and weapons out and prepared for another attack from Rezin as we walk to the portal!" Kaos called over his shoulder. He walked with a straight confident stride, and Amberly wondered if she had ever noticed before how defined Kaos's back muscles were. He wasn't nearly as huge as Trace was, but he was definitely athletic; there was no doubt about that.

Amberly walked close behind Kaos, not wanting to leave his side. He was the only one in the group she felt comfortable being around at the moment.

"So, have we all agreed then?" Kire asked as he walked behind Amberly.

"Agreed on what?" Amberly and Trace asked together.

"We're putting our differences aside? Are we going to be a team and work as a team? Whatever is waiting for us on the other side... it can't be good."

"We have to be a team," Trace said, "That's always been a fact that we've all known; we need to get over the issues we have with each other, and that preferably needs to be done, like, now."

"Okay then," Amberly said, throwing Trace a look over her shoulder. "Is there anything you need to say to me?"

"What?" Trace sounded caught off-guard. "I—this isn't about us; that's not what I am talking about."

So, he just wanted to pretend everything was fine between them?

"He's referring to your issues with me and Rose, Amberly," Kire said.

Amberly rolled her eyes. "I'm over it. I don't have any issues with either of you," she explained. Then the next words, even though she meant them, she had to force them out. "And I'm sorry for how I have behaved toward you. There."

"That didn't sound very sincere," Rose muttered.

"Oh my god, at least I *apologized*, okay?" Amberly snapped. "You're not getting anything else out of me. I cleansed myself of the bad feelings. It's up to you two to do the same."

"Fine," Kire grumbled, "I'm over it."

"Me, too," Rose added, sounding completely dishonest, "I guess."

Finally, they entered the cave. As they all walked through it and made their way to the hidden portal—thanks to Amberly's telekinesis powers of making it look like the drained lake was caved in—the gang had all agreed to get along. Would that make them strong fighters when they got to the Albus realm? Would that help them work better together? Was it the reason Rezin wasn't there trying to attack them now? Because he knew they had put on a united front and were stronger than ever?

In what felt like no time at all, the Unlikely Defenders found themselves once more in front of the glowing blue portal.

And when Amberly came out on the other side, she found herself right smack dab in the middle of an ambush from some of Yash's minions. It was just as Halo had predicted.

At first, Amberly didn't even know who she was fighting or what was happening, but as something slammed into her, her adrenaline immediately kicked in, and already, she was using her telekinesis to get a beast away from her. When she got her footing and was able to step back far away enough to get a good look at what she was fighting, Amberly couldn't believe her eyes.

It looked like a fairy, but not in a good way. Not like the tiger fairy they had run into the first time they came to the Albus realm. This one was clearly evil and dark, clearly one of Yash's many minions. She had jet-black hair, a glowing purple, black, and blue wings that were bigger than the rest of her body. She wore a black leather dress and black, slightly torn mesh gloves that went up to her elbows. She had a look of pure hatred on her face, and her eyes glowed white.

This fairy could wield magic in her hands, and when Amberly saw a ball of light forming, she quickly used her telekinesis to make the fairy fly backward to distract it so that the ball of magic light dimmed. She had no idea what the fairy was capable of doing, but she knew it couldn't be anything good.

She chanced a glance around at the others to see how they were fending off and what they were fighting. Kire was battling a centaur. And when Amberly thought of a centaur, she thought of them as being male. But this one was clearly female: it had longhorns that curled inward, like a ram's, long, purplish hair that seemed to flow in the wind magically, scary yellow eyes, and her chest was bedazzled in purple jewels. The horse part of her was gray and purple-striped and had what looked like electricity sparking from its hooves. In the centaur's hand, she carried a bow and arrow. She was currently aiming her arrow at Kire. Amberly cried out, but luckily, when the arrow released from the centaur's bow, it went straight for Kire but bounced off something. And that was when Amberly realized that Kire had up his protective shield. Then Rose, coming to her boyfriend's aid, manipulated some plants to go after the centaur and try to rip the bow free from her hands. Disarming her would make it easier for them to defeat her.

When Amberly glanced to her other side, she saw a tall, hairy, unpleasant-to-look-at beast. Its body was thick, bulky, and gray. It had a giant beer belly, massive hooves for feet, and massive hands, too. One of them was holding a giant mallet. Its face was made up into a mean snarl and it had beady eyes. There was a hole for a nose in the center of its head. It had pointy ears and no hair and was disgusting to look at. Amberly assumed it was a troll.

Kaos was taking on the troll. He was manipulating the troll's mallet to avoid him every time the troll tried to smash it down on top of his head. It horrified Amberly to watch because she was nervous that Kaos's crown was either going to get knocked off his head or that his gift was going to let him down at some point like it has been doing a lot lately. The last thing she wanted was to see that mallet, with its sharp end, go straight through Kaos's body.

Then, behind her, she saw Trace, and she was what Trace was fighting. A griffin. But not a kind one. This one looked like a daemonic griffin. It was made of black, smoking bones. It had claws sharper than anything she had ever seen. It had a disgusting, huge black tongue and it made a horrendous noise as it went after Trace. It seemed to not care at all that Trace had flames coming out of his sword. This demonic beast seemed to enjoy the flames. He seemed to think of this all as one big fun game to him.

"How is this happening?!" Amberly cried out as she fought against the fairy, who was back to try and throw balls of magic at her some more. Amberly managed to get another one out of her way, and frustrated, the fairy pulled out a short blade from her stockings instead.

"Fine, we will do it this way," the fairy snapped in a velvety, cunning voice to Amberly.

"What are they doing here?" Trace asked as he fought against the griffin with his sword.

The griffin laughed. "You mean to say that you haven't figured that out yet?" it asked as it nipped at Trace once more.

"I think they're here for Yash!" Kaos yelled as he played mind games with the stupid troll, who fell back on its butt.

"Duh!" Kire called.

"No, you don't get it!" Kaos yelled.

"Try to be smart like your friend," the centaur said as it smirked at Rose and Kire. "We're here to protect the portal. We can't let you idiots destroy it. Not when Yash is on his way. He will be here soon." Yash was coming?

Amberly's stomach dipped violently. "If we defeat these guys," she yelled, "are we certain we know how to destroy the portal so that Yash can't get through?" It was hard to talk as she kept fighting the fairy. "The way Albus wanted us to?"

"I know what to do," Kire said. "It's not the way I want it, but it's the way it's going to have to be!"

They had to destroy that portal. And to do that, they had to get through these beasts first.

It seemed as if they were all paired against their own beast to fight. Amberly was against the fairy, she could manage it on her own and she felt confident about it. She and the other Quintets should all be able to fight excellently against these minions of Yash's because they had all agreed to put aside their differences back in the Earth realm. So they had this in the bag, right?

The more Amberly fought with the fairy, using her telekinesis to help her avoid the knife the fairy was holding from going straight into her stomach, she found herself growing weaker and weaker. But how was it possible? How was this happening? She couldn't remember feeling at all this way when the gang had been in this realm fighting the beasts before.

Amberly snuck another peek at Rose, the weakest one in the group, to see how she was doing helping Kire fight off the centaur with its bow. She noticed right away that Rose's nose was bleeding, and when she looked at Kire, it seemed he was having an increasingly difficult time getting Halo to keep the shield up around them.

This isn't right, Amberly thought to herself. *This isn't going well.*

"Argh!" Trace's voice came behind her. Terrified of why her boyfriend had made the noise, she turned around and found that the evil griffin had clawed Trace's arm, and the gashes on him were oozing bright, shiny blood.

"Trace!" Amberly called desperately, worried he was losing too much of it. She wanted to go help him fight off the griffin, but with her back turned to the fairy, she didn't dodge the ball of magic in time, and something hit her square in the back and it sent her flying through the air with a scream. She landed on her stomach, her chin slamming into the ground and causing her to bite her tongue, where she immediately tasted blood. The breath was knocked out of her, but she managed to roll over just in time to see the fairy coming at her with its knife, and she was able to use her gauntlet to get the fairy away from her just in time. But the fairy hadn't been pushed back too far. It barely gave Amberly enough time to get to her feet and keep fighting. She waited for the fairy to get close, and then she threw one of her magnificent punches right into its stomach. By some miracle, it worked well, and the fairy flew back further than she had managed to make Amberly fly back, and out of her hands, the knife went as she did so.

With some time to help another Quintet, Amberly looked wildly around her and saw that it seemed Trace was still holding his own okay. And so was Kaos. It was Kire and Rose who needed the help. So Amberly turned and threw another massive punch right into the side of the centaur. The woman screamed out in pain and fell to the ground, and Amberly pulled the bow from her grasp with her telekinesis and brought it to her hands. Then, with her powerful grip, she snapped the bow in half.

"NO!" the centaur screamed out in rage as it struggled to get back to its feet.

Then suddenly, the centaur was no longer interested in Rose or Kire, so it became the centaur and the fairy against Amberly.

Great.

As Amberly fought against the both of them now, Kire struggled to keep the shield around her and him so that Amberly was better protected as she fought.

"We should be doing better than this!" Kire yelled angrily.

Amberly had just been thinking the same thing. It seemed as if Rose could hardly use her powers now. With Trace's injury and Kaos struggling to keep the troll from coming at him, everything felt all wrong. It wasn't supposed to be this way; it had to mean that some of the other Quintets hadn't meant it when they said they were over their differences with one another. One of them had been lying, so there was still a massive sense of divide in the group. For once, Amberly knew it wasn't *she* who felt the divide; it wasn't she who wanted nothing to do with Kire, Rose, or even Trace. She was accepting of all of them. So, who wasn't accepting, then? Kire or Rose?

It made Amberly realize, as all the Quintets struggled to keep themselves alive against these minions of Yash's, how important it was for them to be united and how they shouldn't have crossed over back to the Albus realm until they were because she wasn't sure if they were going to win this fight.

When Amberly had a spare second to look around, her eyes went to Rose, worried about why she couldn't see her using her powers to fight back and help her against the centaur and the fairy anymore. She was confused when she saw Rose by herself, her nose still bleeding, her face looking pale, as she pulled something out of Kire's backpack. It was a book bound by leather, but it wasn't Halo. Halo was with them, trying to keep the magical shield up.

Kire noticed it, too, and suddenly, he looked even angrier than he had been moments ago. "Rose, what is that?!" he yelled over to her. "Where did that even come from?!" Apparently, he hadn't even known the book was in his own backpack.

That's when Amberly realized what it was. The book from the castle. The one that told them how to complete the sacrifice. Rose had secretly kept it all this time.

But why?

Rose ignored Kire's questions, opened the book, and began reading.

"Rose!" Amberly yelled out in astonishment. What did that girl think she was doing?!

Amberly tried to get to Rose, but then she was hit by another spell, and she felt a crack in her ribs that made her scream out.

"Amberly!" Kaos yelled, sounding worried about her. Trace was too deep into his battle with the griffin to even seem to know Amberly had been hurt. Amberly was quick to brush off the pain; however, she was too concerned about what Rose was doing with that book. Why was she reading it? There was only one way to close the portal regarding the instructions in that book, and it meant...

"Rose put the book down!" Kire yelled at her. He went to go to her, but just the second he left the shield, the centaur was on him, wrapping her hands around in throat to choke him. Amberly quickly raced over to get the centaur off of him.

"Rose, come on, drop it and help us!" she tried yelling at Rose.

But the thing was, Amberly knew that Rose was trying to do just that—Rose thought she was helping them by reading the book. Amberly knew that Rose knew she was too weak to stay in this fight for long and that she had one choice to make, to sacrifice herself to close the portal.

Rose was going to sacrifice herself to save them all.

"Rose, please!" Kire begged as he gasped for air when Amberly got the centaur off of him and was now fighting it on her own.

Rose continued to ignore him and walked over to the small, sharp knife on the ground that the fairy had dropped when Amberly had thrown her backward, Amberly was still in the middle of fighting with the fairy and centaur, and Trace was still fighting off the griffin and trying to protect his bad arm, Kaos's crown had just fallen off of his head, and he was scrambling to get it back before the troll smashed him with his hooves or his mallet.

Rose took the knife in her hand and went and stood in front of the blue portal, the book in her other hand. She looked calm and resolved even though her nose was bleeding heavily, and she looked certain of what she wanted to do.

"What's happening?!" Trace called.

"Rose, what are you doing over there?" Kaos added in, and the two of them seemed to just have noticed what Rose was up to, but neither of them could do anything about it. Amberly felt like she couldn't do anything about it either. She had two beasts she was trying to defeat, after all.

The only person who had the opportunity to stop her was Kire. He just had to leave the safety of his shield to do it.

"Rose, just stop!" he tried. "I can read from Halo, and she will tell us how to defeat these guys! Please don't do this."

Rose completely ignored everyone. She raised the knife into the air. Amberly tried to use her telekinesis to get the knife away from her, but of course, that had to be when the fairy threw a punch right into Amberly's cheekbone, and she was temporarily blinded by the pain so great that she saw nothing for a few moments. And when she opened her eyes again, she was terrified of what she was going to see—the knife inside of Rose from her sacrifice.

However, that ended up not being the case. Instead of Rose having made the sacrifice, she had been shoved to the side, and she was no longer in front of the portal.

Amberly was confused at first, but then she understood what had happened. Kire had left his shield again and had dived to push Rose away at the last moment. He now stood in front of the portal.

Amberly didn't even have time to react to what came next. The centaur pulled one of its arrows out of his it's bag around its back. She didn't have her bow anymore, but she didn't need it. She ran quickly up to Kire and stabbed the arrow straight into his abdomen as she laughed, a loud cackle that pierced the smoke-filled air.

"Kire!" Amberly heard herself and Rose screaming.

Kire fell to the ground, and the centaur stood over him.

So overcome with fear and adrenaline, Amberly screamed out, and she and Rose both used their powers on the centaur, and vines wrapped around it's neck, and Amberly raised the entire creature into the air, and then, as the life was being choked out of it, Amberly slammed the beast into the ground, and it moved no more.

38

lthough Amberly was so relieved that Rose hadn't been able to go through with the sacrifice, she was terrified of the blood that was dripping from the arrow wound in Kire's stomach. Amberly didn't want either of them to die. She didn't want any of the Quintets to make the sacrifice.

Well, that wasn't entirely true.

When Amberly had first learned about the only way—most likely—to close off the portal to just the bad ones, like Yash and his minions, she had felt... intrigued. If that was the word, it had stirred something up inside of her and left her feeling with so many questions. It had made her, without trying to go through the group and determine which out of the five of them, it made the most sense to be sacrificed. First, she thought of Trace and how he had his mom to look after. His mom was sick and had no one else. He couldn't just leave her behind like that; it wouldn't be right. Amberly would never allow it or be okay with it.

Then there was Kaos. He had his whole life ahead of him. He had two parents who spoiled him and loved him, and he was wickedly smart. It wouldn't make sense for his life or his talent to be wasted. He would be missed by so many people, including his peers and his teachers, who all saw so much potential in him.

And with Kire, He had a loving mother. Sure, there were some issues with his father, but at least his father wanted to be in Kire's life at all, right? At least Kire lived in a decent house and had a roof over his head, and he was fed home-cooked meals every night. He was also smart, just as Kaos was. He might even be a little smarter if Amberly dared admit it to herself. He also had a bright future ahead of him. And even if his family wasn't overly wealthy, he likely wouldn't need that much money for college anyway because he would get a full-ride scholarship. And, well…Kire *was* her brother. She didn't want her only sibling in the world to sacrifice himself.

And even *Rose* had a life to live, Amberly could see Rose getting a job protecting the environment in the future, and Amberly knew there needed to be more people like that. Rose had a family of her own that she couldn't just leave. All of them had families.

All of them except for Amberly.

It all made sense to Amberly. Why she had been mentally obsessing over the book and the sacrifice, why she didn't think Trace and Kire should bother wasting their time trying to figure out another way to close the portal? Amberly was all alone in the world, she had nothing to live for and nothing to lose.

She thought of the words her Aunt Lydia had told her. *You need to be bold; you need to be daring; you need to be a fighter.*

You have all three of these qualities inside of you.

Amberly could make the sacrifice; she could save everyone. It made sense for it to be her. This way, her life would finally have some meaning.

This is what Amberly was meant to do. This was her fate.

Rose and the fairy were now at it with each other, the fairy sensing that Rose was a weakling and probably easier to kill off next than Amberly, and it left Amberly some time. Some time to run over to Kire, who lay bleeding on the ground, and she dropped beside him.

"It's going to be okay, Kire," she said to him, tears filling her eyes. "Thank you for stopping her."

"I—it hurts," Kire said to Amberly in a whisper. There was fear in his eyes that he wasn't going to make it.

"You're going to be okay," Amberly told him. Kire had to be okay; he *would* be okay. She just knew it. "Listen, Kire. I... I am so sorry about everything. I am so, so sorry."

"Amberly—"

"No," she interrupted, wanting to get the words out before she could never say them ever again. "I've been a huge idiot and a horrible sister. It was never your fault that I had to live the life I did. And yet, I spent so many years of my life taking it out on you. I spent so many years of my life hating you and resenting you and wanting the life that you have, and for what? 'Cuz you're right, Kire, our dad? He's not that great of a dude."

Kire let out the tiniest hint of a smile as his way of agreeing with her.

Amberly sniffed and continued. "You're a good person, Kire, and a good brother, and I know you'll find everyone a way out of this mess."

"What are you—?"

Amberly smiled down sadly at him, "I have to do this," she whispered through her tears, then she slowly got to her feet. She looked around at Trace, Kaos, and Rose, who were deep in the battle, all fighting to protect their world.

Well, Amberly thought to herself, *you all won't have to fight for much longer.*

She walked over to the knife that had been knocked out of the fairy's hand and then out of Rose's hand, and she stood in front of the portal.

"Amberly!" Kire called out softly, sounding weak.

Amberly ignored him. The beasts of Yash glanced at her, but none of them attempted to come at her. It was as if they had all realized she was going to be dead soon anyway and that none of this would matter; they seemed to realize it before the other Unlikely Defenders did.

When Trace glanced back at her, fear crossed his expression. "Amberly?" he called as he fought against the griffin, "What—are—you—doing?!"

Hearing him, Kaos looked at her, too. "Amberly, put the knife down!" he shouted as he held his crown atop his head, and it looked as if he was trying to use his powers to mind-control her into dropping the knife. It was a lame, pathetic attempt to stop her, as they all knew they couldn't use their powers against each other. "Amberly, come on!" he shouted when it didn't work.

"You guys need to get Kire some help, and as soon as you can!" she yelled at the others, "Save him. That's what matters the most."

"Amberly!" Trace bellowed.

Amberly stared down at the knife in her hand. She looked at the sharp blade and thought about what she was about to do with it, what this would mean for everything. Once she did this, there was no way for Yash to get to Earth, no way for him to destroy all life, and it would have been because of Amberly that their world was saved.

A sense of calmness came over her, even though she could hear that the other Quintets were desperately trying to get her to stop what she was about to do. They were all too busy fighting off their own monsters to knock her out of the way this time, though. And on the ground by her feet, Kire was too weak to do anything about it, either.

"It's going to be okay," Amberly said to her friends. "Trust me."

"Just think about what you're doing!" Kaos called.

"Amberly, you can't!" Rose tried.

And out of the corner of her eye, Amberly saw the hurt on Trace's face. He couldn't stand that she was about to do this and that there was nothing he could do to stop her in time.

Amberly forced herself to look away from him. Instead, she

looked down at Kire again. "They're going to be able to get you some help. I promise. You're going to live, Kire."

"Amberly," Kire whispered. But Amberly was already back to focusing on the book and the knife.

It was time for her to go now.

Slowly, she held the knife's handle with both of her hands and raised it in the air above her head, the blade aimed at herself.

Just straight into the heart, she told herself. *Quick and easy.*

Amberly started bringing the knife down. She was calm and collected. She was certain she was doing the right thing. It had to be her.

When the knife was millimeters away from piercing Amberly's flesh, right in front of her heart, suddenly, she was knocked to the side, and the knife started soaring through the air.

Amberly was confused as to what was happening, why she wasn't dead? How did she end up on the ground like this? Who had managed to get to her in time to shove her out of the way? How could this have happened?! She had been *so* close to saving everyone!

She coughed and sputtered, trying to get the dirt out of her lungs, and when she rolled back over, she saw who had been her unfortunate rescuer.

Albus was here, and he didn't look happy. In fact, he looked the total *opposite* of it. He stood above Kire's body wordlessly and didn't even look at Amberly. He didn't look at any of the Unlikely Defenders. Instead, he used his magical ability to catch the knife that was still soaring through the air. He brought it to himself and held it in his hand.

"Albus!" Amberly shouted out, seeming to be the only one who realized what was happening. She felt she was the only one who even knew he was there. All of the others were too preoccupied. On the ground in front of Albus, Kire looked like he was about to fall unconscious.

Albus still didn't look at Amberly. He didn't say a word. He still looked... angry. Amberly didn't know what to say or do; all she could manage was to sit there on the ground and watch him, paralyzed. It was as if he was using some sort of magic on her to keep her pinned there, unable to sacrifice herself like she had been planning.

How could he do this to me?! Amberly cried internally. *I was supposed to save everyone! It would be what is best for everyone! It should be me!*

She tried to voice this to him. She couldn't wait until this battle was over so that she could corner him and yell at him about it. She told herself she would still make the sacrifice; she would just have to wait until Albus got the heck out of there.

But as she stayed there, down on the ground, while Albus stood in front of the blue, glowing portal with the knife in his hand, it slowly began to dawn on her: there was a reason he was now standing in the spot she had been in. There was a reason he looked so angry or so serious. Amberly couldn't quite differentiate between the two, but she knew what it was Albus was about to do.

"No, don't!" she screamed at the old man. If anyone needed to stay alive, it was Albus.

But Albus didn't listen to Amberly's desperate demands. Instead, he plunged the knife into his own heart, and before Amberly and the others could do anything about it, he plummeted to the ground.

And Albus Bridge was no more.

39

I t was as if time was now standing still. All around them, the creatures that had been trying to fight the Quintets had all stopped moving, and all the fighting ceased. The teens were all staring at Albus's unmoving body with horrified expressions on their faces, except for Kire, who had his eyes closed as he lay on the ground in pain from the arrow that was in his stomach still.

The first person—or creature—to break the silence was the griffin, who looked even meaner and scarier now, if that were even possible.

"NO!" it bellowed loudly. At first, Amberly was confused as to why the beast would be upset about Albus's death, but then it finally seemed to dawn on her what the man's departure from this world meant—he had sacrificed himself. So because of this, the portal was now sealed off to all evil beings, and none of these creatures could use it. Yash could no longer use it, either.

"How could we have let this happen?!" the fairy screeched as she fluttered in the air.

"I didn't even see him arrive!" the troll cried out, his voice booming and making the ground vibrate slightly. "Yash is not going to be pleased to hear about this."

"It wasn't supposed to happen!" the griffin cried out.

Still, all the Quintets could do was say nothing and stare at Albus and at the scene happening in front of them.

Amberly couldn't believe the creatures weren't trying to keep fighting. Why was that? What did it mean? Did they truly no longer see the point of defeating the teens? And if so, was that because it was all over now? Now that Yash didn't have this portal to get to Earth, was he finally going to give up after trying for so long?

"Albus," Rose's voice whispered with a sniffle behind Amberly. She looked over her shoulder and saw that Rose had come to stand near her. Rose held out her hand and helped Amberly, who was able to move again, back to her feet.

"Is he really... gone?" Trace asked, his mouth hanging open in disbelief.

As Amberly looked at the wise old man's unmoving body, she knew it was true. Even though behind him, the portal looked untouched and was still swirling with the glowing blue mist, she knew that Albus was dead. And she could feel it in her bones that the sacrifice had worked.

"What are we supposed to do now?" the troll asked, looking around at the fairy and the griffin and shaking his head. None of them seemed to even care in the slightest that Rose and Amberly had managed to kill one of their kind—the centaur.

"We have no other choice," the griffin said bitterly as he threw a nasty glare in the direction of the teens. "We must go." And in a flash of brilliant white light, the three beasts disappeared at once.

As soon as Rose could see there was no longer any imminent danger, she ran to Kire's side and fell to her knees before him. "We have to save him, or he's going to die next!" she cried.

Trace and Kaos slowly moved toward Kire and Albus, whose body was near Kire. "Albus sacrificed himself," Kaos muttered in utter disbelief.

"He wasn't supposed to!" Amberly cried out. Albus wasn't supposed to die; she was. And on the ground, Kire wasn't supposed to *still* be dying. The others were supposed to have found a way by now to save him. It made Amberly feel helpless. She didn't have any idea what to do. She knew Halo would be able to tell them how to heal Kire, but Kire was the only one who could read from her. So it left the four of them on their own to figure out how to stop him from leaving them, too.

"Kire, just hang on," Rose said, grabbing his blood-soaked hands and squeezing them tightly while tears streamed down her face. "There has to be something we can do!"

"Should we pull the arrow out of him?" Trace asked, going to kneel down beside Rose.

"No!" Amberly and Kaos cried out at the same time. They couldn't pull the arrow out of him until they had something to put on the wound once it was removed, but what could they put on the wound?

"I... I don't know how to help him," Kaos said in disbelief. "I don't know what we can do."

"Kire, stay with us!" Rose begged.

"Come on, dude," Trace added, giving Kire's shoulder a gentle shake. Kire's eyelids fluttered, signaling that he was still conscious, still with them, but Amberly could tell it was barely.

If Albus hadn't made that sacrifice and had let Amberly do it as she had wanted, Albus would be helping Kire right now. He would know just what to do to save him.

She looked over her shoulder at Albus again; his magnificent robes and long hair splayed out around him. She avoided staring directly at the spot where the knife was still sticking out of his body —that was too much to look at.

But then, something on the ground, covered by dirt but glittering slightly, caught Amberly's eye.

"Guys," she said, pointing. "Look."

Everyone except Kire followed her finger and saw what she was seeing. It was a bag. Kaos walked over to it and picked it up. It was a small glittery red pouch that fit inside the palm of Kaos's large hand. He opened its drawstrings, and inside, he pulled out a small, single vial full of a clear liquid.

"What is it?" Trace asked.

"I think I know," Rose said, sniffling some more to hold back the tears as she brought her hand out so Kaos would give her the vial. He did; his eyes were curious.

"Albus must have come to deliver this to Kire," Rose guessed aloud. "Someone else pulls the arrow out of him. I can't do it."

"No," Kire muttered. Amberly couldn't tell if it was because Kire was scared it would hurt too badly, or if he thought it would cause him to die.

"It has to be done so we can save you," Amberly told him confidentially. "Don't be such a chicken." She smiled at him even though he wasn't looking at her because his eyes were still closed. But Amberly figured he would maybe appreciate some sense of normalcy about the way others were treating him right about now, something to ground him.

"I'll do it," Trace said, already by Kire's side. He gripped the arrow with one hand. "You'll be okay soon. It's gonna hurt, but just for a second. You got this, bud." And without a countdown or any warning at all, he plucked the arrow out of Kire's stomach.

Kire screamed loudly in protest, and it was the most conscious Amberly and the others had seen him since he was first stabbed by the arrow.

"Rose, hurry!" Kaos urged.

With shaking hands that still had Kire's blood on them, she opened the cork on the vial and poured the entire contents of it onto Kire's stomach wound. Kire yelled some more and withered around on the ground, seeming to be in complete agony.

"I'm sorry!" Rose cried, tears still continuing down her face and mixing with the blood that steadily trickled from her nose.

Amberly was beginning to worry more. What if they had been wrong about what was inside the vial left behind by Albus? What if, instead, it was a poison that was meant to use on one of the beasts to kill them? What if they had only made things worse for Kire? What if they had just led him right to his death?

"Is it working?" Trace asked, desperation in his voice and his eyes wide.

"Kire, sit still!" Koas demanded, getting on his knees and helping Trace pin him down so he would stop wiggling. Kire continued to cry out in pain, and he continued trying to wriggle and roll, but the other boys restrained him with ease, despite the huge gash on Trace's arm from fighting the griffin.

"What did I do?!" Rose cried out, worried she had just killed her own boyfriend.

"Wait a second!" Amberly called out, getting a look at Kire's stomach now that he was being held still. She was the only one still standing, and she was able to look from a higher viewpoint at the wound, "I—I think it is working!"

Slowly but surely, Kire stopped crying out and shouting so much, and he stopped resisting Kaos and Trace. Eventually, they no longer had to pin him down at all, and Kire stopped yelling entirely and fell silent.

"Kire?" Rose whispered gently.

Finally, Kire's eyes opened again. "Hey," he muttered.

Amberly found that she was crying with relief. Trace and Kaos smiled and high-fived each other. Rose threw her arms around Kire and squeezed him tightly. He was going to be okay. And it was all thanks to Albus.

Albus...

After the gang seemed to get over the fact that a member of the Quintets wasn't about to die, after all, it seemed as if it hit all of them at once, and they found themselves all getting to their feet and looking in the direction of Albus's body.

"I can't believe he did that," Amberly said bitterly, crossing her arms and shaking her head, crying even harder now. She should have been quicker with the knife. She shouldn't have let it get to the point where Albus was able to stop her from being the sacrifice.

Amberly wasn't supposed to be there, alive, right now, but Albus was. And yet, he was gone.

"He didn't want to," Kire pointed out.

Amberly and the others shot him a questioning look.

Kire explained himself, sounding still a little weak from the freshly healed injury. "Did any of you see the look in his eyes? Did any of you notice how quickly he moved and how he said nothing and looked at no one?"

"I noticed it," Amberly said.

"He was angry," Trace said.

"I mean, it makes sense, I guess," Rose added in, wiping tears from her eyes. "He told us *how* many times that we needed to just destroy the portal the way he wanted?"

"I wonder..." Trace trailed off, looking almost like he didn't even want to say what he was about to say, but Amberly had to know.

"What, Trace?" she asked her boyfriend. He looked at the ground, and then he looked back up at the others. "I wonder if he knew this is what would come of it. If we tried to go this route. If he knew that in the end, he would have to be the one who made the sacrifice."

"Well, that's not fair," Amberly bit out. "It didn't have to be him! I had just been about to!"

"And before you, *I* had been about to!" Rose cried. "It—it felt like the right thing to do."

"Not for *you* to do," Amberly argued with her, "You didn't need to do that, Rose. Your life is way more valuable than mine."

"That's not true," Rose said, pouting while also seeming astonished that Amberly would ever say such a thing to her. Amberly was surprised that she had said the words aloud, too.

"This is horrible," Kaos said. He looked angrier than sad. "A great magical being, dead because of us."

"His poor wife," Rose whispered, looking suddenly horrified.

"You guys got what you wanted," Kaos continued, still red-faced. "The portal is sealed off to the bad ones. Great."

Everyone looked at their feet. Amberly could tell everyone felt ashamed of what had happened. Everyone felt terrible and responsible for Albus's death.

"The portal is sealed," Kaos continued gravely. "But at what cost?"

EPILOGUE

Rose turned back to Kire, threw her arms around him, and sobbed loudly. As Amberly stood there and watched, she couldn't help but cry, too, but she was being much more silent about it than Rose was. She didn't turn to hug Trace, either. She just stood there, unsure of what exactly she should do. What exactly were they supposed to do next? What was waiting for them on the other side of that portal?

Kire squeezed Rose back tightly. It seemed like an intimate moment the two of them were sharing, especially when Amberly glanced at him and saw that Kire, too, was crying slightly over the death of Albus.

Wanting to give them a private moment, Amberly turned and walked away from everyone into the cornfield where she could have a moment to be alone, to be away from everyone and Albus's dead body, for herself to process what had just happened, and what she had nearly just done to herself.

Amberly had nearly just died. And at her own hands, not because Rezin or another minion had been close to killing her. But because she had been close to killing herself in a selfless act to save the world. But right before she had been about to do it, she thought about how alone she was and how it made the most sense for *her* to be the one to die. And even though she was still alive now, she still felt it was true. Amberly still felt very much alone.

Behind her, after a few minutes, the cornstalks rustled and Amberly whipped around, worried for a second that the beasts were back to continue to fight. Only instead, it was just Kire coming to check on her, and he was alone.

His eyes were still slightly bloodshot, reminding Amberly of their father, but he wasn't crying anymore. He gave her a weak smile and put his hands in his pockets. "I heard everything you told me before you tried to... ya know," he started.

Amberly could feel herself blushing with embarrassment. "Whatever," she said with a sad smile and an eye roll.

Kire shrugged at her, "You're right; we do have a pretty lame dad."

Amberly giggled, and he chuckled with her. "Yes, we do," she said.

His eyes were kind as they looked into hers. "And... I just wanted to let you know that I forgive you and that I'm sorry, too."

Amberly didn't know what to say back to that. She opened her mouth, but no words came out. Again, it was because she knew she sucked at being vulnerable and sappy. But Kire, her brother, knew this, and he didn't need Amberly to say anything else. Instead, Kire stepped forward, threw his arms around Amberly, and hugged her. It felt weird, but Amberly hugged him back. Her brother!

After, they rejoined the others in the opening by the portal. The first thing Amberly noticed upon their return was the way Kaos was looking at her. It didn't make any sense to Amberly, so she chose to look away from him and ignore it.

Instead, she went and stood directly in front of Albus's body. She couldn't ignore the knife sticking out of it now. And as she looked down at it, and the blood, at his unmoving eyes that stared at nothing, the others joined her, and together, they all stood around the once quirky, majestic, powerful Albus Bridge.

"Man, this sucks," Trace said as he looked down at Albus, standing across from Amberly on the other side of his body.

"Yeah," Amberly agreed as the others nodded their heads.

Trace shook his head as if they weren't understanding him. "Not just that Albus died, I mean, yeah, of course, that sucks. But... we needed him. He was supposed to help us. Now he can't do that anymore."

"You mean because...?" Rose trailed off.

Trace nodded and continued, "Yeah. This isn't over, you guys. It can't be, not when we get back to the Earth realm. When we get back to where Rezin is."

"Yash's most faithful minion," Kire mumbled resentfully.

"Exactly," Trace said, hanging his head.

"We... we need to bury Albus," Kaos said. "Have a ceremony or something. We can't just leave him like this."

"And then after that?" Rose asked.

Everyone looked around at each other. What was clear was that none of them seemed to have the slightest idea of what it would be like once they went back to Earth. What was going to happen next?

"I wish you hadn't done this, Albus," Amberly found herself saying to the man. "I wish you were still here now."

"Me, too," Rose agreed.

Trace scoffed. "Yeah, but if he was still here, what would that mean?"

Amberly raised a questioning eyebrow at him.

He continued. "It would mean that *you* weren't here, Amberly. That's what."

Amberly wanted nothing more than to get the topic of conversation away from her. "You and Kire were the ones who were *so* set on finding a way to close the portal off differently than how Albus had wanted it done."

"We don't need to go throwing blame at each other," Rose said loudly, giving Amberly a look.

"I'm—I'm not trying to blame anyone," Amberly said. She even felt that part of the reason Albus was dead was because of her. She felt that, if anything, they were *all* a little bit to blame for the way it went down and the way the portal finally ended up sealed. "It's funny," she told the others. "You know, I think we wanted so badly to leave the portal open to the Albuses because of *this* Albus right here in front of us. We wanted him to be able to continue to use the portal. And look what happened instead."

"And whose fault is that?" Trace asked. Amberly snapped her head to him.

"Excuse me?" Amberly asked, surprised Trace was talking to her in this way.

"He's right," Kaos said. "If anyone is to blame, it should be you. And you, Rose."

"I thought I just said we shouldn't be throwing blame at anyone," Rose replied as Amberly stood there, too stunned to say anything. She had tried to save everyone, and they were mad at *her* now?

"I can't believe you even tried to pull that stunt," Trace said to her. "How could you do that to me?"

"To us," Kaos added.

"I... I was only trying to help us; don't you get it? I was doing what I thought needed to be done!" Amberly argued.

"Same!" Rose cried. "There was a simple solution, and I just thought I had been the only one who was brave enough to do it."

"But it's not about being brave, though, is it?" Kire asked darkly. "There's more to it than that."

"What do you mean?" Rose asked.

"It was selfish," Kaos said, "On both of your parts, It was like you were trying to take the easy way out. Just end it for yourself and leave the rest of us here to clean up and handle the aftermath."

"Selfish?" Amberly balled her fists, unable to believe what they were saying to her, "How is *sacrificing* myself to save the human race selfish!?"

"There's always some selfishness that comes from sacrifice," Kire added.

"No, there's not!" Amberly and Rose argued together.

"So you were really fine just... dying like that then?" Trace asked Amberly, "Just leaving me behind? How do you think that is supposed to make me feel?"

Amberly let her hands hang loosely by her sides. She was exasperated, "I honestly don't know, Trace. But you know what I *do* know? That we sucked when we were fighting against those minions! We sucked so badly! And I know it's because there are people here who are still harboring bad feelings for another person in the group, and you know what I think? I think it has nothing to do with Kire, Rose, and me. I think it has everything to do with *you*, Trace. I think you're the reason we weren't working well as a team. Even the flames on your sword were weak! It's because you have an issue with me! And you won't just try and work through it with me, and I don't understand why!"

"I didn't have an issue with you!" he complained, "But *now* I do! Because you were so willing to just leave us like that, I have an issue with you!"

"We need to stick together," Kire yelled over both of them. "We *have* to stick together! None of us can do any sacrificing, okay? Because with one of us dead, how will we ever be able to fight at our strongest?"

Amberly closed her mouth. She supposed she hadn't considered that. Would someone else have to take her place? Would someone have to wear her gauntlet if she died and make themselves a part of the group? Or could the four of them become just as strong together without her?

"From this point on, we need to stick together through everything," Kaos said. "Got it? We need to do whatever it takes to keep this group strong and whole. We need to do it for Albus."

"And so we don't get ourselves killed by Rezin," Kire joined in.

"Yes... and that," Kaos said, "but we need to make sure Albus didn't die in vain. We have to stick together, to be the defenders of the Earth and the *realms*. No one dies, and no one tries any stupid sacrifices, okay? We all just need to be united from this point on."

Everyone nodded their heads. But to really solidify everything, Kaos held his hand out, and it hovered over Albus's body, right above his heart. Immediately, Amberly knew what he was doing and what he wanted the other Quintets to do as well and she was the second one to put her hand out, over on top of Kaos's. Kire followed, then Rose, and lastly, Trace put his hand on the top of the group's, but he didn't look satisfied, nor would he bring his eyes to meet Amberly's gaze.

"We're going to go back to the Earth realm, and we're going to defeat Rezin once and for all," Kaos said. "For Albus."

The others repeated after him, a passionate fire blazing through Amberly's body as she said the words with the others, "For Albus!"

AUTHOR'S NOTE

Dear Beloved Reader,

Thank you so much for continuing the journey with The Unlikely Defenders from Amberly's point of view in The Unlucky Guardians. As you may have noticed, Amberly faced tremendous challenges and found herself in a deeply dark and bewildering place. However, it is crucial to remember that this book is a work of fiction, and although it touches upon heavy themes, it is not a reflection of real-life experiences.

If you or someone you know is struggling with thoughts of self-harm or suicide, I urge you to seek help immediately. Life can be overwhelming at times, and it is essential to remember that you are not alone. There are people who care deeply about your well-being and are ready to support you.

If you find yourself experiencing similar feelings of hopelessness, please reach out to a trusted friend, family member, or mental health professional. Additionally, the Suicide Prevention Hotline is always available for immediate assistance. You can call or text them at 988 in the United States. They have trained professionals ready to listen and provide the support you need. If you are in a country outside of the US, please call your local Suicide Prevention Hotline.

Remember, your life is precious, and there is hope even in the darkest of times. By reaching out for help, you are taking the first courageous step toward healing and finding light once again. You matter, and there is a brighter future waiting for you.

On a lighter note, I truly hope that you enjoyed The Unlucky Guardians. If you did, I would be so grateful if you would consider leaving a review. Reviews help other readers find my work, so a review is very valuable to me.

The next book in the series will feature Trace Henderson, and is called The Unseemly Protectors. Also feel free to check out my other books!

https://swiy.co/UnlikelyDefenders

Visit my website at LilySkyy.com and interact with me on social media. Did you know that you could support me directly by purchasing books directly from my website instead of a third party store? There's also awesome merch available for each of my series. Also, make sure to sign up for my mailing list to be the first to know about new releases and special happenings such as previews and give-a-ways!

I love getting feedback from my readers, and if you'd like to stay in touch (or discuss my books), join me over at the Lily Skyy Readers' Group. I'd also love to connect with you on Instagram, TikTok, and Twitter! Feel free to reach out to me directly via email at social@lilyskyy.com.

Again, I thank you for reading, and I can't wait to join you on the next adventure!

With heartfelt sincerity,

Lily Skyy